The Resolute

Legacy of the King's Pirates 7

MaryLu TYNDALL

The Resolute

Legacy of the King's Pirates 7
by MaryLu Tyndall

ISBN: 979-8-9896046-1-6
E-Version ISBN: 979-8-9896046-0-9

Library of Congress Cataloging-in-Publication Data is on file at the Library of Congress, Washington, D.C.

This book is a work of fiction. Names, characters, places, incidents, and dialogues are either products of the author's imagination or used fictitiously. Any similarity to actual people, organizations, and/or events is purely coincidental.

Unless otherwise indicated, all Scripture quotations are taken from the King James Version of the Bible. Scripture quotations marked NKJV are taken from the New King James Version®. Copyright © 1982 by Thomas Nelson, Inc. Used by permission. All rights reserved.

Cover Design by Ravven
Editor: Louise M. Gouge

RANSOM PRESS

Fearing Allard would harm the lady in retribution, Cadan leapt in front of her, daring to offer his unprotected back to the point of her knife. He leveled his cutlass at the man, even as One-tooth followed him with the barrel of his flintlock. "I'll put lead in ye, I swear!"

Boom! Boom! Two more cannon shots sent more birds squawking into the sky.

"I have no time for this! To hell with you and your child!" Allard spat out to the woman. Spinning on his heels, he ordered One-tooth to shoot Cadan, then fled into the jungle.

Cadan started to run after Allard, but One-tooth cocked his pistol.

"Meet yer fate, Cap'n!"

"You better shoot to kill, you traitorous squid, because I will find you and keelhaul you for your betrayal."

A sneer lifted the man's lips, revealing his single tooth. "I'll gladly oblige ye."

Allard was getting away! It was all Cadan could do to remain there and not take his chances and rush the man. But the lady muddled things up. What if the shot missed him and struck her? Or what if it missed them both? Could Cadan chase after Allard and leave the lady behind, unprotected on an island full of pirates? Or even with this cullion?

He groaned. Why should he care? In truth, he still needed her as bait.

One-tooth fired. Cadan dove, taking the lady down with him. They landed with a thump and a moan from the woman.

Leaves fluttered, branches snapped, and Cadan leapt up. One-tooth was gone.

He could pursue him, but the lady cried out in pain.

A strange concern waved over him. Had she been shot? Kneeling, he felt over her body, looking for a wound.

"How dare you?" She slapped him away with one hand and groped for the knife she'd dropped on the ground with the other.

Cadan retrieved it and uttered a bestial growl, pointing it at her. "You've kept me from killing Allard!"

Lady Fox's eyes sharpened to cutlass tips. "I? I have not the power, Captain, to keep you from your wicked schemes." Gripping her belly, she struggled to rise.

Cadan sheathed his blade as more cannon blasts echoed through the jungle.

He must get back on his ship! Perhaps there was still a chance to capture Allard.

He held out his hand for the lady.

She slapped it away again, and with much difficulty, got on her knees and finally stood. Defiant eyes and an upraised nose met his gaze. "Your plan did not work, Captain."

"'Tis not over yet, my lady. Now, make haste." He turned to leave.

"Leave me here, I beg you. You no longer have need of me. You plainly saw Allard wants naught to do with me."

He spun to face her. She might be right, but he couldn't very well leave her here. Growling at his own foolishness, he grabbed her arm and retreated, intending to drag her out of the jungle.

When a shot rang through the air. Intense pain radiated through his head.

Warm liquid dripped onto his shoulder, and he dropped to his knees.

Pain beckoned Cadan, throbbing, pulsating pain, drumming through his veins with every creak and groan of the ship. *Ship*? Where was he? The pain continued, luring him from his slumber, leading the way to consciousness, and though every inch brought more discomfort, he longed to wake up. Finally, he opened his eyes. The deckhead above him told him he was on the *Resolute* in his bed, but the sounds of feminine humming told him otherwise.

He tried to sit, but he was surely tied to an anchor, a *painful* anchor as a spasm of torment made his head spin. And why was it so hot in here? He groaned. Footsteps padded toward him, and an angel appeared in his vision.

Nay, not an angel at all, but Lady Fox, her golden hair tumbling over her shoulder and a look of concern in her eyes.

Taking a seat beside him, she grabbed a cool cloth and dabbed it over his forehead.

With great effort, he stayed her hand and moved it aside. "I have no need of your ministrations, my lady." He heaved a sigh. "What are you doing here?"

She sat back with a huff. "I'm watching over you until Moses returns."

"How did I…?" Ah, now he remembered. Memories returned in shattered pieces. His men helping him through the jungle. Moses and Smity aiding him up the rope ladder onto his ship. His cabin. Moses and Omphile hovering over him...and also Lady Fox.

"You got shot. Do you not remember?"

He closed his eyes. He remembered hearing the shot, then the pain, and then naught much after that.

"Who?" he asked.

The lady shook her head. "We do not know. Moses informed me that none of Allard's men were nearby at the time."

"Allard." He moaned. "He got away."

Pain chiseled a line across her brow. "Aye, I'll let your men tell you what happened." She started to rise, but he grabbed her arm.

She looked at him, alarmed.

Ignoring the pain, Cadan pushed himself up to sit and swung his legs over the bed. He rubbed his throbbing head and touched a bandage wrapped around it. No wonder he'd not remembered much.

"You could have left me in the jungle and run." He glanced up at her, searching her eyes. "When Allard and I were fighting."

She made no reply, but her breathing grew heavy again as it usually did when she was frightened.

"You could have also gone with Allard and left me to die," he added. "Why?"

She lifted her chin. "In truth, you seemed the lesser of two evils, Captain."

Humph. He'd been called many things since he took up pirating, but never the lesser of anything.

The room spun and a rare weakness dragged upon him.

She touched his forehead and all but shoved him to his back again. "You're feverish. You need to rest."

Infuriating woman, ordering him about. He was about to sit up again when everything went black.

A slight tapping on his chest aroused him from his slumber. Agony pulsed through his head, but he no longer felt warm. He opened his eyes to find Zada sitting on his bare chest, staring at him with one dark eye. He breathed a sigh. "Hi there, little one. Worried about me?"

No feminine humming met his ears, only the purl of water against the hull, the snap of sails and the creak of a ship at sea. The eerie glow of moonlight drifted through the stern windows, adding slivers of light to the lantern swaying above. How long had he been asleep?

Picking up Zada, he set him aside and sat, placing his feet on the deck. He felt for the bandage around his head. Still there. But he no longer felt hot and weak. He *did* feel hungry.

His cabin door creaked open and in walked Pell. Following behind him, Omphile carried a bowl. Both grinned when they saw him awake.

The savory scent of fish tickled Cadan's nose. "How long?"

"Two days," Pell replied. "I'll summon Gabrielle."

Gabrielle? He used her familiar name?

Omphile sat on the chair beside the bed.

Cadan blinked away the fog in his mind. "Nay, not the woman. Summon Moses."

"In truth, Captain." Pell scratched the stubble on his jaw. "She knows much about doctoring, especially wounds. She's been the one caring for you."

He wanted to curse, to scream. Instead, he settled himself. "You allowed my enemy to care for me?"

"Quit fussing, Captain. Moses kept a keen eye on her." Pell snorted. "You're alive, aren't you? And feeling better?"

He could not deny it. "Moses," he repeated his command, and with a look of reprimand and a nod, Pell left.

Accepting the bowl from Omphile, Cadan raised it to his lips. "How fares the lady?"

Omphile raised a brow. "Hush now. Thought you didn't care 'bout her. An' she fares better dan you, I'd say." She rose. "Don't drink so fast. You haven't eaten in days." She started to leave but then spun to face him. "Gabrielle's been a big hep since you were shot, Captain. She's not your enemy."

He'd castigate the woman for her insolence...*if* he had enough energy. As it was, he allowed her to leave.

By the time Moses and Pell returned, some of Cadan's strength had returned.

"Yer wound is healin' nice, Cap'n," Moses announced after redressing the bandage. "Lucky ye were. The shot jist grazed yer skull." He tugged upon the red scarf always tied about his neck—the one he used to cover the mark of his slavery.

"If only it had knocked some sense into you," Pell added with a grin.

Cadan ignored him. He had too many questions at the moment to deal with Pell's impertinence.

Gripping the back of the chair beside his bed, he pulled himself up, waited a moment to get his balance, then shuffled to his desk.

Or was it his desk? Documents that had once been scattered now sat in a tidy stack. Quill pens and ink bottles lay arranged neatly to the side. His map had been rolled up like a scroll and tied with a red ribbon while other objects, navigation instruments and trinkets, had been organized according to size, weight, and purpose. Glancing over the rest of the cabin, he saw his clothes had been picked up from the deck, and nary a bottle of rum or glass was in sight.

"Scads! Who touched my things? And where is my rum?"

Moses moved to a sideboard cupboard and opened it.

Pell appeared to be having trouble suppressing a grin. "Gabrielle must have cleaned up a bit while you were sleeping."

"Cleaned? She's made a muck of things. How am I supposed to find anything now?" He shifted a stern gaze at Pell. "And why is everyone calling her by her common name!? Am I to discover next that she has taken over the ship?"

Pell chuckled.

Moses set a bottle of rum and a glass on the desk. "I best get back t' work, Cap'n."

"Aye." Cadan popped the cork and poured himself a drink as Moses marched out, no doubt wanting to avoid Cadan's temper.

"That's the name she gave us, Captain." Pell shrugged. "She's harmless. Been helpful, even in her condition." He fingered the wooden cross around his neck.

Cadan slapped the rum to the back of his throat and closed his eyes as the liquor warmed its way down to his belly.

He had more important things to deal with at the moment. "Pray, who is sailing the ship? And do not tell me it is *Gabrielle*."

"Durwin, Smity, and myself." Pell chuckled as he took a seat.

A wave of dizziness struck Cadan, and he leaned back to sit on his desk. "Where are we heading? And what happened to Allard?"

A knock on the door sounded, and Durwin entered with Soot and Smity. "Heard ye were awake, Cap'n."

"We damaged 'is ship pretty good, struck 'im below the waterline." Excitement flashed through Durwin's eyes as he fumbled with his hat. "A few o' 'is shots hit the *Resolute*."

The ship rolled over a wave, only adding to Cadan's nausea. He gripped the edge of his desk. "Damage?"

"Repaired, Cap'n." Smity's eye drifted off to the right. "At least till we can get t' port fer a few supplies."

"And Allard? If his ship was damaged, why didn't you capture him?"

Soot's eyelid began to twitch. "As soon as Allard an' 'is men got on board, they raised all canvas t' the wind an' sped off."

"We could have given them chase, Captain." Pell thumbed the arm of the chair he sat in. "And probably caught him, but with only a quarter of our men, including our captain"—he raised a brow toward Cadan—"we would not have been able to board and finish him off."

"So we sailed back t' the cove," Durwin slid a finger down his hawk nose. "Which is when we found out ye'd been shot."

Pell laughed. "You wouldn't have believed it if you'd seen it. Gabrielle ran out of the jungle hysterically shouting for help, and once we came ashore, she brought us to you."

Why the woman would do that and not try to escape made no sense. Pain throbbed across Cadan's temples, and he sighed, glancing out the windows onto the dark raging sea.

"This was after Allard's ship set sail?"

"Aye."

Cadan shook his head, suspicion rising along with his anger. If all of Allard's men were on his ship, who had shot him?

Chapter 10

Gabrielle once again entered the captain's cabin, but this time, the beast was not unconscious on his bed, weak and feeble. Nay, the man who stood in the sunlight pouring in the stern windows was no sickly creature, but strong, virile, fully conscious…and in control.

He turned to face her, dismissed Moses, and after the door slammed shut, he stared at her for what seemed an eternity. The iguana—what was its name again?—scrambled across the deck, halting before Gabrielle, and reaching down with difficulty, she swept him into her arms.

She thought she heard the captain growl. Hard to tell over the mad dash of water against the hull.

Glancing about the cabin, she was quick to note that all her work had been in vain. Once again, piles of discarded attire—shirts, boots, doublets, and belts—lay across the deck like ant hills. A clutter of parchment, pens, weapons, and trinkets covered every inch of his desk, while bottles of rum, glasses, and plates of half-eaten food lay strewn over sideboard and shelves.

"Why did you not go with your lover?" he asked, bringing her gaze to him. Circling the desk, he grabbed an open bottle.

Petulant cad! "As I have told you, Damien is not my lover."

He stared down at her belly, a sarcastic grin on his face.

Anger boiled within her. "He ravished me, if you must know." She swallowed a burst of terror as memories assaulted her. She hated even the mention of the vile act.

A ray of sunlight piercing the stern windows oscillated over him. He didn't flinch, didn't move a muscle. Yet something softened in his eyes—a flash of sympathy, perhaps? A look that indicated he might believe her? But then his gaze hardened again with disdain.

For both her *and* her child.

The *Resolute* lurched over a wave, and Gabrielle steadied herself lest she fall.

"Yet you willingly went aboard his ship." He poured rum into a glass and downed it in one gulp, staring at her.

How did he know that? Her brow wrinkled. She stroked Zada's head, then set the iguana down. An ache swelled through her feet, and she moved to sit in a chair. "I was deceived."

He cocked his head. "The only women who willingly board a pirate ship are whores."

She'd stand and strike the man if she had the energy. But the babe had been moving about in her womb, causing pain in her back and legs. And he was heavy. 'Twas like carrying a cannon ball around. "Have you summoned me to assail me with insults? Or pray, is there another purpose?"

At this, a small grin appeared on his lips.

Crossing arms over his chest, he leaned back against his desk. "Nay, I wished to thank you for your help in my care."

"A compliment, Captain?" She placed a hand on her chest. "Why, my heart is all aflutter."

He frowned, eyes narrowing as he moved toward her, his black Cordovan boots thumping over the deck. Placing both hands on the arms of her chair, he leaned in until he was but inches from her face.

Her pulse raced, her breath crashed, but she forced herself to return his gaze with brazen indignation. Loose hair hung about his stubbled chin. He smelled of rum and the sea with a hint of spice...nutmeg?

"You will never again touch anything in this cabin without my permission. I've sent men to the gallows for less than what you did here." His rum-drenched breath saturated the air between them as he pushed from the chair and studied her with eyes that shifted from dark brown to green and back again. Only then did she notice that half his right earlobe was missing.

Was he mad? One minute thanking her and the next threatening her life? She would not allow him, or *any* pirate again, to feast on her fear.

"I merely made some sense out of the chaos and squalor you obviously enjoy living amongst." She hated the tremor in her voice.

He flattened his lips, his hand resting on the hilt of his cutlass as if he would thrust her through for her infraction.

"'Tis *my* squalor and it will stay the way I like it."

"Fine. If you wish to live like a pig, what is that to me?" The words flew out of her mouth before she thought of the consequences. This was not a man to be trifled with. There was an intensity about him, a depth, and a restrained power that both frightened and excited her.

His grip on the cutlass tightened and for a moment, she thought she might have finally overstepped the limits of his patience.

But he released a heavy sigh and returned to his desk. "Your tongue, Lady Fox!" he said with both acrimony and a bit of humor.

She gave a nervous laugh. "Lady Fox?"

He ran a hand through his hair, or attempted to, around the bandage. "It suits you." He poured more rum into his glass. "For you are as shrewd as a fox and yet just as deadly."

She gave a ladylike snort. "And you are naught but a heartless kidnapper."

His eyes narrowed as he consumed the rum. Then slamming down the glass, he walked back to the stern windows and stared out upon the sea, aglitter in sunlight.

She feared she'd once again over spoke, inflamed his anger overmuch. Perhaps a change of topic, something that interested him. "The large map on your desk, Captain, the one full of strange markings and signs. What is it for?"

Instead of soothing his temper, he spun around, his face reddening, his eyes aglow. "What did you see?"

"Nothing." Zada shifted by her feet, and she picked him up again, if only for the comfort he brought in the face of this man's anger. "I was merely trying to make conversation."

This seemed to settle him as he moved to his desk to stare down at the map in question, the same one she had rolled up in a scroll but was now laid flat before him. "This map will bring me the wealth, power, and prestige I desire."

From one map? she wanted to say but thought better of it. The man was as volatile as a drunken gunner during battle.

After several seconds, she asked, "What are you to do with me now, Captain?"

"Nothing has changed, my lady. 'Tis obvious Allard harbors some affection for you and his child. Ergo, you will remain on board as bait."

Gabrielle's throat went dry. Was she never to be free again? Foolish girl. *What have I done?* It would do no good to challenge the man. "May I at least have the freedom to wander about the ship? 'Tis not good for me or the babe to be confined all day and night below deck."

He stared at her, fisting hands on his waist. "Very well. But not alone. Omphile can accompany you."

"Thank you, Captain." Setting Zada down once again, she pushed against the chair to rise, ignored the pain in her legs and back, and started for the door. Truly, she didn't wish to burden Omphile further with her care. "Why not have that guard you assigned to me on the island watch over me?" For she'd also seen him in the jungle before Allard had found her. She assumed he'd been the one to go get the captain.

Cadan shook his head, confused. "Once again, you speak nonsense, Lady Fox. I assigned no such guard, save Moses."

How could a woman so ripe with child turn every male eye upon her all at once? Yet this was no ordinary woman. Even Cadan's loathing of her could not prevent him from staring when she emerged from the companionway onto the main deck. With child or not, the woman was a beauty, like a pearl one searches for among the rare queen conch shells, and upon finding it, all other pearls are discarded.

He suddenly regretted granting her permission to come above, for such a distraction would only hinder the crew's tasks. Especially should they encounter an enemy.

Bracing his feet on the heaving quarterdeck, he followed her movements to the larboard railing, Omphile on her heels. It wasn't simply her natural beauty. He'd known women just as lovely. But 'twas the way she held herself like a princess, her courage, her kindness, her wit. Nay, this was not some doxy to be cast from man to man. This woman fit no mold he was aware of. She surprised him, intrigued him. And he wasn't sure he liked that one bit.

If what she'd told him was true, if she'd been ravished, then she had suffered more than most. Yet she was no weak flower to fade at the first strong wind. She possessed more fortitude and courage than most of his crew. All bundled up in a rather alluring package.

"See something you like, Captain?" Pell smiled from the tiller.

Cadan shifted his gaze to the sails above. "Unfurl tops and gallants!" he shouted to Durwin on the main deck, who repeated his orders, sending men leaping into the ratlines.

Blocks creaked and sails rattled as the *Resolute* slung a-weather, her snowy canvas catching the wind in a hearty snap. Close hauled and running northwest on the trade winds, she crested a wave. White foam exploded over her bow and showered the deck with spray.

Cadan gripped the quarterdeck railing and thrust his face into the wind. The scent of salt, sodden wood, and freedom blasted over him as he gazed over the turquoise sea, rippling gold beneath the noon sun. Freedom. Freedom and power, two things he had lacked most of his life. But no more.

Feminine laughter sprinkled the air, and his gaze unavoidably landed again on Lady Fox. Wind blew her flaxen hair behind her as she stared over the waves, not the least bit bothered by the heave of the ship. Oddly, Soot ambled over to speak to her. What could be the master gunner's purpose?

"Where are we heading again, Captain?" Pell asked.

"Nevis. There's something I need to retrieve there, and we need supplies." Shielding his eyes, he shouted aloft, "Haul taut! Sheet home to weather. Hoist away the topsail."

But his eyes were on the lady.

Gabrielle was not immune to the salacious glances of lusty pirates. She'd grown accustomed to them on Allard's ship, even endured a few on her father's. But for some reason when she stepped onto the main deck of the *Resolute,* she felt like a thousand arrows pierced her from all directions. Surely these men must be starved of female affection to be so interested in a woman with a belly as large as a whale.

"Jist ignore dem," Omphile said as she gripped the railing beside her. "Dey'll do nothin' against de Captain's orders."

Sunlight glinted white over the mulatto's teeth and glittered over her ebony skin.

"Is that why you feel safe?" The ship rolled over a wave, and Gabrielle tightened her grip on the railing.

Omphile's gaze wandered across the deck to Moses. She smiled. "Yes. An' I have a protector."

"Ah, Moses." Gabrielle nodded. "He's sweet on you, eh?"

"I dunno 'bout dat, Miss, but seems de crew thinks so, an' dat be enuf to keep 'em at bay."

Gabrielle smiled and shifted her gaze to the sparkling turquoise waters. Would that she had a champion on board. Would that she'd had one on Allard's ship. Would that God had not abandoned her so quickly. She drew a deep breath of the salty sea air, so familiar to her. In truth, she knew naught else but the smell of the sea and the heave of the deck beneath her, having been born and raised aboard the *Redemption.*

Deep sorrow threatened to flood her eyes with tears. She missed her father and mother, her sister and brother. What were they doing? Where were they sailing? Were they safe? Did they think of her at all?

The babe kicked—hard! Gabrielle pressed a hand over her belly, struggling to breathe. He was a strong one, a real fighter. He'd need to be in order to survive this world.

Wind blasted over her, spinning her hair and cooling the perspiration on her neck and chest. She closed her eyes for a moment, pretending she was standing on the *Redemption*, safe in her father's arms.

"'Ello, Miss."

The scratchy voice snapped Gabrielle from her fantasy, and she opened her eyes to see the man the captain called Soot standing beside her.

"Good day to you, Mr. Soot," she responded, gauging the man for any nefarious intent.

But he wore a kind expression beneath his mass of red, stringy hair.

"I want t' thank ye agin fer savin' me rabbit, Hellfire, on the island. Not like 'er t' run off like that."

"My pleasure. She's quite friendly. Nor skittish like most rabbits."

"Naw, she's been on a pirate ship 'er whole life." Soot placed arms on the railing and gazed over the sea.

The man was not much taller than she, but wide as a barrel. He smelled of gunpowder and sweat, but there was a kindness in his blue eyes. Still, all manner of weapons were stuffed in his baldric and hooked on belts strapped about him. She'd learned long ago never to trust a man who made his living thieving on the seas. She glanced over at Omphile, but the woman was whispering with Moses, who had joined her.

"How did you come to sail with the captain?" Gabrielle faced Soot again. A wave splashed against the hull, showering her with sea spray. Ah, but it felt wonderful on her hot skin.

"That'd be a long tale, Miss." He scratched his neck beneath a filthy blue bandana.

Gabrielle glanced over her shoulder at the quarterdeck and found the captain's gaze focused on her. Uneasy beneath his scrutiny, she faced the sea once again. "I have all day, Mr. Soot. I'd love to hear it."

He chuckled. "I'll give ye the jist of it, Miss. I am a deserter from the royal navy. Should they find me, I'll be hung fer sure. The captain brought me on board, made me master gunner, an' keeps me safe from capture."

Gabrielle huffed. The captain seemed in the business of rescuing the downtrodden. "May I ask why you deserted?"

He shook his head. "Weren't the life fer me. Too strict. Pure slavery it were fer most seaman."

"What position did you hold?"

"Gunner."

Shielding her eyes from the sun, Gabrielle smiled. "I'm impressed, Mr. Soot. Many able seamen never move up in rank to petty officer. Must have taken you awhile."

"Four years at sea." His right eye began to twitch, and he pressed a thumb to it. "Me parents were so proud o' me. Now I'm disgraced."

Sails thundered above, drawing Gabrielle's gaze to the men in the yards. "Where are you from?"

"Dartmouth. They was good people. Godly people. Raised me right, but I've been nothin' but heartache fer 'em since birth. In an' out of trouble. They finally sent me to sea to straighten me out, an' I let them down again." He frowned and rubbed the back of his neck.

Gabrielle could relate. Her parents had been the best parents anyone could want. They'd raised her right, but she was the one who had gone astray. "Perhaps there are some of us who are destined to be the black sheep of our families, Mr. Soot."

He smiled and nodded. "Aye, I figure both my parents an' God are done wit' me now."

Odd that she had more in common with this master gunner on board a pirate ship than most people she met.

He glanced toward the quarterdeck. "But the captain gave me purpose again. Had faith in me."

"Soot!" The captain's shout stiffened the man, and he tipped his fingers upon his forehead at Gabrielle and scampered off.

She would not grant Cadan the privilege of gazing his way. Instead, she watched Soot leap upon the foredeck and speak to a pirate cleaning one of the carronades.

"Watch your Luff, Mr. Pell," the captain shouted then added, "Lay aloft and loose the mainsail!"

Lazy-eyed Smity marched across the deck, shouting orders to the men in the tops to adjust sail. His gaze focused back on the captain, and for a brief second, Gabrielle thought she saw hatred in his narrowed eyes. But how could that be? From what she was seeing, Captain Hayes inspired naught but loyalty among his crew.

Chapter 11

A loud rap sounded on the door to Gabrielle's cabin, jarring her from her rest. Not that she was able to sleep with her babe doing flips in her belly and her heart doing flips in her chest. Childbearing and fear made horrid bedfellows. After two hours above deck trying to balance on a heaving ship, her feet had swollen to the size of melons, and every muscle in her back ached. Besides, she'd grown weary of the lecherous stares of the crew—including the captain's.

Omphile rose from the chair beside the bed, where she'd been reading, and slowly opened the door. Moses slipped inside, though Gabrielle doubted the large man slipped anywhere. After smiling at Omphile, he nodded toward Gabrielle.

"The cap'n wants you to join 'im an' 'is officers for dinner in 'is cabin at sunset, Miss."

What? Surely she was hearing things. Reaching for Omphile's hand, she allowed the woman to help her to sit. "Why?" She rubbed her temples where an ache had formed. "What could he possibly want?"

Moses shrugged. "Dat's all 'e said."

"It'll be alright, Miss, you'll see." Omphile patted her leg. "We'll get you cleaned up an' I'll fetch another one o' my gowns. I knows jist de one."

"I care not for my appearance!" Gabrielle snapped, instantly regretting her tone. "Forgive me, Omphile. I know you're only trying to help."

The mulatto gave a gentle smile. "Dat's all right, Child. I knows you are scared."

Gabrielle stared up at Moses. No way she could stand, for the man consumed the entire cabin. "You may tell Captain Hayes that I decline his invitation."

Moses scrunched his nose as if he smelled something foul. "I would not say dat, Miss, if I was you."

"Then tell him I'm not feeling well."

Moses's expression remained stoic, though his eyes drifted to Omphile and then to the book still in her hands. Sunlight angled in through the window and landed on a mark on his neck, peeking above his ever-present scarf. A brand? Aye, it had to be, for no doubt Moses had once been a slave. She tried not to stare, but it looked like a lion in the center of a shield.

"Do you have time now?" Omphile asked him, to which he nodded, the first flicker of excitement crossing his eyes.

Gabrielle stared between them. "Time for what?"

Omphile bit her lip and studied Gabrielle. "Don't tell no one, but I's teaching Moses to read."

Gabrielle's brows shot up. "Indeed? And where did *you* learn such a skill?"

"My last benefactor, afore he became violent, taught me. Wanted an educated servant to hep run his estate."

The deck shifted and Moses put a hand on the bulkhead.

"I won't say a word. I think it's marvelous." Gabrielle's thoughts drifted to Jackson, a freed slave on her father's ship. Her mother had taught him to read, and it had opened up the world to him. Still, some of the crew had protested against a Negro being educated. "Surely, this does not please some of the pirates."

"Which is why I teach him in private." Omphile shared a loving glance with Moses.

"Stay here, then." Gabrielle said. "I can rest while you read."

Moses offered a rare smile and managed to lower himself to the floor as Omphile opened the book.

Hence, Gabrielle lay back down and slowly drifted to sleep to the words of *The Pilgrim's Progress*.

Before the lady even arrived, Cadan was full of rage. First of all, how dare she deny his invitation as if she were some princess sitting in her palace and he a mere courtier? He had put a quick end to that by threatening her should she not make an appearance. Now, she was late. *Very* late. And his men were getting deep in their cups awaiting her arrival. He'd throw himself to the devil before he wasted any more time waiting for a female.

Sipping his port, Cadan raised his hand for the two pirates standing off to the side to fetch the food from the galley when the door creaked open and in strode Lady Fox herself—more like waddled—one hand on her back and one hand at her throat as if the thought of having dinner with him was already making her nauseous. Her lustrous blue eyes glanced over each of his crew sitting at the table, then at the table itself, set with pewter plates, silverware, fine glassware, and flickering candles, and finally onto him before she proceeded to the empty chair to his right.

She wore a faded but clean gown of purple trimmed in lace, that spread out from her waist over her enormous belly. The curves of her breasts peeked over a tight bodice, and he found himself wondering what her figure looked like before…Scads! What was he thinking?

Pell rose from his seat and pulled out her chair, which earned him a smile. A twinge of envy caused Cadan to pour more port into his glass.

"Forgive my tardiness, gentlemen," she said with the grace of a woman attending a soiree. "I fear my condition oft slows me down."

His men stared at her, confused. No doubt they'd had little dealings with genteel ladies.

Cadan had. And he'd vowed never again to be fooled by the polished, mannerly exterior that so oft hid a deceptive, cruel interior. After sending his men to bring the food, he introduced his crew to her. Smity, his boson, Durwin, his first mate, Pell, his quartermaster, Soot his master gunner with Hellfire in his arms, and Moses, his carpenter and surgeon.

The lady nodded and smiled at each one, though he could tell from her expression, she'd rather be anywhere but here.

Why had he invited her? He sipped his drink as two of his men brought in platters of food and set them on the table—fresh biscuits, peas, rice, and a plate of roasted fish. The savory scents moistened his mouth, but he found he had little appetite.

He had been trained by his mother and father to treat women well, to honor the weaker sex. Surely that was the cause of his present madness. Or perhaps 'twas her little snooty nose she kept lifting in the air that made him want to prove to her that he and his crew were not savages.

There was, however, the slight possibility that she had been ravished, in which case, she deserved more care than he'd thus far shown her.

The ship crested a wave, shifting plates over the table and serenading them with the creak and groan of its timbers.

His men leapt upon the food like starving pigs at a trough, grabbing biscuits, shoving spoonfuls of peas onto their plates and making a muck of things in the process. It never bothered Cadan before, but as he watched Lady Fox cringe at the display, he hated the flush of embarrassment that passed through him.

Only Pell waited for the initial onslaught to cease before he served himself, and Cadan always wondered if the man was praying a blessing over the food.

The preacher passed Lady Fox a bowl of steaming rice, and after she declined, he handed it to Cadan. Grabbing it, he plopped a spoonful onto her plate.

"Eat," he ordered her. "Omphile is quite a good cook."

"I told you, Captain, I was not feeling well." She gave him a tight smile. "Yet you insisted on my coming or, how shall I put it, I would suffer consequences too harsh for a lady to bear."

Pell's chuckle was silenced with one look from Cadan, while in between bites, Smity eyed her with disdain from across the table.

The port spread a comfortable haze through his thoughts. "And now I insist you eat. We can't have any harm come to your child, can we?"

Arrows shot from her eyes and her breathing increased, but she accepted a platter of fish from Pell and eased a small piece of roasted squid onto her plate.

"Is that all you care about, Captain? Your revenge? What exactly did Allard do to you to warrant such ill treatment of an innocent babe?"

Both her sharp tone and the pointed question snapped an instant silence over the cabin as all eyes shifted to Cadan.

Gabrielle had eaten many a meal with pirates on her father's ship. Never had she eaten with such begrimed, uncouth animals. Well, save for Pell and perhaps Soot, both of whom seemed to have retained a smidgen of manners from their youth. The captain drank his dinner, and despite his insistence on her eating, he barely touched his meal.

Now, at her question, his jaw tightened, his eyes darkened, and a scowl marred his lips. He stretched his fingers, then balled them into a fist, then stretched, then balled. Gabrielle's stomach twisted into a similar knot. Surely, he would do her no harm in front of his men.

Finally, he leaned back in his chair. "Any child of Allard's is naught but a spawn of hell."

His sharp words cut her deeply, igniting her fear. She'd never seen such hatred in a man's eyes. Tearing her gaze from his, she began fidgeting with her silverware, lining it up perfectly beside her plate, then easing her glass to the top right corner of her knife. 'Twas the only thing she could think to do that would bring some comfort in this mayhem.

The crew started eating again, slapping their lips and tongues, as if their captain had not just threatened to kill an innocent babe.

"You're frightening the lady." Pell gave a look of censure to the captain. "Let us enjoy the meal and this rare female company."

"Aye, aye," Durwin added, smiling at her, as did Moses and Soot. All save Smity. Why the man still hated her, she couldn't say.

Finally, the lines on the captain's face faded, and he exhaled a deep breath as if ridding himself of whatever demon had taken him over. Demon, indeed. In truth, the entire crew seemed possessed.

Hoping to settle her own nerves, she turned to Mr. Pell. "You are the quartermaster?" Her gaze was immediately drawn to the wooden cross around his neck. Odd.

"I am, Miss." Smiling, he bit into a piece of crusty bread.

"How long have you been sailing?"

Surprise lit his face, and he shook his head. "A few years with the captain. Off and on my whole life."

"Don't let 'im fool ye. He's a preacher," Durwin said, spitting out food in the process.

A preacher?

"Not anymore," Pell said sharply.

"Well, ye act like one," Smity added. "Steerin' clear o' wenches an' drink whene'er we go ashore."

Preacher or not, perhaps the man had a shred of honor left within him. "Noble pursuits," Gabrielle interjected, "and no doubt you do not kidnap women with child either, Mr. Pell." She cast a spiced look at the captain.

Laughter roared over the table. All save the captain, who sat back in his chair, hazel eyes smoldering.

She flattened her lips and faced Pell. "What changed your course in life, Mr. Pell?"

He shoveled in another bite of food, refusing to answer.

Soot fed Hellfire a handful of peas. "His wife an' child died."

"'Tis not for you to say!" Pell shot back. "Nor for any to mention." The authority in his voice stilled them all. The man held some power here, even with the captain, 'twould seem, who allowed him some measure of freedom with his tongue. Short cropped light hair, he stood nearly as tall as Captain Hayes, yet had to be at least ten to fifteen years older. With his influence, he might be an ally of hers.

Which was why, despite the captain's threat, she had finally conceded to come, to mayhap discover a friend aboard this ship of fools.

"I'm sorry," she said as the deck slanted to larboard. Her glass of what had to be grog started to slide, and she steadied it.

Pell glanced at the captain. "I learned the hard way that God doesn't honor His promises."

Gabrielle swallowed. She quite agreed. At least not to *all* His children. Grabbing her fork, she tasted the squid. A fishy but pleasant flavor filled her mouth, and she eagerly took another bite, noting the captain's eyes were upon her.

A breeze swept in through the stern windows, flickering the candles and casting ghoulish shadows over the bulkhead. *God has favorites.* Gabrielle glanced behind her, seeking the source of the words, but no one was there.

"Tell 'er 'bout how ye an' the cap'n took t' swords," Durwin gestured to Pell with his fork.

Swords? Gabrielle raised her brows.

Pell chuckled. "Aye." He shared a glance with Cadan. "I was working on a merchant ship when the *Resolute* came upon us fast, all guns blazing. We were quickly overtaken, and Cadan and his men came leaping over the bulwarks to board us."

Cadan smiled. "You were quite the swordsman, Pell. For a preacher."

"Preacher or not, I almost beat you." Pell winked.

"Your execution was exemplary, I'll grant you. But in the end"—Cadan raised one brow—"not enough."

Silence invaded the room, save for the crash of water against the hull and the slurp and slap of the men eating.

"What happened?" Gabrielle finally asked.

Pell plopped a spoonful of rice in his mouth and nodded toward Cadan. "He gave me an offer I could not refuse. Be stranded on an island or become his new quartermaster."

Cadan lifted his glass toward Pell. "You chose wisely. For both of us."

There could be no denying the friendship that existed between the two men. Gabrielle tucked away the information for later use should the need arise. She looked over at Durwin. "I know your story, Mr. Durwin. You were in the navy, correct?"

Nodding, Durwin ran a hand beneath his nose and began piling more food on his plate.

Soot snickered. "Poor Durwin were sich an addle-brained boosy, he were tossed from the royal navy!"

Slamming down the spoon, Durwin leapt to his feet, drew his blade, and leveled the tip at Soot's rabbit. "Take that back, or I'll slit the vermin's throat!"

The squid soured in Gabrielle's stomach. Not that she hadn't seen pirates threaten each other over nothing, but carrying a child in her womb seemed to heighten her fears over everything.

Soot remained still, eyes slits of anger, drawing his pet closer to his chest.

"Enough!" Cadan shouted. "We have a guest. Can you not for one meal behave as though you were not born and bred in a brothel!?"

Durwin's blade remained. "Make 'im take it back, Cap'n."

"Burn it, Durwin." Soot gave a humorless snarl. "You cut Hellfire, an' ye'll be the one gutted."

Cadan rose, pushing back his chair. "I said enough! Sheath your blade at once, Durwin."

Pell eyed the men with caution, Smity grinned as if enjoying the entertainment, while Moses stood, hand on his own blade, in case his captain needed him.

Finally, Durwin withdrew his blade and slammed it into the sheath with a metallic scrape.

Pressing a hand on her churning stomach, Gabrielle attempted to settle her nerves. She should leave, but she was learning so much about these men and their captain. "Did you not tell me, Mr. Soot, that you deserted the navy? Why then so much anger toward Mr. Durwin?"

"Aye. Left o' me own accord, Miss. Not tossed." He fired a look of hate toward Durwin.

Gabrielle sipped her drink. Grog, a mixture of mostly water with a small portion of rum. Perhaps it would aid in settling her nerves. She glanced around the table at the pirates who were either shoving food into their mouths or pouring more rum into their cups. All save Moses who merely stared at his half-eaten plate of food, arms crossed over his chest.

"Moses, and pray tell, what is your story?"

His eyes shot to the captain with a smile. "Nothin' as excitin' as dese, Miss. De Cap'n bought me at a slave auction on Saint Lucia. Set me free an' gave me a position on de *Resolute* if I wanted it."

She couldn't help but glance at the captain. Such an enigma. So cruel to her, so filled with hate toward Allard, but kind to so many others.

His eyes met hers and for a brief second, she saw them soften, perhaps even a hint of affection—or mayhap sympathy in them. Uncomfortable beneath his gaze, she looked away.

"And you, Mr. Smity?" She dared ask the man who had not stopped scowling at her the entire dinner.

She wondered at the scars on the right side of his face and his wandering eye. She wondered at the pearl in his right ear, but mostly she wondered at the hatred radiating off him like heat from a furnace.

Pell sipped his grog. "Smity sailed with the great pirate captain, Avery, didn't you, Smity?"

For the first time since she'd known him, a tiny smile curved his lips. "I did. A great pirate he were too. Got us a fair amount o' treasure, says I. Went missing jist last year afore I met up wi' Cap'n Hayes."

"And let me guess," Gabrielle said. "Captain Hayes found you starving at some wayward port and offered you fame and fortune aboard his ship."

Smity glared at her. "Nay. I approached 'im on St. Kitts. 'Eard he were a fair captain who kept 'is crew in coin." He rubbed the scars on his face and never once made eye contact with the captain.

In truth, he rarely looked at Cadan, and when he did, Gabrielle sensed his disdain. She wanted to ask about his scars but thought better of it. "And your family, Sir?"

He snorted in disgust and sat back in his chair, his left eye a blade slicing through her while his right one wandered off to the side. "Me mother were a whore, me father a seaman. As soon as she gave birth t' me, she tossed me in the gutter."

Despite the man's hostility, a sudden sorrow crept over her. She'd been privileged to have two parents who had loved and cared for her. It appeared that no one here, save perhaps Soot, had that same blessed childhood. Even Omphile had shared her horrid upbringing. Why then did Gabrielle find herself in such a dire situation? Why had the God she believed in and followed since birth allowed such cruelty? Omphile had said that God was good and faithful. Perhaps she'd find a way to ask Mr. Pell. He'd been a preacher, after all.

The men continued pouring rum as if it were water and guzzling it down just as fast. All coherent conversation ended, replaced with slurred words, insults, salacious comments about women they'd known, ostentatious boasts, and at one point, Smity and Soot drew knives.

All the while the captain sat back watching as if this were a normal occurrence at mealtime.

Gabrielle lost what little appetite she had and sought an opportunity to excuse herself. From the looks in the pirates' eyes, she might well become the dessert, ripe with child or not.

She was about to do just that when the iguana dropped from the ceiling onto the table and began hobbling across the now mostly empty platters and bowls. Hellfire leapt from Soot's lap and took chase after the lizard, unending bowls, tipping over glasses, and splattering food scraps over the pirates.

Horrified, Gabrielle struggled to rise and back away before Zada, now covered in rice and fish broth, slithered onto her lap. Too late. He landed on her chest, then crawled around her shoulders, yanking at her pinned-up curls. The rabbit followed.

She caught her by her hind feet and gripped her tightly as Zada dropped to the deck with a plop and scrambled under the captain's bed.

Restraining the demon rabbit tightly in her arms, Gabrielle rose and glanced around the table. Both Pell and the Captain stood as well.

"Well, gentlemen, I thank you for a most entertaining evening," she said politely.

At this, the men laughed so loud, it rattled the silverware. All save the captain. Scowling, he ordered everyone to leave. *Thank heavens*! She skirted the table to return Hellfire to his owner when the captain's slurred command rang through the room. "Not you. Stay, my lady."

Chapter 12

Rising with difficulty, Cadan ordered his raucous crew to leave. He'd had enough of their besotted blustering and raucous behavior for one night. Despite her attempts to act unruffled, 'twas obvious Lady Fox had her fill as well.

"Stay, my lady," he ordered her as she handed the rabbit back to Soot and started to follow the men out.

Halting, she faced him. "Is that a command, Captain? Or a wish?"

Stopping at the doorway, Pell gave Cadan a look of disapproval as if to say *you're besotted and better do the lady no harm.*

"Close the door, Pell." Cadan brooked no argument. Not this night.

Frowning, the man obeyed.

The door slammed with a thud that pounded Cadan's head.

"Both," he answered the lady.

"Regardless, I see I have no choice." She released a sigh and stared at him, unflinching.

Pell was right about one thing. Cadan had consumed too much to drink. The lovely Lady Fox swayed in his vision. Or was that the ship moving? He couldn't tell.

Blinking, he lumbered to the stern windows and stared out. The inky sea rose and fell in his vision while a sprinkling of stars winked at him from the night sky. The evening had not gone as expected. For some reason, his crew behaved even more barbarically than usual. Why, then, had he asked her to stay? He couldn't remember, save that he found her company intriguing. She fascinated him. A highborn lady who did not swoon, nor even cower, in the presence of such vulgar behavior. A lady who drew the affection of both lizards and rabbits. A woman who, if she had been ravished, did not reveal any terror at finding herself alone with a pirate captain in his cabin.

Not like any woman he'd known.

Several minutes passed in which only the whistle of wind against windows and the splash of water against the stern could be heard.

"Seems you are in the business of rescuing misfits, Captain. To procure their loyalty perhaps?" Her sweet voice, so sharp with sarcasm, made him smile. Not that he would allow her to see it.

"Has it not worked, Lady Fox?"

"Aye, perhaps. All save for Smity."

At this, he turned to face her, arms crossed over his chest. "Scads! Smity's as loyal as any of them."

"Is he?" She moved to the table and began picking up the bowls that had been overturned by Zada and Hellfire. "He bears no affection for you, Captain. The look in his one eye betrays him."

Cadan rubbed the stubble on his chin. "He's a mean cur, I'll grant you, but he's more than proven himself in the year he's been sailing with me."

She began stacking empty plates atop each other. Flickering candlelight sent shimmering waves over her golden hair pinned up behind her, though a few lustrous curls, released by Zada, dangled about her neck. Splotches of broth stained her gown, and once again shame struck him hard in the gut. What a disaster the night had been.

"How did he come by those scars on his face and his injured eye?" she asked. "Was it with Avery?"

"My men will clean up the mess, my lady. Sit."

Eyes of ice sliced through him for but a moment before she returned to her task.

Groaning, Cadan grabbed a bottle of rum from the table and took a swig, then leaned back onto the stern seat, angry at her defiance, but too besotted to act upon it. "Nay, Smity suffered injuries from an incident aboard the *Resolute*."

At this, she looked up. "Indeed?"

Guilt knifed Cadan with a dozen wounds. He'd gone over the event a thousand times in his mind, wondering how he could have done things differently. Sipping the rum, he welcomed the numbing haze spreading across his mind and heart. "We were at battle with a French merchantman," he began. "A tough, seaworthy captain who refused to give up." Cadan shook his head, staring out over the sea. "We'd taken a couple of good blows to our mainmast, our head braces were shot away; the fore topmasts were gone. Men were injured. Everything was in chaos. Even though it wasn't his job, I sent Smity down for more gunpowder." He hesitated, trying to retrieve the memories of that day he'd attempted to bury, but they were as foggy as his mind at the moment.

"And?" He heard her say.

He shook his head. "A shot set the gunpowder ablaze. Smity caught fire. It took ten men to put out the flames." All because Cadan had miscalculated the enemy's range and skill.

"Ah, so he blames you?"

Cadan spun around to find her standing before the table, a plate in hand, a look of genuine concern on her pretty face.

"Nay. Could have happened to anyone, he told me."

One of her beautiful eyebrows rose. "I wouldn't be so sure, Captain. Was it not one of your own who shot you on the island?"

There was no censure in her gaze, no anger, no fear…to what purpose would she mention her suspicions of Smity? "You wish to cause division among my crew, Lady Fox," he hissed. "You must take me for a fool."

With a heavy sigh, she continued cleaning the table, stacking plates, picking up platters, wiping the mess with serviettes.

Rising, Cadan slammed down his bottle, circled the table—with difficulty he might add, for the cabin started to spin—and grabbed her wrist before she could retreat from him.

Her breath caught short.

"Be still, my lady," he ordered a bit too sharply. "Cease this foolish cleaning."

She stared at him, her eyes shifting between his, her chest rising and falling rapidly. He stood so close, he could feel her breath on his chin and smell her sweet scent of sunshine and rose.

The shock in her gaze changed to fear but finally settled upon anger as he continued his grip around her wrist.

In truth, he didn't want to let her go. Every inch of his body came alive at her touch, at her closeness, alive like he'd never known before. And he hated himself for it. She was everything he loathed in a woman.

Not to mention she carried his enemy's child.

Flames shot from her eyes. She tried to shake off his hold. He held her firm for a moment longer if only to prove his command over her, that he would have his way whene'er he wished. Finally, he led her to a chair and released her. "Sit."

Pressing a hand on her back, she eased onto it, clearly distraught by the encounter. "I beg you, Captain. Allow me to leave."

Gabrielle did not look at him, could not look into those eyes that so often changed from brown to green when he was overwrought, for what she saw past the glaze of alcohol disturbed her more than anything. Sorrow, intense, deep sorrow and pain, the depth of which she could not fathom.

And yet, a spark…a spark of something else that unnerved her, sent a shiver down her, and not in a bad way.

That was before the hatred returned.

She rubbed her wrist where he'd held her, if only to inspire guilt in the man, *if* he possessed the ability to feel such an emotion. For he hadn't hurt her. Even when she'd tugged from him, he'd not squeezed too tightly.

Men. Physically superior to be sure. Yet rather than use their God-given strength to protect, most used it to control, to harm, to subjugate. This man was no different. In truth, she wondered if the only reason he hadn't had his way with her was due to the child in her belly.

"Why do you hate me so, Captain? Is it only for the babe I carry, or do you have some other maniacal reason?" The words fired out before she remembered this volatile man was benumbed with alcohol, and she'd learned with Damien 'twas always best to keep one's tongue when spirits were active.

He huffed, started to walk, but stumbled slightly. Then shoving plates and cups aside, he sat on the table, hoisted his legs onto a chair and leaned forward, staring at the deck as if fascinated by the deep rivets in the wood.

She waited, listening to the wash of water against the hull and the creak of wood. Above deck, one of the pirates played a fiddle, a sad tune that seemed to fit the mood that had flooded the cabin.

"Did Allard have something to do with the stripes on your back?" she dared ask.

His gaze lifted to hers. A strand of his dark hair fell across his cheek, and he eased it behind his ear—the one missing half the lobe. He pressed it in passing. "Aye, though not directly. 'Twas his doing that sent me to Barbados as a prisoner-slave."

"For what crime?"

He gave a sad laugh and plunged a hand through his hair. "Suspicion of treason."

Shock sped through Gabrielle. "Suspicion?"

"Her word against mine."

"Her?"

His eyes narrowed. "Does your tongue never rest, Lady Fox?"

Gabrielle bit her lip and glanced over the cabin. The heap of dirty dishes and food-splattered table beckoned to her. Sorting things, cleaning things, soothed her nerves, set life in order, as much as was in her power to do so.

He grabbed a nearby bottle and drew it to his lips. If she was lucky, he'd pass out. If she wasn't lucky, the rum may loosen what moral restrictions restrained him from taking liberties with a woman with child. "Did you?"

"Did I what?"

"Commit treason."

His lips slanted. "Nay."

The baby kicked, and Gabrielle rubbed her belly, desperate to know this man's full story. She might not have another chance to be alone with him so besotted. Yet she walked a fine line between his rage and lust.

"How long were you a prisoner?"

"Five years." He slammed the bottle down and kicked out the chair, leaping to his feet. "Five years of hell."

"But you paid the price and were set free."

He spun to face her, chuckling. "Nay, my love. I escaped."

Again, this man shocked her. Escaping from a Barbados prison was no easy task. "And you became a pirate."

"Not just any pirate, Lady Fox. One of the best who e'er sailed the Caribbean." He crossed arms over his chest and raised his chin. The bombastic stance, however, immediately faded as the deck tilted, and he stumbled to the side.

She smiled. He'd said a woman betrayed him, but what did that have to do with Allard? "So, 'twas Allard who falsely accused you. 'Tis why you hate him so."

"He and my…" He halted and the muscles in his jaw bunched as the all-familiar loathing knotted his face.

"My?" But she already guessed the answer. Hadn't Allard mentioned the captain's wife in their exchange on the island? Something about leaving her bed? She'd forgotten that until now. Forgotten he was married.

Fingering his clipped earlobe once again, a fieriness rose up in him that defied his inebriated state, and picking up a bottle, he threw it across the cabin. It crashed onto the bulkhead and shattered onto the deck.

Gabrielle's heart lurched into her throat, and she pressed a hand to her chest. She'd been at the brunt end of Damien's temper, and she'd rather die than be at the brunt end of this man's. Best to either stop speaking or change the subject.

Or wait until he fell to the deck, unconscious.

For now, she waited for his temper to cool, studying him as he stood, arms fisted at his waist, staring at the mess he'd made. Or mayhap not staring at anything in particular as memories of his past further inflamed him.

Gabrielle glanced at the door. Could she slip out without his notice?

Nay. He faced her, his chest rising and falling, his hair dangling about his face. "She was highborn, a proper lady like you." He spat the words *proper lady* with such contempt Gabrielle could almost touch the hate floating in a dark cloud her way. So, that was the reason he loathed her so. 'Twas her voice, words, and mannerisms that gave away her status. If the man knew she was the daughter of an earl, he may have no qualms about tossing her and her babe overboard on the spot.

Rubbing his forehead, he seemed to regret revealing that fact as he made his way to a chair, plopped into it, and dropped his head into his hands.

Best to shift his thoughts from the cause of his fury. "May I ask where we are going, Captain?"

He huffed but did not look up. "To Nevis for supplies and a clue."

*A clue to wha*t? His elusive treasure no doubt.

"I implore you, Captain. Leave me ashore. As I said, Allard has no interest in me or his child."

He sat back, a grin on his face as he eyed her up and down a bit too freely. "You think your lover will give up? Nay. Not when he knows I have you and his babe."

Gabrielle straightened her spine and tightened her tone. "He is not my lover. And 'twas obvious to even an ant on that island that Damien cared not a whit for me or his child."

His lips slanted. "Mayhap not, Lady Fox. But he cares a great deal that 'tis *I* who have you both and not him. You must consider the male pride."

"I consider the whole lot of you buffoons."

A deep chuckle bubbled up from his chest as he struggled to rise and stumbled to the table for another sip of rum. "I ought to flog you for your sharp tongue, my lady."

From the slur of his words and the clumsiness of his motion, Gabrielle knew 'twas the best time to make her exit. Surely in his condition, he'd be unable to stop her.

Pushing against the chair with one hand and with the other holding her belly, she rose as gracefully as she could and began inching her way toward the door.

Grabbing a bottle, he hoisted it to his lips, but then lowered it back to the table before he took a sip.

Gabrielle took another step, keeping her eyes upon him.

Even in his condition, he was like a panther ready to strike. Standing to his full height, he snapped back his hair and seemed to be having trouble keeping his balance on the tilting deck.

Gabrielle moved closer to the door.

"Allard will pay for what he has done," he ground out. "And I shall join the ranks of the rich and powerful."

To whom was he making this grand announcement? Perhaps to no one in particular. Which is what she was counting on as, heart racing, she took the final step to the door and gripped the handle.

He was on her in seconds. His grip around her arm tight, his rum-laced breath suffocating her. He dragged her back into the cabin.

Terror pulsed through every nerve.

She pushed from him, attempting to jerk her arm from his grasp.

"Nay, Lady Mi—" he slurred out before he fell against her, shoving her back with the weight of a sack of sodden rice. Struggling to keep her balance, she slammed against the bulkhead, his unconscious body pressing against her. An ache welled up in her belly. His face dove, or rather sunk, against her breasts, his thick chest an anvil keeping her pinned.

"How dare you?" She attempted to scream but instead gasped for the air that was being squeezed from her lungs.

Finally, gathering her strength, she managed to shove him away. He dropped to the deck like the aforementioned sack of rice. Right beside his bed.

"Besotted fool."

Hand to her chest to still her thrashing heart, she stared at him. Even unconscious, there was a danger about him, an anger, nay, a fury that if left unchecked, would eventually destroy him.

She understood fury. She understood betrayal. She understood a life that had given naught but pain and heartache.

A surge of sudden pity caught her off guard. Now, she knew she'd gone mad. Pity for this monster?

She kicked his leg to make sure he was not awake, then grabbed a blanket from his bed and gently laid it atop him. Why, she could not say. Perhaps because they had both suffered a great deal in this pathetic life. She turned to leave. The pirate who had guarded her before stood in the corner. Or did he? She rubbed her eyes, and he was gone.

Chapter 13

A broadside fired in Cadan's head. *Boom boom boom!* Each explosion sent ripples of pain through every inch of his body. His pulse raced. His mind spun. Were they at battle? If so, he must get to the quarterdeck at once.

But he couldn't move.

The booming started again. He tried to speak, but his mouth was a desert, his lips so parched, he couldn't open them.

The deck swayed beneath him, the water gently purled against the hull. No shouts or cries or thundering footsteps of dashing pirates met his ears. No, not a battle. A war.

In his body.

He'd drank too much. Again.

He moved his hand. His fingers met the hard deck. Not his bed. With great effort, he pried open his eyes, blinked, and finally his cabin came into focus. Sunlight speared through the stern windows, bouncing circles of light up and down over the bulkhead. How long had he been out?

With great difficulty, he pushed to sit. A blanket fell from him onto the deck. *Blanket?*

Lady Fox.

Ignoring his nausea and pounding head, he stood, caught his balance on the pitching deck, and stumbled to the table in search of rum—the only antidote for the agony wracking his body. His glance took in the dirty plates all stacked neatly together, the silverware sorted by knives, forks and spoons, and the empty glasses arranged by size standing in a row. He smiled. The lady who possessed the manners and speech of nobility worked as efficiently as any servant. He could make no sense of it.

A knock on his door sent throbbing through his head. "Enter and be quiet about it!" Even his own shout caused a thousand knives to pierce his brain. His stomach revolted, and he plunged into a chair before he lost what was left of last night's repast.

Pell stood before him, a look of castigation on his face. "You're needed above, Captain. A storm brews on the horizon." He quirked his lips. "But I see another storm brews within you."

Cadan rubbed his temples. "If you mean I enjoyed myself immensely last night, you are correct."

"Do you even remember last night? The lady was here quite late." His gaze sped to Cadan's bed. "Pray, tell me you did her no harm."

"Bah! What do you take me for?" Though now that Cadan thought about it, the memories of the evening peeked in and out of the fog in his brain. He did remember disclosing far too much to the lady, and…blast, he'd dragged her to his bed! 'Twas the last thing he remembered.

"I take you for a besotted man who despises the lady," Pell retorted.

"I'll admit to frightening her a bit." Which was his intention at the end. "But the woman's tongue is as deadly as a sea serpent." He reached for a bottle on the table.

Pell grabbed it first, corked it, and set it back on the sideboard along with the other bottles not yet empty. "You've had enough."

"Take a care, Pell. I am your captain, and I'll not be ordered about."

He faced Cadan, one cynical brow raised and sunlight glinting off that blasted cross of his. "Then act like one."

Cadan studied him, this man who had once called him out to swords, but who had become his good friend. There was a wisdom about him, a rational calmness Cadan envied. He'd suffered nearly as much at the hands of an unscrupulous man as Cadan had, yet he let justice lie dormant. "Why do you not wish revenge on those who killed your wife and son?" 'Twas a question he'd asked the man before, the answer to which Cadan desperately needed to know, but Pell always gave a shrug and changed the subject.

Agony etched across every inch of his face, betraying his usual calm demeanor. The man could be in no less pain than Cadan.

"What good would it do?" he finally said. "What's done is done." He circled the table and headed for the door. "I'll send some men to clean this up and have Omphile bring you some tea and something for your head."

Cadan nodded, devoid of the energy to argue. "Very well. I shall be on deck shortly."

Pell left, shutting the door a bit too loudly, and Cadan leaned over, head in his hands if only to lessen the throbbing.

Zada slithered out from under his bed and crawled onto his boot. He reached to pick him up, but he took one look at Cadan and scampered away.

Traitor. No doubt the lizard was angry at him for his treatment of Lady Fox. Perhaps he was right. He would seek her out today and assure her that no harm would come to her whilst on his ship. She did, after all, put a blanket on him.

His heart suddenly tightened. She could have killed him! In his benumbed condition, she had every opportunity to bash his head in with a boarding ax. Why hadn't she?

Gabrielle was getting married! 'Twas the most wonderful day of her life! The sun shone brightly from an azure sky, sprinkling glitter atop the foamy crests of wavelets in the bay. Her parents had erected a canopy of white sail cloth on the main deck of the *Redemption* as the ship swayed and rocked at anchor in Kingston Harbour.

Tropical flowers were festooned over the canopy and spread across the deck, mixing their sweet scent with the salty breeze. Her family had ne'er looked so good. Charlisse, her mother, dressed in a blue silk dress with belled sleeves veiled in gossamer lace, smiled at her. Her father, Captain Edmund

Merrick, cut a fine figure in his suit of black camlet, richly embellished with gold braid. Alexander her brother, his wife, Juliana, and their four-year-old son Caleb stood beneath the quarterdeck. Reena, her sister held hands with her husband Frederick across the main deck, and Juliana's brother, Rowan, assisted his wife Morgan in comforting a crying one year old Rose. All dressed in their finest, all smiling joyfully at her.

To her left stood her father's loyal crew, Jackson and Sloane among them, grinning like cats who'd just feasted on a platter of ship mice. And up on the quarterdeck, two pirates played a happy tune upon their fiddles.

Facing the port railing that overlooked the growing town of Kingston, the preacher stood beneath the canopy, smiling her way. She could hardly stop the leap of her heart. She'd waited all her life for this moment! More than anything she wanted to marry a Godly, wonderful man who would cherish her forever. And she'd finally found him. Now she could start the family she'd always wanted—at least a dozen children, some her own and others, orphans she hoped to rescue.

Unlike her sister Reena, who was an adventurous risk-taker, and her wild pirate brother Alex, so strong and brave, Gabrielle had always been the shy, well-behaved daughter who stayed home with her mother and father and had no desire for frightening exploits upon the sea. She'd been the good daughter, the one who followed all the rules, who loved God and had never strayed from her faith. Nay, her only dream was to be a wife and mother. A somewhat docile and uninteresting dream compared to her siblings, but her parents had told her it was the noblest pursuit of all.

So, when she met Jonas, the physician aboard her brother's ship *Ransom,* and he took a fancy to her, she knew she'd found the right man. Godly, honorable, kind, and absolutely devoted to her. Their engagement was longer than she would have liked, but finally the day had come.

Her gaze scanned the docks reaching out upon the crystalline turquoise waters. Jonas had spent the night in town, hence, any minute now, he should be rowing out to the *Redemption*. Any minute now…

Gabrielle gasped for air. Pain spun through her belly. Heart thumping wildly, she sprung from her pillow, striking her head on the bulkhead. *Ouch!*

Sweeping her legs over the edge of the cot, she moaned, unavoidable tears filling her eyes and spilling past her lashes down her cheeks. The same dream. Over and over. Why must she continually be reminded of that day?

Jonas had never arrived. No sign of him was found after several weeks of searching. Finally, two months passed when her father learned from a pirate at a tap room that Jonas had run off with another woman.

Ah, the humiliation! The shame. Left at the altar. Was she not even worthy of a good husband? Why had God allowed this to happen to her? When she'd spent her entire life serving Him, devoted to spreading the Gospel and saving others? This was her reward. The mockery of friends and family, the shame of being unwanted…unworthy.

That's when she had stopped praying.

More tears came, and she released them in full force. Now look at her, unmarried, carrying an illegitimate child, and a prisoner tossed from one ruthless pirate to another. God had surely abandoned her. What good did it do to serve a God like that?

Another throbbing pain pulsed through her belly, and she bent over with a moan. She'd been having these spasms all night. In truth they'd stolen much of her sleep, save for the last few moments when her nightmare had returned. She hoped they'd dissipate, but they'd only gotten worse.

A knock startled her, and she wiped her eyes. "Come in."

'Twas the quartermaster, Pell. He stared at her for a moment, then entered and shut the door.

Her pulse sped. Was she to suffer another attack?

Yet genuine concern crossed his brown eyes. "Are you all right, my lady?"

"Aye. As good as I can be." She feigned a calm expression, devoid of pain.

"Did the captain harm you?"

She shook her head. "Nay, he lost consciousness before he could."

He frowned and released a heavy sigh, staring at the deck below. "He is not himself when deep in his cups."

She gave a ladylike snort. "'Tis no excuse for what he is doing to me."

"Nay," he quickly answered. The man's intense gaze locked upon her. Broad in shoulder and muscled, she wondered what kind of preacher he'd been, for he looked not the part.

"Omphile will be here soon." He turned to leave.

"What caused you to choose piracy over preaching, Mr. Pell?"

Halting, his entire body seemed to tighten. "God forsook me."

"Because your wife and child died?"

He faced her, his expression stern yet oddly empty. "I devoted my life to His work, sacrificed all, but still my wife died of fever and…" He swallowed and his lips flattened. "My son was murdered by the lieutenant governor."

Gabrielle gasped, both shocked and horrified at both the man's words and the matter-of-fact way he voiced them. "Why would he do such a thing?"

He looked down, his fist squeezing the door handle until his knuckles whitened. "He wanted no missionaries on the island. He threatened me many times, yet I believed God would protect me. Matthew was eight." A bell rang. A muffled shout came from above. "I must away, my lady."

And with that, he left, closing the door. So she was not the only one God abandoned after a life of service. Even a preacher doubted in His goodness. Perhaps her parents had been wrong about this God of theirs all along.

A breeze swept in from the small window, oddly chilling her. She rubbed her arms.

Serving God is useless. A whisper, words in her ears, yet not in her ears.

Rising, Gabrielle moved to the bowl, poured water into it from the pitcher and splashed it over her face. She was glad for no looking glass in the cabin, for she must look a fright. Taking a cloth, she dabbed it in the water and did her best to remove the stain on her gown from last night, but 'twas no use. Instead, she removed the pins from her hair and attempted to brush out the tangles. By the time Omphile arrived with grog and a bowl of oatmeal, Gabrielle felt ill. The throbbing in her belly continued, and she feared something was terribly wrong.

"You must eat, Child." Omphile held out the bowl and urged her with concern. "For the babe."

A kick stabbed her belly. "I fear should I feed him any more, he'll have the strength to break through my womb." Her chuckle faltered as another pain carved across her belly. She leaned over, moaning.

"Miss?" Omphile laid a hand on her shoulder.

"I'm fine." She breathed out and sat up as the pain subsided. "Perhaps some fresh air?"

"Only if you eat."

Reluctantly, Gabrielle took a few bites while Omphile braided her hair behind her.

Hence, no sooner had she stepped on deck to a blast of salty wind and the caress of the warm sun, than Gabrielle felt slightly better. The babe must have fallen asleep for his movements stopped as she made her way with Omphile's help to the port railing.

She felt the captain's eyes on her from the quarterdeck, but she would not give him the satisfaction of returning his gaze. Not after the way he'd treated her last night. Had he intended to ravish her? She couldn't be sure.

Gripping the railing, she drew a deep breath and glanced over the sea, surprised to see dark clouds swallowing up the sun in the distance. Omphile took a stand beside her. "Looks like we's in for a storm."

Not that Gabrielle hadn't sailed through many a tempest in the Caribbean, but with child? A gust of salty wind struck her. The sails flapped above, and the captain's voice thundered over the deck.

"All hands wear ship! Stand by to raise storm sails!"

Smity repeated the commands while Durwin ordered the topmen to task, and soon pirates flew into the tops to adjust sails. She faced the sea again. Waves that merely rolled when she'd first come above now leapt and dove, spewing white foam from their tops.

"Two points to port, Mr. Pell!" the captain ordered. "Head for that island!"

Gabrielle followed his gaze to a speck of land in the distance. Aye, should be large enough to offer them shelter until the storm passed.

Another pain etched across her belly, starting low and rising in ripples of anguish, this one far stronger than those prior. Fear heightened her breath as she schooled her expression. The throbbing passed and she loosened her tight grip on the railing, blowing out a breath. Thankfully, Omphile was too busy staring at Moses, who was repairing a gash in the larboard bulwarks, or surely the woman would make her go below.

The ship bucked over a rising wave. Gabrielle gripped the railing tighter, balancing her feet on the heaving deck. Thick, black clouds tumbled across the sky, stealing all remaining sunlight and casting a gray hue over the sea. Wind blasted over her, and she closed her eyes, relishing the strength of it, the feel of it caressing her skin.

She sensed rather than saw the captain standing behind her. Despite the gusts of wind, his unique scent mixed with stale rum assailed her.

"My lady." The deep, smoky voice caused a slight tremor to course through her as he slipped beside her.

She glanced his way but said naught. No need to encourage the beast. Though she thought she saw a speck of, dare she say, humility on his expression. Nay, couldn't be.

"I did not behave well last night."

The understatement of the century. "Truly?" she retorted with sarcasm.

"'Twas not my intention to frighten you."

"Captain, if this is your attempt to apologize for nearly ravishing me, 'tis a poor effort, indeed."

His jaw tightened, and he rubbed the stubble on his chin. Gripping the hilt of his cutlass, he shook his head. "I assure you that was the last thing on my mind."

"'Twas not your rum-flooded mind that concerned me."

Anger flared in eyes that now shifted from green to brown as his dark hair blew behind him in wild abandon. The ship crested a wave, and he shifted his boots on the deck, obviously having difficulty holding his tongue.

"I came to inform you, Lady Fox"—he began in a strained tone—"that you will not be harmed on board my ship, but I see now 'twas a waste of my time. Why do I bother?"

"I am curious about that as well." She dared to peer into his eyes where his fury remained, but something else lingered there…sorrow.

"The seas roughen. Go below," he ordered.

She did not respond. She *could* not respond, for another spasm racked through her, and it took all her strength to not reveal her discomfort.

Lightning streaked a white fork across the sky. Gazing up at the sails, he pushed from the railing, issuing commands as he went.

The pain subsided as wind blasted over Gabrielle, filled with the sweet sting of rain and charged with the power of the storm. Unlike her family, tempests at sea terrified Gabrielle, but what terrified her more at the moment was that something was amiss with her baby. 'Twas too soon to be giving birth, wasn't it? But what could she do? Either way, she didn't wish to endure it below deck in a tiny cabin. Hence, when Omphile returned and asked her to go below, she pleaded to remain a few more minutes.

The ship heaved over a particularly large wave. She squeezed the railing even as Omphile clasped her arm to give her additional support. What a kind woman.

Soon, they approached the small island, no larger than a navy dockyard, but covered in trees that would offer them safety from the storm.

Something red caught Gabrielle's attention. Through the trees on the north side of the island. There one second and then gone. But she knew those red and blue colors. The unique ensign was forever imprinted on her mind.

"I must speak to the captain at once." Pivoting, she held out her arms for balance and made her way to the quarterdeck ladder.

Omphile dashed after her, gripping her arm. "Miss, I wouldna bother him now."

Ignoring the woman, and the sudden pain gripping her belly, Gabrielle mounted the ladder and staggered to where Pell manned the tiller and the captain stood at the binnacle.

"I ordered you below!" he shouted, then nodded for Omphile to take her away.

"Allard is here!" Gabrielle shouted over the din of the rising storm.

The captain's eyes met hers. Determined, yet full of doubt.

"I saw his ensign, his colors. I know it!" She gestured toward the north end of the island. "He waits behind the trees."

His gaze snapped in that direction; his look intense. A myriad of emotions brewed in that one look. Finally, he plucked the spyglass from his belt and held it to his eye. Before he even lowered it, he began spouting orders. "Battle stations! Reduce to battle sail. Bear off, haul your braces, ease sheets, man the guns, clear the deck!"

The prow of a ship peeked from around the island. A plume of yellow light burst from her hull.

"All hands down!" the captain shouted. Leaping in front of Gabrielle and Omphile, he shoved them to the deck.

Heart pounding, Gabrielle closed her eyes, waiting to be torn apart by the shot, aware of the captain's body surrounding her like a shield, his warmth, his scent.

The ship continued to rise and fall. The shot must have landed in the sea, for no crunch of wood, no blast, no moans of pain were heard.

As quick as he had covered them, the captain leapt up. "Ready about! Rise tacks and sheets! Hard aport, Mr. Pell!"

With Omphile's help, Gabrielle stood and staggered over to grip the quarterdeck railing, gazing up at the sails snapping in the wind. Cadan was tacking a-weather to return fire.

Omphile tugged on her, terror streaking across her face. "Let's go below, Miss."

But Gabrielle's gaze was on the captain. He'd leapt down onto the main deck and was issuing order after order, sending the men scrambling to task. He marched with authority, confidence, and from what she knew of sea battles, expertise. No fear. No hesitancy in his voice or demeanor, which inspired the same in a crew that was quick to obey him.

"Mainsail haul! Bring our guns to bear, Mr. Pell! Starboard guns standby!" Cadan issued a stream of rapid-fire orders.

Soot and his gun crew worked furiously to ready the guns, both on deck and below, as men brought up powder cartridges and shot from the hold. The creak of blocks and rattle of slating sails filled the air as wind fluttered impotently in the sails before shifting in the tack.

Smity shouted orders for the topmen to "haul taut, take in foretopsail!"

Confused, Gabrielle watched as the sailors in the tops hesitated but finally obeyed. But that would not allow the *Resolute* to make the quick turn needed to return fire.

Pain gripped her belly, radiating out in waves of torment. Ignoring it, she clambered down the ladder toward the captain.

He barely glanced her way. "Scads, woman, get below!"

"The foresail." She pointed aloft. "It should not be taken in or you'll not be able to tack enough to fire a shot."

He followed her gaze. Confusion turned to anger as he marched to Smity and began shouting.

Another flash from Allard's ship sent the crew dropping to the deck. *Boom*! reverberated through the air.

This time, the ship staggered beneath a blow that smashed her bulwarks at the waist, sending splinters across the deck.

Another spasm struck Gabrielle. Had she been hit? She spread hands over her stomach but felt no moisture from blood. Still the pain grew worse. She cried out.

Omphile clasped her arm. "What is it, Miss?"

Thunder bellowed. Or was it a broadside? The sky unleashed a torrent of heavy rain that pelted her like grapeshot.

The captain dashed toward her. "Are you hurt, my lady? Moses!" he shouted.

"No, Captain," Omphile screeched out. "She's having her babe!"

Chapter 14

aving her babe? Cadan growled. After ensuring the woman had not been injured by the last shot, he sent her and Omphile below. 'Twas just like Lady Fox to have her baby during a battle! Could she not wait for a calmer moment?

He could not think of it now. Omphile assured him she knew what to do. Cadan's focus was on defeating Allard! The moment he'd been waiting for, dreaming of for the last seven years.

The fool must have spotted the *Resolute* seeking shelter near the island. No doubt the storm had kept him from their view and given him time to hide like the coward he was.

The little minx had saved him by spotting the blackguard's colors. Then she did so again by pointing out Smity's error.

Cadan leapt onto the quarterdeck, pressing the spyglass to his eye. Smity never made mistakes, not when it came to sails. It would have been a deadly one if the lady had not spotted it.

But how would she know such a thing?

Still, as his gaze landed on Smity, a twinge of suspicion pricked him. Gabrielle's words from last night had shot holes in Cadan's trust of the bosun. Or mayhap that was her goal. Nevertheless, he would keep his eye on him.

"She's comin' round on our starboard side, Cap'n!" Durwin shouted.

Good. Just as Cadan had hoped. Lowering his scope, he wiped rain from his face. Black clouds broiled above them, but at least the rain had lessened.

The *Resolute* veered, and her sails caught the wind with a violent snap. Bracing his boots on the quarterdeck, Cadan balanced while leveling the spyglass once again to his eye. The

Nightblood's sails flapped impotently in their tack, giving Cadan a chance to fire.

"On my order, Mr. Soot!" he shouted, glancing at the master gunner standing at the head of the companionway. Snapping his gaze back at Allard's ship, he waited…"Fire!"

"Fire!" Soot shouted to his gunmen below, and the *Resolute's* broadside boomed, shaking the ship to its keel. Thick gray smoke swept over the deck.

Batting it away, Cadan peered through his scope. Pirates scrambled over the *Nightblood*'s deck. Black smoke poured from a gaping hole on her hull between wind and water. Not enough to cripple her.

"Scads!" Cadan cussed, then fired off another round of rapid orders. "Brace about! Veer to starboard! Bring larboard guns to bear!" If he could turn in time, he'd rake Allard's stern before he could swing about.

Thunder bellowed, followed by another flash of lightning.

The *Resolute* swung to starboard, wind flapping thunderously through the sails as black squalls of frothy water swept over the deck.

Before they could complete the tack, red flashes belched from the *Nightblood,* and the eerie zip of a cannon ball filled the air. One punched a hole through the *Resolute*'s main mast and shattered her yards, sending canvas and rigging to the deck. The other crushed the foredeck railing. A piercing scream drew Cadan's gaze to one of his men, fallen to the deck with a splinter in his leg.

He turned to order Moses to task, but the large man was already heading toward the injured pirate.

"Ready the larboard guns!" Cadan ordered as the *Resolute* veered about on the Nightblood's stern.

Wind tore over Cadan as he marched to the railing and eyed his enemy, his nemesis. This was his chance to destroy him, to get his revenge.

He waited…waited…watching the lift of the ship, the waves, gauging the wind…

"Fire!"

Gabrielle was dying. 'Twas no other explanation for the excruciating pain wracking her body. Each wave ripped apart her insides as if someone was gutting her like a fish. She screamed and squeezed Omphile's hand for dear life.

The pain lessened, but only slightly. Enough for Gabrielle to catch her breath and shoot Omphile a look of despair. "If I should die, please watch after my baby."

Freeing her hand, Omphile winced and shook it in the air. "You aren't gonna die, Miss. Though I knows it feels that way."

A knock rapped on the door, and the mulatto shot up and opened it.

Gabrielle heard Moses' low voice.

"Water, rags, a clean blanket, and a bottle of rum," Omphile responded before shutting the door.

The ship heaved, nearly tossing the woman to the deck before she reached her chair. Shouts and thundering footsteps above told Gabrielle they were still at battle with Allard. She'd seen Damien command his men in action. He was skilled, yet nothing like her father, the infamous Captain Merrick. And what little she'd witnessed of Cadan's skill, he had a good chance against Allard.

Still, a battle? Perhaps she would be having her babe at the bottom of the sea, or worse, the child would be blown to bits before he took his first breath.

She wanted to cry, but the pain started up again. "Is it supposed to hurt this much?" she screamed.

"Yes," came Omphile's only response, though just from the shakiness of that one word, Gabrielle could tell she was as nervous about delivering this baby as Gabrielle was.

Sitting on the edge of the cot, Omphile adjusted Gabrielle's skirts. "Lemme check on things, Miss. All right?"

But Gabrielle was once again in such torment, she neither cared nor could answer. Howling, she gripped the edge of the cot, digging her nails into the wood until she felt blood drip over her fingers.

"Now, now, Child." Omphile took her hand. "No need to hurt yourself. Looks like de babe be coming soon."

The thunderous roar of a cannon shook the ship, trembling the cot on which Gabrielle lay. *Please, God. Please. If you still care at'll for me, please deliver my baby safely.* 'Twas her first prayer in years and one said in between screams of agony.

Moses must have brought the supplies, for by the time the last pain subsided slightly, a piece of sailcloth had been placed beneath Gabrielle's legs and Omphile was dribbling rum into Gabrielle's mouth from a rag.

"Do you know how to do this?" Gabrielle panted out.

The woman smiled nervously. "Better dan anyone else on board dis ship. 'Sides," she added, "women been birthin' babies for thousands o' years without any help at all."

An overwhelming urge to push consumed Gabrielle. "He's coming!" she shouted, sending Omphile to the end of the bed.

"Push, Miss! Push wit' all your might!"

Raising the spyglass to his eye, Cadan focused on the smoke spewing from Allard's ship. He smiled.

"Good work, Soot!" he exclaimed. "A direct hit."

"'Twere by yer command, Cap'n," the gunner replied with a smile and a shrug.

Indeed. Cadan had timed it perfectly, taking in the direction of the wind and the rise and fall of the waves, waiting…waiting…until that precise moment when he'd shouted "Fire!"

The broadside raked the *Nightblood's* stern, crushing her timbers at the water line and shattering her bulwarks. Smoke gushed from below deck, where a fire must have started.

Pirates dashed back and forth across the ship, lowering and raising buckets into the sea to put out the rising flames. All the while, Allard's commands sent men to the tops to raise all sail and flee as fast as they could.

The villain had the audacity to leap onto the quarterdeck, remove his plumed hat, and sweep it before him in a mock gesture of deference.

Cursing, Cadan gazed up at his damaged mainsail. Even if he raised the remaining sails, he'd never catch up to Allard's smaller sloop. Aye, the *Nightblood* was on fire for now, but her sails were intact.

Cadan could only stand there, hands fisted at his waist, wind whipping through his hair, and groan in frustration. How many chances would he get to battle this blackguard?

"Orders, Cap'n?" Durwin shouted from the main deck. "Should we try an' catch 'im?"

"Nay." Cadan plowed a hand through his hair and cursed. "Another time."

Dark clouds retreated on the horizon. As quickly as it had come, the storm passed.

"Anchor in the shelter of the island and make repairs on the sail and mast. We'll have another chance at Allard."

"I hope yer right, Cap'n." Durwin spit to the side before he turned and began ordering the men to task. Smity nodded and went to work, avoiding Cadan's gaze.

If the man hadn't made that error, Cadan might have had the advantage quicker and not allowed his mainsail to be damaged. He'd talk to him later. For now, he must check on the wounded.

And on Lady Fox.

Leaping down the companionway, he stormed toward his cabin. He needed rum. Lots of it, but he needed to know how the lady fared first.

Stopping at her door, he listened. No moans of pain, no screams came from the cabin, though he'd heard plenty during the battle.

He knocked.

The door creaked open and Omphile's face appeared. Surprise swept over it at the sight of him.

"How is she?"

Glancing over her shoulder, she opened the door further. "See for yourself."

Cadan slowly stepped into the room, only then smelling his stink of sweat, blood, and gun smoke.

But the sight before him sent a lump of burning into his throat.

Lady Fox, sitting upright in bed, her back leaning against the bulkhead, her golden hair tumbling about her, and a tiny, swaddled babe in her arms.

So absorbed with her child, she barely noticed him until he halted beside the bed.

She glanced up. Gone was the usual hatred, fear, angst, and hauteur. Instead, she had the face of an angel filled with love and hope, a very *tired* angel.

"It's a boy, like I said." She gazed back down at her child.

He nodded, unsure of what to say. He should hate this child, should despise its very existence, but instead, he found himself mesmerized. A tiny pink face, complete with perfectly formed lips, nose, and eyes stared up at his mother as if she were an angel. The babe reached his tiny chubby hand up and his fingers clasped onto one of hers. She smiled.

'Twas a life, a person, a miracle that had emerged from the lady's womb.

But it is Allard's bastard.

He tore his gaze away. Bloody blankets were heaped in the corner, evidence of the lady's pain.

Omphile slid onto the seat, clearly exhausted. "She done good, Captain."

"As did you, Omphile, Thank you. See to it you get some rest."

The mulatto nodded.

He turned to leave.

"Did you sink Allard?" Lady Fox asked.

"Nay," he ground out. "Your lover lives to fight another day."

Looking up from her babe, she frowned. "Now you have your bait in plain sight, Captain. You should be pleased."

Chapter 15

"There is no excuse for your error, Smity!" Cadan glared at his bosun, who stood before him, eyes downcast and jaw bunched.

Pell and Durwin stood on either side of Smity, and two of the topmen cowered behind him.

Smity thumbed to Kipp over his shoulder. "Were 'is mistake, not mine, Cap'n. I gave no such order." He dared to glance up at Cadan, his one eye drifting off to the side.

The topman in question fidgeted, his face turning red. Cadan would talk to him privately later.

"Matters not. You are the bosun and hence, responsible for your men," Cadan ground out. "Your mistake could have cost lives, maybe even the ship." *If Lady Fox had not noticed it.* But he wouldn't add that. 'Twould make him seem weak. And weakness, even *perceived* weakness, was the ruin of any captain.

Sunlight angled in through the stern windows, shifting over the man's face with each roll of the ship. He rubbed his scars, as he always seemed to do when being chastised or ordered about. Was he trying to make Cadan feel guilty, to soften whate'er punishment would come?

"Like I said, it weren't me order."

Frowning, the topman Kipp heaved a deep breath.

"You have one more chance, Smity"—Cadan shoved his face toward his—"or you will be removed as bosun. Is that clear?"

"Clear as fresh ale, Cap'n." But the man's tone was anything but conciliatory.

"Dismissed. Pell, Durwin remain."

Smity and his men marched out, Kipp shaking his head at Cadan before he left.

"Aye, Moses." Cadan nodded toward the man who entered as the others slid out.

"You asked 'bout Barnett, Cap'n. He's doin' well. Healin' good an' should be back on deck wit' in a few days."

"Thank you, Moses. And the babe?"

"I's don't know nothin' 'bout babes, Cap'n. But I checked 'im out like you asked, an' he looks healthy t' me."

"Good. That'll be all." He gestured for the carpenter to leave.

"So the lady had her baby?" Pell said with a smile after Moses left.

"Aye, a boy." Cadan circled his desk and stared at the map. The chirp of birds filtered in from the island as hammers sounded from above. "As soon as the repairs are finished, we are to get back on course for Nevis."

Durwin rubbed his hands as he approached, a gleam in his eyes. "Fer the next clue?"

Cadan nodded, studying the lines and circles drawn on the crude map. "I seek the final clue Captain Dempster was said to have left. It should lead me right to the treasure."

Durwin ran a hand beneath his hook nose. "Where be this last clue, Cap'n?"

"For me to know," Cadan answered, eyeing the man. "You'll get your share, Durwin, like I promised."

The man licked his lips, staring at the map as if he wanted to grab it and run.

Pell crossed arms over his chest. "Wealth is a trap. What profit is there if a man gain the whole world and lose his soul?"

Snorting, Cadan grabbed a bottle of rum. "My soul was lost a long time ago."

"Not until the day you die, Captain."

"What now?" Cadan chuckled. "Are you taking up preaching again?"

Pell shrugged. "Just hoping to save you some heartache, Captain. Riches never fulfill."

Durwin stared at Pell as if he'd said mermaids had taken over the ship. "Tush, man. If not, then what does?" He fingered the speck of beard on his chin, his brow wrinkling. "'Tis wealth, Cap'n. Ye be right in that, says I." But his gaze remained on the map. "Wealth. Wealth brings power an' women. Wealth brings the only happiness one can find in this world."

Cadan gestured with his head toward Durwin. "Wise words."

Pell huffed. "From such a proven sage."

Missing the insult, Durwin grinned. "Why, thank ye, Pell." Then turning to Cadan, "How much we talkin' about?"

"Enough." Enough to give the crew their share and Cadan to retire to the colony of Virgina and buy himself an estate that would put the local gentry to shame. Then he would have the power he craved. The power to run his life the way he pleased and enact justice where justice was needed.

Cadan turned to Durwin. "As soon as repairs are finished, weigh anchor and set all sails to the wind. Pell, set a course south by southeast toward Nevis. Unless we run into further difficulties, we should arrive in a week."

Three days passed and Gabrielle was still having trouble walking. And sleeping! As it turned out, little Matthew had quite the appetite and insisted on being fed every two hours. Aye, she'd called him Matthew, for she remembered her mother telling her the name meant gift of God. Not that she was speaking to the Almighty, but He had given her a safe delivery and a healthy baby boy. Besides, she'd always loved the name. 'Twas a strong name, and she knew her son would grow to fulfill its meaning.

The door creaked open, startling Gabrielle, and in flew Omphile, the ever-present smile on her face and a tray of food in her hands. "De captain wishes to see you when you are done breakin' your fast, Miss." Setting down the tray, she placed hands on her hips. "Look at you, now. We needs to make you more presentable. Get up. I'll take de babe."

Rising, Gabrielle handed Matthew to Omphile. "And why should I care if I'm presentable to that beast?" Though in all honesty, she knew she'd feel better with a little water and fresh undergarments.

"Aw, Child, he isn't dat bad." Omphile cradled little Matthew in her arms, easing a finger over his soft, smooth skin. "He is so beautiful, Miss. You are blessed."

One hand on the bulkhead, Gabrielle balanced against the shifting deck and stared at Omphile, remembering that the poor woman had lost her unborn babe due to her owner's beatings. "I'm sorry if it pains you to hold him after…after you…"

"Lost my own?" Omphile looked up, naught but joy sparkling in her eyes. "No. What a joy to hold dis precious child o' God in my arms! 'Sides, mine is wit' Jesus now. I'll see her again."

Baffled, Gabrielle made her way to the basin of water. Nary a speck of jealousy appeared on the sweet woman's face. In truth, she'd been more than helpful these past days, bringing food, grog, cleaning soiled linens and clothing, even showing Gabrielle how to nurse. "I don't know what I would do without you, Omphile." Gabrielle poured water into a basin and splashed it over her face.

"Oh, go on… I's jist doin' de Laud's work."

How anyone could do the Lord's work on a pirate ship was beyond her.

Still, an hour later, Gabrielle, babe in her arms, knocked on Captain Beast's door. At his "enter," Moses nodded and strode away, leaving her to walk alone into the lion's den.

More like pigsty as she glanced around the cluttered chaos he called a cabin. Zada sat on the stern window seat, enjoying the warm rays of sunlight spearing through the window—rays that rippled over the rest of the cabin, landing on the captain's bed. Torn sheets and a crumpled blanket appeared to have fought a war during the night.

Cadan looked up from staring at the map spread across his desk and gave her the oddest look. She drew Matthew close, sudden fear rising that he meant him harm.

He must have noticed, for he said. "I have no intention of harming you or your child, Lady Fox."

"Merely offer us up as a sacrifice," she retorted.

He huffed and touched his nicked earlobe. "I will do anything to defeat Allard, 'tis true, but I will do all in my power to keep you and the babe safe in the process."

Gabrielle stared at him, incredulous. "And what, pray, has brought this change of heart?"

"No change. 'Tis always been my goal. Just not one I've put a voice to."

"It would have been nice to know, Captain."

He grinned, studying her. "I rarely disclose my plans to my enemy."

She raised her brows playfully. "Am I no longer your enemy, then?"

At this, he merely stared at her, as if searching her eyes for the answer.

"Sit, Lady Fox." He gestured toward a chair once again covered with a cross-staff, leather belt, a half-filled decanter of some sort of spirits, and a Gunter's scale. "Ah." Circling the desk, he swept the items into his arms and tossed them onto a pile littering another chair, then gestured toward the seat.

Gabrielle moved past him—far too close—and lowered to sit.

He smelled better than he had the last time she'd seen him after the battle. For once, the sting of rum was not on his breath. Instead, the scent of the sea covered him like a blanket, along with a spice—a pleasant nutmeggy smell.

Her breath caught in her throat, and she tried to focus on the silken rustle of the sea against the hull, which always soothed her.

He stood back, examining her, his gaze taking in the flatness of her belly. Wild, dark shoulder-length hair dangled over an open-collared white Holland shirt. Leather breeches that clung to every muscle in his legs were tucked into boots of black Cordovan leather. A baldric was slung across his chest, hooked onto his belt where a cutlass rested idly upon his hip.

His gaze remained upon her. She swallowed at the intensity *and* at her body's reaction. He was a force, a rather handsome force, a leader of men, and yet a deep sorrow encased him like a tomb.

"How ever can you function in this mayhem?" she said nervously, hoping to break the spell between them. "Why not bring your wife aboard? Surely, she could make some sense of this chaos."

No sooner did the words slide off her tongue than she realized her error, for he immediately stiffened and headed for the nearest bottle of rum. Why had she mentioned the wife? Hadn't he implied she'd betrayed him? She supposed she was curious whether the woman was still in his life and, more importantly, how was Allard mixed up in all this.

Uncorking the bottle, he took a long draught. "My wife is dead."

A lump formed in Gabrielle's throat. "I'm sorry."

Matthew began to fuss, and she gently rocked him back and forth.

The ship lurched over a wave, its timbers creaking and groaning as the *Resolute* flew through the waters with all sails set to the breeze. Obviously the captain was in a hurry to get to Nevis for his illusive treasure clue.

Slamming down the bottle, Cadan leaned back against his desk and gripped the edges. "Tell me, my lady, how do you know so much about sailing?"

"I've been on ships my entire life. In truth, I was born on one." She slammed her lips together. She must not say any more lest she give away the identity of her parents. This man, who was as greedy for wealth as he was for revenge, would think nothing of demanding ransom from her family for her safe return.

He cocked his head, his eyes narrowing. "A noble lady, educated, mannerly and raised on a ship? I can hardly credit it."

"Credit what you will, Captain. 'Tis the truth."

"You pique my curiosity, my lady.'"

A soft whimper escaped Matthew's lips, but quickly intensified into a wail.

Rising, she took up a pace while humming a tune. After several moments, the babe settled. When she looked back at the captain, he was staring at her with the oddest expression. Not a malevolent look, but one that held…a deep yearning? Did the captain lose a child as well? Perhaps if he grew to care for Matthew, he'd be less inclined to use him in his nefarious plan.

"Would you care to hold him?" she asked against every motherly instinct within her.

At first shock pinched his expression. She took a step toward him, holding Matthew out.

He held up his hand. "Nay! I hate children."

The shout woke up Matthew, and Gabrielle retreated, heart racing. What kind of man hated innocent children? "They don't bite."

"Nay, but they fuss, they toss their accounts where they will, they soil their undergarments, and they whine. A lot."

She couldn't help but smile. "I perceive you've had some experience with children, Captain."

"Too much." He snorted. "Brothers and sisters."

"You come from a large family?"

He crossed arms over his chest. "Three brothers and two sisters, all younger than me."

"How lovely." She glanced down at Matthew. "I've always wanted a bevy of wee ones."

He uttered a curse. "Sounds like a nightmare."

A deep sorrow penetrated his voice and burned in his eyes. So painful, it almost brought tears to her own. "Why? Family is the only source of real joy."

"Is it?" He pushed from the desk and went to the sideboard for another drink. "My mother died when I was eight. My father was a tenant farmer, gone from dawn to dusk. Hence, I was left to care for my siblings. I assure you there was little joy to be found in our house."

Despite Cadan's hate-filled tone, Gabrielle's heart grew heavy at the tale. Though her father was an earl and had thus inherited an estate, they gave away much of their wealth to the poor. Still, they never lacked for anything. Indeed, she'd grown up in a loving home with Godly parents who loved each other and with a sister and brother whom she adored. "No joy to be found at all? Was your father a Godly man?"

Taking another sip of rum, he faced her, brows drawn. "Aye, he and my mother both. And me, if you can believe it." He gave sharp snort. "Until my mother died."

Anguish churned behind hazel eyes that quickly darkened to brown, and Gabrielle thought it best to change the topic. Besides, what comfort could she offer for she, too, believed God had done her an injustice.

Zada jumped from the stern seat to the captain's desk and skittered to the edge where Gabrielle stood. "Greetings, little one." Gripping Matthew tighter in one arm, she petted the iguana, who stretched out his neck for her touch.

Cadan huffed. "'Twas me who rescued him from drowning in a swamp and yet he prefers your company to mine." A jovial tone penetrated his feigned anger.

She smiled. "I've always heard that iguanas are quite smart."

Instead of barking some insult at her or running for his rum, he returned her smile, his gaze remaining on her far too long.

Zada darted away, creating even more chaos on the desk, and Gabrielle reached to pick up an overturned ink pot—thankfully corked—then lined up a compass and divider on the left side of the desk and moved two scrolls beside each other on the right.

"Cease, woman!"

The captain's shout startled her, and she halted, glaring at him.

Matthew began to wail.

"Now, look what you have done." She took up a pace, bouncing the baby in her arms.

The ship leapt over a wave, catching her unaware. She stumbled to her right, tightening her grip on Matthew lest he fall from her embrace. Normally, she'd have no trouble steadying herself, but she was still sore from the birth. She continued to totter and would have fallen to the deck…

If the captain hadn't caught her in his arms.

Chapter 16

Cadan was as shocked as the lady seemed to be at finding herself suddenly in his arms. Shocked, aye, but *not* displeased. At least not on his part. Her feminine scent flooded him even as his fingers touched her soft skin, far softer than it looked. His body reacted. His blood heated, and he found he didn't wish to release her. She pressed the babe closer to her chest. Her blue eyes shot to his, terror sparking across them…followed by indignation and horror.

They were but inches apart. He lowered his gaze to her lips, full and pink, and oh, how he longed to kiss her, to sample her sweet taste. If only for a moment. Unable to resist, he pressed his lips to hers…not forcefully, not lustfully, but gently, warmly, caressing, tasting.

At first she responded, accepting his touch, returning his kiss as a moan of pleasure escaped her throat…

Before she kicked his shin, sending pain coursing through his leg.

"Let me go at once!" She struggled, clinging to the babe, whose eyes had opened and latched upon Cadan.

He fully expected the child to let out a horrified wail, but instead, he merely blinked and continued to stare at Cadan with an innocent dependence that did something strange to his insides.

Lady Fox shoved against him all the more forcefully, this time, real fear on her face. He released her but kept a loose grip on her arms to ensure she was steady on the rolling deck.

She backed away from him, eyes alight with fear, her chest rising and falling rapidly. Had she felt the same yearning, the same excitement during their brief kiss as he had? Whatever she'd felt, clearly it unnerved her. Mayhap even repulsed.

"How dare you take such liberties!"

A sarcastic quip rode on his tongue, but the look of real terror on her face halted it. If she had indeed been ravished by Allard, then Cadan's kiss had no doubt alarmed her.

"Why did you summon me, Captain?" She glanced at the door as if planning her escape.

Hmm. Why had he? Ah yes. "To discover how you came to be so well versed in seamanship."

She raised her chin. "Since I have answered your question, may I have your leave?"

"Aye, Begone with you," he said a bit too harshly. But 'twas for the best. The last thing he wanted *or needed* was to form any attachment to the lady. Not only was she too much like Elyna, but if need be, he must be strong enough to sacrifice her and the babe to get his revenge.

Ah, but that kiss… He strode to the stern windows and gazed out. Like none he'd ever experienced.

Gabrielle stood at the larboard railing on the main deck, raising her face to the warm sun. She closed her eyes and pretended for a moment she was back on her father's ship, the *Redemption*, safe with her family, back in their good graces. *And in God's.* Back when she believed in a God who rewarded those who served Him. Life was simple then. Filled with joy and purpose and the love of family. Did they know how far she had fallen? If so, how utterly disappointed they must be.

"Lay aft the braces. Starboard main and larboard head!" the captain's strong voice bellowed over the deck, repeated by Durwin, sending men leaping into the shrouds. She risked a glance in his direction, then snapped her eyes back to the sea lest he see her looking at him.

His kiss had been unexpected, shocking, yet so gentle and loving, she'd not resisted him. Not at first, anyway. In truth, her lips still tingled when she remembered his touch. Not like Damien's harsh, lustful, greedy kisses. Those, she'd fought with all her might. But the Captain's…his was different, even pleasurable.

How dare he?

And with her holding her babe in her arms! The audacity, the brazen impudence!

Yet her reaction was even worse, proving her growing fear that she was indeed a wanton woman. All she could hope for was that he hadn't noticed *and* that he, henceforth, would keep his distance.

Inhaling a deep breath of the sea, she wondered how Omphile was faring with Matthew. Perhaps she should not have accepted the lady's offer to watch over him whilst he slept and give Gabrielle a much-needed break. But the woman used the time to further teach Moses how to read. The two made a happy couple, indeed. Omphile deserved it after all she'd been through.

A white blur caught her eye, and Gabrielle spun to see Hellfire hopping across the deck, Soot lumbering on her heels.

Reaching down, she scooped the rabbit into her arms and gently rubbed between her floppy ears.

"Ah, Miss. Thank you." Soot halted beside her and smiled, revealing two missing teeth. "She sure 'as takin' a liking to ye."

Gabrielle returned his smile, enjoying the feel of the rabbit's soft fur beneath her fingers. "She's precious. How ever do you keep her from hopping overboard?"

Soot brushed what looked to be ashes from his waistcoat, then ran a hand through his hair as if he were trying to make himself presentable. "She's a wise one, that. She seems t' know 'er boundaries. Well"—he quirked a grin—"'cept coming to me when I need t' put 'er in 'er cage."

A waft of wind brought the smell of gunpowder and lye to Gabrielle's nose. "I'd say she's the smartest bunny I've ever met, then." She chuckled and Soot joined her, his face turning as red as his hair as he gazed sheepishly at the sea.

Smity slid down the backstay and landed with a thud on the deck, drawing her gaze. Did the man ever smile? The pearl in his right ear glimmered in the sunlight, so at odds with the sneer he gave in her direction.

"Here." Gabrielle held out Hellfire. "Her name, however, does not seem to suit her. She's more a Seafoam, don't you think?"

Taking the rabbit, he drew her close. "Aye. I agree, Miss. But it wouldna be fitting fer the master gunner t' 'ave a bunny wit' sich a winsome name."

She laughed. Shielding her eyes, she glanced up at the mountains of snowy canvas catching the wind and the topmen balancing on yards. With topsails furled and a considerable list to larboard, the *Resolute* rippled through the sea on a southeast course, rising and falling over waves that sent spray over the deck.

"In royals, down flying jib." The captain's shout echoed over the deck.

Gabrielle faced Soot. "I heard 'twas your expert gunner skill that saved us, Mr. Soot."

Another blush blossomed on his cheeks. "Weren't nothin', Miss. Cap'n Hayes were the one what told me when t' fire."

"You're far too modest. I know being a master gunner takes a great deal of skill. A God-given skill." For she'd seen many a man attempt the position and fail over the years.

He squinted in the bright sun, his right eye twitching. "I don't think the Almighty 'as much t' do wit' me. I weren't worthy o' the post in the navy. Weren't worthy o' my good family name. An' surely not worthy o' such a gift from above."

She placed a hand on his arm. "That is not true, Mr. Soot. God loves all his children. None of us are worthy of that love, but God loves us none-the-less." She repeated the things she'd heard all her life from her parents and siblings, if only to comfort the man. Yet in truth, she doubted she'd ever truly believed them.

"Surely 'E does a goodly woman like yerself." Soot smiled.

"I am far from goodly, Mr. Soot." She reached up to rub Hellfire again, then glanced at the captain who was busy talking with Pell. "Tell me of the captain's wife. How did she die?"

He shifted his stance and stared over the sea. "No one knows fer sure. And it be best I not say." He leaned toward her. "But I 'eard she killed herself."

Gasping, Gabrielle closed her eyes. "How utterly horrible. Do you know why?"

"Nay. T'were some scandal that ruined her." He glanced up at the quarterdeck and a flicker of unease swept over his eyes. "I best be back to me duties, Miss." After nodding in her direction, he sped off.

She knew before she turned around that the captain was staring at her. His penetrating gaze seemed to spear her heart even from the distance. Pivoting, she leaned on the railing and glanced across the sea, admiring the deep rolling waves in every shade of blue imaginable.

Kiss or no kiss, the man still intended to use her and Matthew to gain his revenge. That much she knew.

Her chest grew tight, not only from fear but because 'twas time to feed Matthew. Drawing one last breath of fresh sea air, she glanced to her left where the man she'd once assumed the captain assigned to guard her sat on a barrel tying a rope. He neither looked her way nor spoke. Odd.

Pushing from the railing, she grabbed her skirts and shuffled over the deck to go below, only noticing then that nearly every pirates' eyes were upon her.

Cadan was the biggest fool to ever live. For there was no other explanation for the plethora of emotions battling within him. Raging, insane emotions, and worst of all, completely unexpected! The woman was everything he loathed, everything

Elyna had been—highborn, educated, mannerly, beautiful, fastidious, deceitful, arrogant—a strumpet. Hence, he must not believe a word she said. Nor could he trust her.

Then why could he not keep his eyes off her? It wasn't just her lustrous golden hair blowing like silk in the wind. It wasn't the way the sunlight glistened over her flawless skin. It wasn't her alluring feminine curves, more evident now that she was no longer with child. Nor was it even the sound of her laughter drifting like sweet music on the salty breeze or the kind way she spoke to Soot and gently caressed his infernal rabbit.

Nay, there was something about the woman that went beyond her appearance, beyond even her upbringing. And that something had taken ahold of his heart.

Hence, the reason he was the biggest fool ever to live.

To make matters worse, his men seemed equally enthralled with the lady. More than once, he had to command them back to task. More than once, he had to shove down a rare burst of jealousy at the ease with which she laughed with Soot. Soot? He'd have to have a chat with the master gunner and order him to keep his distance.

He glanced at Pell standing at the tiller and found even the preacher's eyes upon her. "You as well, Pell?"

He shrugged with a grin. "Just admiring the scenery, Captain."

Finally, Soot let the lady be, but only after Cadan had given him his worst scowl. And after casting him a disapproving glance, the lady left too. Thank the stars, for now Cadan could focus on task. They would anchor at Nevis tomorrow, and he'd finally have the last clue to the location of Captain Dempster's treasure. Not only that, 'twas highly possible the ship they'd had glimpses of far behind them was Allard's.

Cadan knew the man would ne'er give up on his babe. If everything went according to plan, Cadan would have both the treasure and his revenge. Finally, he could start the life he was meant to live.

Picking up his backstaff, he positioned it toward the sun, making adjustments, then gave Pell the order to veer one point to starboard. "Inform me at once should the lookout spot sails behind us again."

"Aye, Captain."

"I'll be in my cabin." Marching to the companionway, he dropped below, fully intending to go to his cabin for a much-needed drink.

But he could not shake the woman from his mind. Perhaps he should castigate her for her flirtatious behavior with Soot. He'd have none of her dalliances aboard his ship. Perhaps he should let her know that no matter how many of his men she lured in with her beauty and charm, he still intended to use her and her babe as bait.

A little cruelty would, no doubt, solve his temporary infatuation.

Not waiting to knock, he burst through the door of her cabin.

To find the lady sitting on her cot with Matthew at her breast.

Instantly, the harsh words he'd intended to speak froze on his tongue. In truth, everything within him froze at the tender sight of a mother nursing her babe.

Though a portion of the lady's breast was exposed, Cadan found his body did not react at all. Nay, instead, his heart melted in places long since hardened.

Until she looked up in horror and the innocent vision of Madonna and child transformed into a dragon and its whelp. "How dare you!"

While still holding the babe with one arm, she grabbed a nearby chamber pot and tossed it at him.

He ducked, but not before whatever was inside the pot splattered all over his shirt.

Chapter 17

Well, Captain, you certainly smell better than the last time I saw you." Gabrielle took the captain's extended hand while offering him a sarcastic grin. Light from a nearly full moon showered them in silver, giving her a good view of his face.

Instead of his usual growl or insulting retort, he returned her smile, his gaze lowering to her chest. "I find 'twas worth the sight, my lady."

"Cad!" she snapped back, tugging from his grip in order to slap him. It had been two days since he'd barged in and seen her nursing Matthew. Two days and she'd not seen or heard from him. She'd assumed he was furiously plotting her demise for soaking him with the contents of her chamber pot. Apparently, however, like most men, he had only one thing on his mind.

She continued to pull her hand from his, but he refused to release her. A good thing, that, for she would have most likely fallen over the bulwarks into the water below instead of into the cockboat that awaited her.

Wind blasted over her, pulling strands of hair from her pins and showering her with the fishy scent of Bath Bay. Across the dark moonlit water, lanterns blinked among taverns, shops, and warehouses that lined the small city of Charlestown, Nevis.

She glanced behind her to see Omphile, a bundled Matthew safely tucked into a sling flung across her chest. Why the Captain had insisted they bring the babe could only mean one thing. He intended to use him to trap Allard.

"Release me at once," she ordered with a huff. Yet his grip was firm, not harsh or painful, but warm and strong.

He gazed at her with an intensity in his hazel eyes she'd not seen before. Whether he plotted to kill her or kiss her again, she could not tell, though both impulses could be seen in his brooding gaze. And that unnerved her most of all.

Finally, he aided her over the bulwarks and down onto the rope ladder to Pell's open arms below.

Omphile descended after her. "Hope you knows what your doin', Captain," she said as she passed him, which only caused further tightness in Gabrielle's belly. Wobbling in the unsteady boat, Gabrielle finally settled on the thwarts. The mulatto sat beside her and squeezed her hand as more men jumped into the craft, Durwin and Smity, among them.

The captain gave orders for Moses and the remaining pirates on board the *Resolute* to guard the ship with their lives before he leapt into the cockboat and commanded his men to shove off.

The slap of oars hit the water, stirring up swirling foam as each lurch of the boat brought her and Matthew closer to whatever doom awaited them. Perhaps she deserved her fate, but not her innocent child. She reached over and stroked the soft skin of his cheek and whispered a prayer. "Lord, allow no harm to come to him, I beg you. Not for my sake, but for his."

Omphile smiled and squeezed her hand tighter as if to say, *it will be all right.*

To her left, the cannons of Fort Charles could barely be made out in the milky moonlight, making Gabrielle wonder why a pirate would venture here. Yet, she supposed many of them held privateering papers due to the war with France, thus granting them leniency.

As they neared the town, the rattle of carriages, sounds of voices, laughter, and the twang of an off-key harpsichord drifted on the wind. How many port towns like this had she ventured into with her father and mother, witnessing about the love of Jesus and feeding the poor? Too many to count. Though they were often shunned, those memories brought a smile to her face.

She'd had a purpose then. She was doing good in the world. And her parents were proud of her.

This time, she'd not be feeding the poor nor spreading the Gospel. This time, she and her son would be bait to lure in an evil, loathsome pirate. She looked at Cadan as he faced the port, his jaw tight with purpose, dark hair blowing in the wind.

All because of one man's greed for revenge.

The metallic taste of fear filled her mouth, and she longed to jump into the dark rippling waters. To end all this madness here and now.

But she had more to think about than herself now. She would never leave her son.

Though Charlestown boasted a small Royal Naval Base, protected by Fort Charles, recently it had become a haunt for pirates and nefarious seamen, particularly when the sun set. No doubt the need for privateers forced British officers to not only look the other way but to allow their fellow combatants their nightly debauchery. Hence, 'twas no surprise to find bands of savage buccaneers roaming the streets, deep in their cups, seeking a fight—*any* fight. Good thing Cadan had a reputation as an expert swordsman and heartless avenger, one he'd spent years fostering for such a time as this. For he had no time for foolish braggarts and useless pompous challenges.

He glanced over his shoulder at Lady Fox and Omphile, protected on both sides by two of his largest men. The lady glanced about with more curiosity than fear. Odd. Durwin and Smity walked behind them and two more of his pirates took up the rear. Pell strolled beside Cadan, hand clenching the hilt of his blade. Perhaps he should not have brought Smity, wanted for desertion as it was, but the man had insisted, and he promised to keep his head down. It also helped that he was a good fighter, should Cadan run into trouble. Besides, Cadan had a special mission for the bosun, a small test of his loyalty.

"Not the best place to bring a lady, Captain," Pell said.

"A necessary evil," Cadan replied, casting a stern eye on a group of pirates stumbling down the street to their left.

Music from a bagpipe chimed from within the walls of a tavern, along with off-key singing, shouting, and swearing. Men, arms around doxies, spilled from the door like vomit into the night. A pistol shot cracked the air.

Halting, Cadan listened for another, but the sounds of revelry returned.

Lanterns flickered atop poles, spreading spheres of gold over the cobblestones as wind brought the scent of the sea, roast pig, and men's sweat to Cadan's nose.

A band of pirates crossed the street in front of them. Halting, their leader narrowed his gaze upon Cadan. "Shiver me soul, if it ain't the bilge-sucking cap'n o' the *Resolute*. What brings ye 'ere, Hayes?" He snorted as his hand fingered the hilt of his cutlass.

Cadan huffed a sigh. "Naught to concern you, Deadeyes. Move along." The aged pirate was big of head and paunch and of less than mediocre intelligence. A roaring, quarrelsome, hard-drinking, hard-gaming scoundrel, and Cadan had not the time to deal with him.

The men with Deadeyes stared at the ladies, licking their lips.

"So's ye remember me, eh?" Oddly, pride permeated the man's drunken tone.

Cadan smiled. Who could forget a man who'd stolen—or attempted to steal—a pouch of coins from him? "I remember slicing off two of your fingers."

The man winced. His men chuckled. The empty look in his eyes grew darker, if that were possible. His remaining fingers grew tight on his cutlass. "How's about a rematch?" He gestured toward Lady Fox standing behind Cadan. "Fer the lady?"

"Come on, Karn," the man standing behind him slurred and tried to tug him away. "Leave 'im be."

Laughter and the sound of female voices lured the rest of Deadeye's companions to head toward a punch house across the way.

"I suggest you take your friend's advice or lose the rest of your fingers."

Deadeyes spat to the side, then belched. "Another time, Cap'n. Another time."

Cadan smiled. "I shall await the moment with great anticipation."

Turning, old Deadeyes stumbled away, flinging curses in his wake.

"Making friends, I see," Pell remarked as Cadan continued forward.

"More like keeping the animals at bay." Hastening his footsteps, Cadan drew a deep breath as they left the main part of town behind, giving way to shops and warehouses and avenues leading to homes and farms. Now, to find the church. It shouldn't be hard. There weren't many places of worship on this spit of an island, and this one was said to be along the main thoroughfare.

The babe squealed behind them, and he glanced once again at the ladies. Omphile handed Matthew to his mother, and after drawing him close, she gave Cadan a scathing look.

Was he the monster he saw reflected in her eyes? Perhaps. For what kind of man used a baby to get what he wanted? Bitterness filled his mouth, despite his attempt to swallow it. Yet what other choice did he have? Allard was no mewling poltroon to be easily defeated. Nay, trickery was the only way. And Cadan *must* have his revenge. For Elyna. And for the torturous years he spent as a slave on Barbados. Pain held memories too, as he shifted his back against the stripes he'd received.

The sounds of music and drunken laughter faded, replaced by night birds and the *whish* of wind through leaves. There. He peered through the darkness at a stone structure perched near the road. A steeple rose into the black sky like a beacon of hope. A good sign?

Halting, he spun about. "Smity. You know what to do." The bosun uttered an "Aye" and sped off into the night.

"Pell," Cadan continued, "with me. Durwin, bring the ladies. The rest of you stay out here. If you see anyone, alert me."

"Aye, Cap'ns" shot into the night as Cadan headed for the church.

The heavy wooden door creaked open, and he stepped inside. The smell of beeswax, mold, aged wood, and holiness swept over him, sending an odd chill across his shoulders.

Beams of silvery moonlight speared through a large open window at the back wall, revealing rows of wooden pews leading up to an altar at the front. He'd been told the church was rarely used, as evidenced by the dust tickling his nose.

The ladies entered behind him, the babe making cooing sounds as Durwin led them to sit on a pew in the back.

"Whatever are we doing here, Captain?" Lady Fox's tone, filled with both alarm and annoyance, echoed through the church. "Come to repent of your sins?"

He chuckled, then retreated to a table by the entrance. Grabbing flint from a timber box and a candle and holder from a basket, he lit the candle and started toward the front of the church. "Stay with the women, Durwin."

"So the last clue is here?" Pell eased beside him, frowning as he glanced around the empty church.

"Aye. If ole Barnacle Bill was telling the truth." Weaving around the altar, he halted and stared at his friend. Sweat lined his brow and upper lip and his normal tan complexion had blanched. "You look like you're about to meet your Maker."

Pell cast a wary glance around the sanctuary. "Just haven't been in a church since…" He gripped the cross around his neck. "Just memories, I guess."

"You preached behind one of these?" Cadan gestured toward the pulpit.

Pell nodded, his gaze absently scanning the pews. "I used to do some good back then. People said I had a gift at making the Bible easy to understand."

Cadan didn't know whether to feel sorry for the man or chastise him for remembering his former occupation with such fondness in his voice.

Instead, all he said was, "Lot of good it did you." Kneeling, he set down the candle and plucked the pickax from his belt. Probably not the kindest thing to say, but the last thing he needed was for his best friend to become a weak-kneed bumbling preacher again. "A worthless profession, that," he added. "Serving a God who tossed you to the sharks."

Memories of his mother surfaced. She would clap him upside the head for even thinking such a thing. Oh, how she had served God and loved Him. That was before He robbed her of her health and put her six feet under.

Groaning, Pell knelt beside him as Cadan counted four planks from the left. "Help me lift the altar."

"You're not going to break it," Pell said with more authority than he should use with his captain. "'Tis sacred."

"Scads, man. 'Tis just furniture. Nothing sacred about it. Besides, thought you were done with this God of yours."

Still the man hesitated, flattening his lips.

"I won't damage it. Just help me lift it."

Dropping back down, Pell slid his fingers beneath the altar and together with Cadan lifted it off the floor.

Reaching under the fourth plank, Cadan groped for the small indention he'd been told was there.

There! His heart felt like it would burst.

"Hurry!" Pell groaned beneath the strain.

Cadan pressed it and instantly a small wooden plank along the top of the altar flipped open.

"Okay, set it back down."

Grabbing the candle, he held it up to the narrow opening. Something was in there. Reaching in, he grabbed what felt like a tiny scroll. A surge of elation swept over him. He could hardly breathe as he gently undid the scarlet cord and opened it.

"Here." He handed Pell the candle.

Aye. 'Twas the final clue he'd been searching for!

"Is that the clue?" Durwin's excited voice blared behind them. "What do it say? Do it tell ye where the treasure be?"

"Scads, man!" Cadan growled, trying to keep his voice down. "I ordered you to stay with the women." Rising, he quickly rolled up the small piece of parchment and eased it into his waistcoat pocket.

At first startled at Cadan's angry tone, Durwin took a step back. But then he merely shrugged. "They's in no danger 'ere, Cap'n."

"That is for me to say," Cadan seethed out. The man's interest in the treasure was natural, but his greed caused him to overstep Cadan's authority, and he couldn't have that among his crew.

"You got your clue," Pell said. "Let's get back to the ship."

"Nay." Cadan started for the door, still angry at Durwin. "The night has only just begun. We're off to The Kraken's Grotto to wait for Smity. And if he bears good news, to set a trap."

Chapter 18

"What do you have for me?" Captain Damien Allard stood, feet spread apart, arms crossed, staring down at the slimy varmint who would betray his captain. He hadn't been sure the man had spoken the truth about Cadan going to Nevis in their brief meeting on that spit of an island. But as soon as he appeared out of the darkness, Damien found both delight and disgust brewing in his gut.

Lazy-eyed Smity, for that is what they called him, shifted his feet in the sand, and scanned the beach as if looking for an escape.

But it was too late for that. Damien had already paid the man well for the information he was about to give. And he'd not take no for an answer. Neither would the eight pirates, fully armed, standing behind him, his best and most loyal men.

He wrinkled his nose, both at the smell of fish coming from the warehouse they stood behind and the stench of betrayal radiating off the man before him.

"Told ye 'e'd come 'ere, Cap'n." Smity grunted, shifting his stance.

"Aye, and it was wise of you to choose this meeting place ahead of time. No harm will come to you, as I promised," Damien tried to reassure him. "A bargain is a bargain."

A cloud moved, revealing the rippled flesh on the right side of Smity's face. "Do you not wish to punish the man who caused that?" Damien gestured toward the hideous scars.

The man's good eye locked upon Damien. He nodded. "After ye get the woman and 'er child, ye'll 'elp me take o'er the ship?"

"As I said. The *Resolute* will join my fleet under your leadership as captain." *For a brief moment, that is.* What a little split-tongued weasel. "Now, where is your captain and the lady?"

A gust of wind stirred the fronds of the large palm they stood beneath as wavelets lapped against the shore to their left.

"Alls I know is 'es off to find a clue t' the treasure. Then I'm to meet 'im at the Kraken's Grotto and tell 'im whether yer ship arrived." Smity snorted in derision. "'E's got a plan to trap ye. I just ain't privy to it. If 'e tells me at the tavern, I'll slip out an' let ye know. If not, jist follow us."

Damien huffed. So Cadan hoped to trap him. What a fool.

"And"—Smity smirked—"'e's got the wench an' the babe wit' 'im."

Delight soared through Damien, and he couldn't help but smile. Perfect. He would steal Cadan's ship, obtain the final clue to the treasure, and get back Gabrielle *and* his son. All in one night!

"Off with you now." Damien waved at the dung-souled bungler.

Smity started away.

"And if you betray me," he called after him. "I'll eat your liver for breakfast."

Smity's one eye widened before he skittered away.

For any lady to set foot inside such a vile establishment was reprehensible enough, but to be forced to bring an innocent babe into such a wicked pit of hell was beyond the pale. However, the captain had insisted, assuring her that she and Matthew were safe with him. And from the way she'd seen the pirates on the street making wide berths around him as he walked down the center, and the particular one, Deadeyes, who'd scrambled off at Cadan's challenge, she might believe it. Yet he was only one man with a mere six of his pirates against a tavern full of miscreants.

And by the smell, sights, and sounds—all of which slapped her in the face as she entered—the customers of this particular tavern were well past the point of rational self-preservation and decent decorum. Some men lay on the floor unconscious. Others were draped over chairs and tables. Those that remained somewhat alert played cards, slammed down jugs of ale, or fondled scantily clad women. Curses, along with a few chairs, flew through the air, while the eerie twang of a violin accompanied it all.

Cadan leaned to whisper in her ear, no doubt seeing the horror on her face. "We shan't be long, my lady. Stay close."

And for the first time since she'd met the man, she thought being close to him was a good idea.

He strode forward, shoulders back, head held high, hand resting lightly on the hilt of his cutlass as if he owned the place. With a commanding gaze, he surveyed the crowded room, eyes halting here and there…assessing any danger or looking for someone?

Pell marched beside him.

Omphile slid her arm through Gabrielle's and pulled her tight as the rest of the captain's men surrounded them. The scent of sour spirits, sweat, and evil filled her lungs even as lantern light transformed men's faces into demons as they passed.

Whistles and lewd invitations soiled her ears, and she covered Matthew's face with his blanket and drew him closer.

Her chest rose and fell with each rapid beat of her heart. She'd graced a few sordid taverns like this before, but always with her father. She'd felt safe with him, for much like Cadan, he was rarely challenged, even as he aged. People feared him, revered him almost, not because of his ruthlessness or cruelty, but because of the power of God that so easily rested on him like a cloak.

Longing welled up within her to see him, to feel his fatherly arms around her. To feel safe once again.

They passed a long bar full of dirty glasses, bottles of spirits, and several patrons shouting and singing. One man fed pieces of cheese to a plump rat sitting beside his mug of ale.

Finally, Cadan halted and gestured for her and Omphile to sit at a table in the corner.

"What now?" Pell asked.

"We wait for Smity."

Durwin took a seat beside Omphile while Pell sat next to Gabrielle, offering her a smile and nod that said there was naught to fear.

She wanted to shout at him, scream that there was everything to fear, but the noise in the room and her good sense kept her quiet. Omphile, who normally was a bastion of peace, cast a worried glance at Gabrielle.

Cadan took a seat but kept his gaze over the room. The rest of his four men took up positions around the table. Wait. Now there were five. The fifth was the same pirate who often guarded her. When had he joined them? Tall, built as sturdy as a mast, with long light hair tied behind him, he merely stood behind her, not saying a word.

Men and women alike cast glances at them from all around, but none dared come near.

Durwin leaned toward Cadan. "Since ye got yer clue, why not just leave, Cap'n? Go get the treasure? Why risk Allard killin' us or, worse, stealin' it?"

"Have you so little faith in me, Durwin?" Cadan snapped his fingers at a passing barmaid, and she nodded and headed off, only to return within moments with two bottles of rum and several glasses.

Leaning back in his chair, Pell folded arms over his chest. "Money isn't the only treasure worth having."

Removing his hat, Durwin scratched his head and scowled at the preacher. "Says ye."

Cadan poured rum into a glass, then handed it to Pell, but he shook his head.

Good. At least one of these fools would remain sober this night.

Matthew shifted in her arms, and his tiny hand extended from the bundle. Kissing it, Gabrielle quickly slid it back where it would be hidden.

The captain's other men greedily grabbed the rum, pouring themselves glasses. All save the man standing guard behind Gabrielle.

"You do not partake, Mr. Pell?" she asked the quartermaster.

"Not usually. I suppose I learned restraint when I was a…" he halted and sighed.

She gave him a sad smile. Of course.

Pain and regret flamed in his dark eyes. Regardless of his defiance of God, this ex-preacher seemed completely out of place in this wicked tavern, as if the evil therein caused an irritating rash to cover his skin. Then why had he chosen such an opposing profession?

"And are you happy being a pirate?" she asked.

"I am pleased to be of service anywhere."

"Even in thievery?"

"'Tis not what you think, Miss. Besides, I have suffered no misfortune as a pirate, whereas as a man of God, I suffered immensely."

Though he'd had to raise his voice over the din, his tone bore the same anger and sorrow she often saw marring his expression, and she wondered if her own face bore such scars, for the same was true for her. The only difference? Her bitter misfortune had continued long after she'd stopped praying.

Cadan tossed another shot of rum into his mouth, scanning the raucous mob.

Omphile nudged her arm. "D'ye want me to take him from you? He must be gettin' heavy."

"Thank you, nay." Gabrielle smiled at her friend. "I cannot let go of him in this place."

The woman nodded her understanding.

Finally, Lazy-eyed Smity materialized out of the crowd, like a man emerging from Hades, an uneasy grin on his face. "Cap'n. There ye are." He grabbed the bottle, took a big swig, and wiped his mouth with his sleeve. "Ye were right, Cap'n. Allard sailed into the harbor jist a few minutes ago. Saw 'im meself, did I."

Gabrielle couldn't quite discern why, but Smity seemed a bit over-anxious, more enthusiastic than his usual irritable demeanor.

The captain took no note. Instead, he slapped the table with a grin, then motioned the barmaid over who'd served them. Not that she'd been too far away, for the poor lady's flirtatious glances oft found their way to Cadan.

She rushed over to him and promptly perched on his lap. Though the captain attempted to nudge her off, she began showering his neck with kisses.

Oddly, irritation clawed up Gabrielle's throat. Or was it jealousy? Absurd! She was only shocked to see such blatant behavior in any woman. Pursing her lips, she wanted to look away, but found she could not. No doubt the captain was enjoying the trollop's attentions.

Then why did he suddenly rise, shove her from his lap, all the while gripping her shoulders to prevent her from falling?

She gave a childish pout, clearly upset at his rejection. However the gleam returned to her eyes when he reached inside his waistcoat and placed two gold coins in her hand.

Then leaning, he whispered something in her ear, to which she smiled and nodded. A plan for a future assignation?

What did it matter to Gabrielle? Men. All the same, the lot of them.

The woman sashayed away, drawing the gaze of every man at the table, including Cadan's. Yet when he spun back around, his glance found hers. And for the briefest of moments, a flash of something crossed his eyes, but what she couldn't tell. "Stay here," he ordered, then pivoted and approached the man pouring ale behind the bar.

Gabrielle couldn't hear what he said, nor did she care. She was only glad when he returned and announced they were leaving.

Thankfully Matthew had mostly slept through the entire ordeal. What a good boy.

No sooner did they walk out into the night air than she peeled back the blankets to check on him.

Omphile leaned over. "His first trip to a tavern, and he slept the whole time."

"His *last* trip to a tavern," Gabrielle said emphatically.

"Is he to be a preacher then?" Pell slipped beside her.

She glanced down at her son's sweet face. Her father was a preacher of sorts. But how could she recommend such a profession when she believed God had let her down?

"Perhaps," was all she said, as a sudden ache spread across her belly. No doubt her body was still recovering from childbirth.

Thankfully, the captain didn't go far before he stopped at the same church they'd been at before. Only this time, they inched around the brick building to the back. Gravestones rose from the misty ground like the tongues of the dead, screaming for help.

A chill scraped over her. There was only one thing left on the captain's agenda and that was trapping Allard. She looked over to ask Pell the plan, but he was already moving toward Cadan.

They skirted around several tombstones and a few wooden crosses before halting in the far corner near a copse of trees.

The captain gestured for her and Omphile to stand by one of the grave sites. "Remain here, my lady. You, as well, Omphile."

He then commanded two of his men to hide in the nearby brush and two more to dig on the other side of the tombstone. The pirate she assumed was her guard, despite the captain's denial, took up a position beside her.

Clinging tightly to Matthew, she glared at Cadan, the blood in her veins turning to ice. "Your trap is set, Captain. How appropriate that you are to dig my grave here in a graveyard."

Cadan drew a deep breath of the night air, ripe with the loamy scent of overturned earth and the putrid odor of decaying bones. A mist clung to the ground as tightly as death clung to this place, penetrating his skin with the hopelessness of the eternally damned.

Two of his men pretended to dig at the back of the tombstone, whilst Lady Fox and her babe remained in full sight before it. Hidden in the shadows of a batch of Ficus trees to his left stood two of his men, blades drawn, pistols primed, at the ready.

Unease prickled on Cadan's neck. Not simply due to the mist and the eerie place, but because something wasn't right. He didn't know how he knew or why, but something was amiss. Perhaps 'twas Smity's odd behavior. Cadan had never seen the man express any emotion save sullen peevishness, yet he seemed overly anxious when he'd arrived at the tavern. Odd. Perhaps Durwin's greed had dribbled onto the bosun, eliciting an excitement over the treasure they would find. And then there was the strange observations of Lady Fox.

Yet Smity had no way to know whether Cadan had found the final clue.

Which was why Cadan had sent Pell and Durwin to hide in the shadows beside the church while keeping Smity close by. No doubt Allard was at the Kraken's Grotto by now, discovering from the barmaid and the owner Cadan's whereabouts, and more importantly, the whereabouts of the lady and his child.

If all went according to plan, Allard would come upon them, see that Cadan only had three men, and attack. Then the rest of Cadan's men would emerge from hiding and surround them.

Cadan smiled. He'd finally have Allard! Finally, after seven long years, he'd have his revenge. He'd draw it out of course, make the man suffer as much as he'd made Cadan. Ah, sweet, sweet vengeance!

In addition, he glanced down at Lady Fox, babe snuggled against her chest, he'd ensure the lady would be unharmed, and afterward, he would sail her to any port she desired and put her safely ashore.

A slight twinge pricked his heart at the thought he'd not see her again. Ridiculous.

She glanced his way, and even in the lantern light, he saw fear and loathing twisting her expression. But how could he blame her?

Regardless, 'twas a good plan. Then why did a wave of guilt suddenly assail him? He shifted his stance and studied the gravestone before them.

Here lies Sir Thomas Maine
Thought he could lie and cheat for gain
But God took him out in a burst of pain
Cadan snorted.

"A word of wisdom for you from above?" Lady Fox commented with sarcasm.

"We shall see."

A noise pricked his ears, and he held up a hand to silence her. The sound of bootsteps on dirt, the crunch of gravel, the stealth movement of men. They were coming!

With a nod to the two men to keep digging and a glance at the trees to his other men, Cadan slid his hand to the hilt of his blade and waited.

Chapter 19

Gabrielle was more determined than ever not to show an ounce of the terror squeezing every nerve within her. From the captain's face, she knew Damien approached, knew there would be a skirmish at best. At worst, a deadly battle.

And she, Matthew, and Omphile would be caught in the middle.

Not to mention that if the captain's plan failed, she'd once again be Allard's prisoner. Only this time she doubted he'd ever let her go.

'Twas a fate worse than death, not only for her, but for her precious son. Father or not, she would not have her son raised by that vicious, heartless, swine.

Clinging to Matthew, she shared a glance with Omphile who looked as frightened as she did. Entwining her arm with hers, the mulatto attempted a smile. "Have faith," she said. "We will be all right. I knows it."

Ever the encourager. Even when things seemed hopeless.

Bootsteps crunched over gravel, then thudded on soft soil. The chime of blades being drawn rang through the misty night— an omen of the grim reaper's arrival.

Cadan glanced up.

Allard's voice stabbed Gabrielle in the back. "Ah, Captain Hayes, we meet again so soon."

She turned to see Damien, rapier extended before him, victorious grin lifting his thin mustache. His glance shifted from Cadan to her for the briefest of moments, then to the bundle in her arms, and his grin widened.

Four pirates surrounded him, some burly, some thin, all dressed in dark breeches and colorfully embroidered waistcoats with scarves tied around their waists. And all brandishing weapons—flintlocks, muskets, swords, and long knives.

Allard wore his usual posh attire, complete with a red feather fluttering from his cocked hat.

"I believe you have something I want." Allard pointed at her with the tip of his rapier. "And"—he craned his neck to look at the two men who had stopped digging—"I'll take that clue as well."

Cadan chuckled. "I believe you have underestimated me, *mon ami*. I am not the boy you once defeated." He absently touched his clipped earlobe and gave a nod toward the trees.

Heart tight as a drum, Gabrielle clung to Matthew in one hand and to Omphile with the other, hoping…waiting for the remainder of Cadan's men to emerge from the trees and surround Allard and his men.

"Are you not?" Allard lowered his blade and leaned on the hilt, that ever-present smirk on his thin lips.

No men appeared, none from the trees and none from behind Allard, where Gabrielle assumed Cadan had ordered them to approach. Something was wrong. Terribly wrong.

She felt Cadan tense behind her, could hear the slight outtake of his breath.

Rustling brought their gazes back to the trees. The two pirates finally appeared, but not with blades drawn and bloodlust in their eyes. Nay, with scowls of defeat and shame as they were brought out at blade point by four of Allard's men.

Terror scraped across every nerve. Her breath caught. Her knees wobbled, and for a moment Gabrielle thought she'd faint. As if sensing her fear, Omphile drew an arm around her waist for support.

A scraping sound sliced the air, chilling her to the bone as Cadan, Smity, and his two remaining men drew their blades.

"Come now, Cadan. As you can see, I have your men *and* the advantage. You are four. We are nine. Do you wish to die this night?" Damien hesitated, shifting his gaze to her. "All I want is the woman, my child, and the clue. A fair price for your life and the lives of your men."

Cadan moved to stand before her, leveling his cutlass at Allard. "Omphile, take the lady into the church," he ordered.

"You would fight us?" Allard chuckled. "But you will die, and I will have her regardless."

"Let us play this game and find out." Cadan's tone held no fear, only a misplaced arrogance, coupled with hatred.

Omphile tugged her away. Nay. She would not be the cause of this! Halting, she faced Cadan.

"Captain. Please. I will go with him. I do not wish anyone to die on my account." And, oddly, she did not wish to see him die either.

"Ah, my sweet." Damien's silky voice hissed. "You see, she wishes to be with me."

Nausea bubbled in her stomach. *This can't be happening*!

"Take her now, Omphile!" Cadan shouted.

With more force than the little mulatto appeared to have, Omphile took hold of Gabrielle's hand and dragged her to the church.

Tears burned in her eyes. Why, Lord, why was this happening? Had she not caused enough pain that she now would be the reason these men would die?

Omphile nudged her against the back wall of the church. The cold stones sent a chill down her as she gripped Matthew close.

Thumps and groans filled the air, and Cadan's men who'd been at blade point, instantly swerved. One of Allard's men fell to the ground, gripping a bloody wound. Two others swung about to face their attackers, while the fourth hurried to find the weapon that had been knocked from his hands.

Cadan's men quickly pounced, and the fighting began. Wasting no time, Cadan heaved his blade down upon a surprised Allard.

But the villain raised his rapier at the last moment. Their blades rang together in a bone-scraping sound that would likely raise all the dead from their graves.

Releasing Cadan, Damien rushed blindly at him, but the captain quickly dipped his cutlass in defense. Behind them, Pell and Durwin emerged from the trees, where they had snuck up on Damien's men. Rushing into the melee with blades in one hand and pistols in the other, they quickly engaged Damien's men.

Gabrielle had seen sword fights before, but never ever had she been the prize. Nor had there been so much at stake.

Matthew began to wail.

Cuddling him close, she attempted to shush him as best she could, but the babe surely sensed her stress.

A pistol shot cracked the humid air, followed by a cry. Matthew screamed. Omphile drew closer to Gabrielle. One of Damien's men fell to the ground. Durwin tossed the pistol down, and drawing his cutlass, leapt over a gravestone and charged the nearest man. Pell held his own with another, swords whirling aloft, while Cadan's other men did the same.

With an ominous growl, Cadan met Damien's low thrust with a counter-parry, expertly done. Then slashing his blade left and right, he forced Damien back, step by step. Damien heaved, breathless, sweat shining on his forehead. He was no slouch at sword fighting, but he had clearly met his match with the captain.

"What are we doing?" Omphile shouted over the violent din. "We should leave."

What? Gabrielle glanced around. No one was guarding them. None save the one pirate she always saw. Confusion spun a cyclone in her mind. Why was he not fighting alongside his captain? Or at least, why was he not helping her and Omphile escape?

Gabrielle drew a deep breath, glancing once more at Cadan as he slashed his cutlass over Damien's arm, drawing blood.

To the right, one of Cadan's men tumbled to the ground, clutching his bloody side. Having dispatched his own opponent, Pell rushed to his aid.

There was no guarantee Cadan and his men would win. Omphile was right.

Bundling Matthew close, she nodded. "Let us go."

Grabbing her hand, Omphile led the way along the back of the church, keeping to the shadows. They had just turned the corner, just made their way onto the pathway that led to town…and freedom…when Lazy-eyed Smity appeared out of the mist.

"Now, where d'ye two think yer goin'?"

With a snap of his blade, Cadan thrust Damien's rapier out of the way and sliced the snake's right arm. Red etched a trail over his white shirt. Smiling, Cadan took the chance to glance at the women. They stood in the shadows of the church, safe for now.

Gripping his wound, Damien's face wrinkled in pain. Anger took its place, and hefting his rapier with a mighty growl, he swooped it down upon Cadan.

Cadan quickly leapt out of the way and thrust his cutlass low toward Damien's leg. If he could prevent the man from standing, he'd have him.

Damien jerked to the left, nearly tripping over a tombstone, but then spun around, and brought his rapier toward Cadan's neck. Matching his blade hilt for hilt, Cadan pushed him back, then released his blade and shoved him.

Stumbling backward, Damien's hot breath filled the air as his chest rose and fell like angry waves at sea.

To Cadan's left, Pell, with a flick of his cutlass, sent his opponent's blade flying into the brush, then leveled his own at the pirate's throat. The man raised his hands in defeat.

Durwin and Cadan's remaining men fought with the skill and ferocity he'd taught them, blades clanging, grunts and groans filling the air. Though outnumbered, 'twould not be long before they'd defeat these miscreants. Where was Smity? He scanned the graveyard.

Cadan faced Damien again. He'd allowed him to regain his strength, a foolish thing, that. Yet he could see from the slight twitch of his jaw that he, too, realized he'd soon be overcome.

Pointing his cutlass at the man's chest, Cadan huffed. "You are done for, Allard. Admit defeat like a man and come meet your fate."

Allard pursed his lips, shifting his eyes over the scene.

Cadan licked his own. 'Twas the moment he'd dreamt about for so long.

But then an odd grin contorted Damien's face. Cadan knew that grin. 'Twas a grin of victory. But how could that be?

Only then did movement catch his eye, and he turned to see one of Allard's men dragging Gabrielle forward. Omphile tugged upon the burly pirate, screaming, "Let her go!" but he paid her no mind.

"Lower your cutlass or I'll order him to snap her neck." Allard sneered.

Catching his breath, Cadan shifted his gaze between Allard and the lady. He knew the man was more than capable of fulfilling his threat. Hence, he lowered his blade.

Sheathing his rapier, Allard took Gabrielle's arm and tugged her and Matthew close while the other pirate grabbed Omphile. Before Cadan could move, Allard plucked a knife from his belt and held it to the lady's neck.

"I can see this wench has wormed her way into your weak heart, Cadan. Your eyes betray you."

Rage threatened to strangle Cadan. "Let her go, Allard! Would you keep a woman who despises you? A child born from naught but your violent lust?"

"Ah, that's where we differ, *mon ami*. That makes it all the sweeter."

Cadan knew the man was evil. What he hadn't known was that he was also mad. He glanced behind him at Pell, Durwin, and his other men, all standing with blades drawn, their opponents cowering before them.

Gabrielle wrenched from the man's grasp, eyes flashing terror.

Allard gripped her all the tighter. "Let us go peacefully, or I will kill her here and now."

"You're mad," Cadan spat.

"Indeed."

"Tell your men to lower their swords, and we will do you no harm."

Cadan blew out a bitter laugh. "Us no harm? Clearly, we defeated you and your men. 'Tis you who should beg us for your lives."

"Perhaps. But once again, seems I have the upper hand. And with a woman again, ha!" A breeze swept over them, stirring leaves and tossing strands of Damien's hair across his cheek. "Do as I say!" His tone hardened as he pressed the knife until a drop of blood trickled down Lady Fox's neck.

"Lower your blades!" Cadan commanded.

"Very good." Allard began backing up, then ordered his man, "Take the mulatto as well."

"What need have you of her?" Cadan said, taking a step forward. "She's but a maid."

Allard shrugged. "For the babe, for I'll not have my sweet burdened with his care."

Blood surged through Cadan's veins—red, hot blood.

"If you follow us," Allard said, "if you attempt anything. If I so much as see you behind me, I will kill her. And now, I bid you *adieu*." Retrieving his hat from the ground, he swept it out before him in a flourish, then plopped it on his head and continued to back away, never taking his eyes off Cadan. One by one, his men fell in behind him, leveling blades their way.

"Oh, I almost forgot," Allard shouted. "Your ship is mine. Even now, my men are taking it over. Don't bother dashing to save it, for I am sure it is too late." And with that, he spun around and disappeared into the darkness, dragging Lady Fox beside him.

Alarm rammed into Cadan, thrusting and poking and stabbing. In one dastardly moment, he lost the lady, her child, Omphile, and his ship! He could not lose his ship, not to this man! He could not!

Sheathing his blade, he clenched his fists until blood dripped down his palms. Pell, breath heaving and blood running down his arm, moved beside him. "We will get her back, Captain."

"The ship or the woman?" he asked, though he suddenly wondered which one was more important to him.

"Both."

Cadan rose to his full height and stretched out his shoulder where he'd been struck with the hilt end of Damien's rapier. A pain stretched down his leg, no doubt from a wound he didn't remember getting, but he could still walk. "Indeed." He would not be defeated by this blackguard. Not again.

"Orders, Captain?" Durwin approached as did Smity and his other men, one of them holding a bloody hand to his waist.

He surveyed the two pirates Allard had left unconscious in the dirt, bloody and bruised. The craven cockroach abandoned his men like so much refuse.

His own crew had fared much better. Out of the seven men, only two were injured, one with a blade to his side and the other a bloody gash on his head. "Olin, take Hawk and Kipp into town. Seek out a physician posthaste, then meet us on the ship." That last order was more one of hope, but it seemed to infuse confidence in the remaining men as Cadan set off to follow Allard.

His plan? He had none. Except to rescue the woman and take back command of his ship. But which to tackle first?

Pell, Durwin, Smity, and Barnett took to his heels as he crept down the muddy street, clinging to the shadows, careful to not make a sound. Allard and his men were easy to spot, for they cackled on like a group of lusty hens, not to mention the occasional blue flash of Gabrielle's skirts.

By the time they reached town, a strip of gray light lit the horizon, pushing back the darkness, not only in the sky but in town where the debauched revelry of just hours earlier had crawled back into hiding. Light and dark. Good and evil. Cadan rarely thought of such things, but he'd seen pure evil that night in the empty eyes of Allard. Pure insane evil. Did such wickedness, such debased corruption truly exist? And if so, was it a spirit, as his mother had told him? For if evil did exist, then so did good.

And hence, God.

Peering through the gloom, he spotted Allard once again, still maintaining his tight grip on Lady Fox. Another of his pirates had Omphile in his clutches, dragging her along as if she were a stuffed doll.

Fury boiled in Cadan's stomach.

Halting, Allard looked behind him.

Cadan slammed against the side of a wooden building that no doubt served as a chandler, for the scent of beeswax filled his nose. His men followed suit. A cough rose in his throat, and he slammed his hand on his mouth to stifle it.

After a few moments, Allard continued on his way.

Cadan and his men hopped from building to building, keeping to the shadows in stealthy pursuit until there were no more structures to hide beside.

Docks stretched out to the rising sun like baby tongues awaiting their morning milk.

Rays of gold rippled over the incoming waves as the scent of fish, salt, and fresh baked bread swirled in the air around them.

The masts of ships poked high into the gray sky like boney fingers, reaching for heaven.

Cadan sought out the *Resolute.*

He'd purposely anchored as far from town as possible should he need to set sail quickly, but even from this distance, and even in the remaining shadows, he spotted flashes from muskets and pistols, and could hear the faint shouts and groans of men at battle.

He should forget the women and row out to the *Resolute* as fast as he could, save his ship! Though he trusted Moses and the men he'd left, good fighters all, no doubt Allard had sent a swarm of pirates to overwhelm them.

But Gabrielle? His gaze sought her out as Allard and his men disappeared around the dockmaster's station. He could not forget the fear in her eyes nor her willingness to sacrifice herself to save their lives. What kind of woman did that for her captors? For a man who used her as bait?

Creeping out from the fish house, he followed, stopping behind the dock house and peered around the side. Allard and his men lumbered down a wooden dock toward a jolly boat tied at the end. Cadan swung his head back and glanced at Pell.

"The men must sheath their weapons when they enter the boat. That's when we'll get them," he whispered.

Pell and the others nodded. All save Smity who fingered the pearl in his ear and stared off into town.

But Cadan had no time to ponder why. Timing was everything.

"Pistols at the ready, men," he whispered, plucking his flintlock from his belt before peering once again at his nemesis.

As he suspected, each of the pirates put away their weapons, and with moans and groans, clambered into the boat. Omphile was all but shoved onto a seat. She let out a squeal that nearly sent Cadan charging forward.

Finally, after Allard cast one last glance behind him, he sheathed his knife and held out a hand for Gabrielle.

The lady shoved it aside and must have said something rude, for he scowled, grabbed her hand, and roughly pushed her onto the thwarts beside Omphile, a good two yards from where he stood.

Now!

Hefting his flintlock, Cadan charged down the dock, his men behind him, pistols at the ready.

"Halt there!" Cadan yelled. "Halt or be killed!" He stopped at the edge of the dock and glanced down at Allard and his men. For a brief moment, his gaze locked with Gabrielle's and surprise and relief appeared on her face.

On the contrary, alarm squealed across Allard's—alarm and then fury. He had no chance and he knew it. His men would have no time to draw their weapons before Cadan and his men shot them all.

"Release the women and the babe and I'll let you live!"

A knot traveled down the snake's throat, the only indication of his fear before he leapt toward the women, grabbed Gabrielle, and shoved her in front of him.

Cadan had no shot! Even if he did, and even though he was a good marksman, flintlocks were not always accurate, and he would not risk the woman so close to Allard.

She wrestled against his fierce grasp, but he tightened his grip. She cried out in pain. Cadan longed to dash to her aid, but the boat was full of Allard's pirates, and they were looking angrier than ever.

At least she prevented him from pulling his knife.

"If you fire one shot, I'll slice her! Now, row!" Allard shouted.

"Always hiding behind a skirt! You coward!" Cadan growled.

"Do ye want us to shoot the rest?" Durwin asked.

"We can kill the rowers," Smity added.

"We'd have to kill them all." Cadan shook his head. And he was not prepared for a bloodbath, nor to risk the women. But what to do?

The men put oars to oarlocks and plunged the paddles into the water, all staring anxiously at Cadan and his men.

Gabrielle's wide, pleading eyes reached for Cadan, and it took everything in him to not jump into the water and rescue her. But they'd both be easily overcome by Allard's men.

All he could do was stare at her, feeling as though his heart were being ripped from his chest.

Then with a loud groan, she jabbed Allard's chest with her free elbow, struggled from his grip, and leapt to her feet in the wobbling boat.

Shocked, Cadan could only watch as, without hesitation, she threw her baby toward him.

The bundle swooped through the air, teetering and gliding on the morning breeze, blanket unraveling as it went—heading for the rippling waters of the harbor! Dropping his pistol, Cadan jumped into the bay, shallow enough for his feet to barely reach bottom, and flung out his arms to catch him.

Chapter 20

What was Cadan going to do with a baby? And a wailing one at that? Especially when he had a battle to fight. He attempted to bounce the babe up and down as he'd seen Lady Fox do, but the child would not cease. How could they sneak up on the *Resolute* undetected with such an annoying racket!?

Water bubbled down the side of the cockboat as his men shoved off from the dock and headed toward the ship. He'd know soon enough whether the *Resolute* remained under his command or whether his most hated enemy had taken that from him as well. First his wife, then his freedom, and now Lady Fox. He'd be damned if he'd also lose his ship to that spineless squid.

Morning sun caused him to blink as water from the oars splashed his breeches, cooling his skin. If only it would cool his fury.

"Here." He handed the infant to Pell, sitting beside him. "Quiet him."

Pell snorted. "Do I look like a nursemaid?"

Cadan's eyes drifted down to Pell's cross. "Maybe pray to your God."

"Humph." Pell swung the babe back and forth in his arms, only causing young Matthew to scream all the louder. "I think he's hungry."

Smity chuckled. "Looks like yer out o' luck in that department, Cap'n."

Durwin smiled, but his eyes were seeking out the *Resolute*.

As were Cadan's. It remained at anchor, bobbing in the incoming surf, which was a good sign, indeed, for if Allard's men had taken her, she'd be setting out to sea.

Sharp rays of golden sun speared her three bare masts, set her lines aflame, and angled across her deck. She was a beauty. The only woman who had never betrayed him. And he would not lose her.

Wind whipped him, cooling the sweat on his neck and flapping his shirt as they rounded the hull of a nearby schooner. The chime of swords and shouts of battle finally met his ears. Good. They were not too late.

Yet the element of surprise would be lost to them with both the daylight and the incessant howling of the babe. But it couldn't be helped. He would not stand by and allow his ship to be taken.

But what to do with the child? He glanced around the boat, and his eyes landed on a wooden chest that carried knives, pickaxes, and extra rope.

"Empty the box," he ordered Durwin.

Pell arched a brow. "You aren't thinking…?"

"I am. What else can I do?"

Pell frowned but offered no alternative.

After the box was emptied, Cadan coiled the rope to form a cocoon, then laid Matthew inside and shut the lid. A few holes on the side would provide air.

Oddly, the baby ceased screaming.

"See?" He shot Pell a satisfied smirk. Then facing forward, Cadan checked his flintlock, and gripped the hilt of his sword.

They were but yards from the ship now. Shouts and grunts, along with the crash of blade and pop of pistol serenaded the squawk of birds and slap of waves. A distant horn blared from the fort.

Over the starboard rail, a pirate spotted them and shouted over his shoulder.

"Faster!" Cadan ordered. They had to reach the hull, or they'd be peppered with gunshot.

Too late.

Two of Allard's pirates fired upon them. *Pop! Pop!* Spurts of water flung into the air on the right side of the boat. The men disappeared, no doubt to reload just as the cockboat thumped against the hull.

"To the fight, men!" Cadan leapt onto the rope ladder with one hand and clambered above, drawing his blade with the other before he even reached the deck. Leaping over the bulwarks, he took on the pirate who was furiously reloading his pistol for another shot. The poor man never knew what hit him. The other man dropped his gun and drew his blade, and Cadan advanced on him with confidence.

Pell, Durwin, Smity, and Barnett rammed into the battle-weary mob, blades in hand.

Moses, engaged with his own pirate, shot him a rare smile before quickly dispatching his foe and charging toward another. Bodies of slain pirates littered the deck. Cadan searched for any that were his as another pirate sliced at him from his left.

Spinning, he parried right, then left, ignoring the ache in his shoulder and leg. Finally, Cadan whirled his sword aloft and brought it down upon his opponent, toppling him to the deck.

Wiping the sweat from his brow, he spotted Soot on the foredeck. He knifed his enemy in the gut, then shoved him backward over the railing. The pirate landed in the bay with a mighty splash.

Cadan spun around, ready to take on another foe, but there was no one to fight. Moses slammed the hilt of his blade atop his opponent's head and the man crumpled to the deck. Pell, Durwin, and Barnett quickly dispatched their assailants, and the remainder of Allard's men, realizing they were defeated, ran for the railing and leapt overboard.

"Should we shoot 'em, Cap'n?" One of his men rushed to the railing, pistol in hand.

"Nay. Let them go." Bending to place hands on his knees, Cadan caught his breath and smiled. He'd thank God for saving his ship if he thought He had anything to do with it. Nay, 'twas his men's loyalty and skill.

A hard clap on his back brought him up to see Moses, the whites of his teeth brilliant in the rising sun. Sweat glistened on his bald head, his chest heaved, and a bloody slice marred his thick arm, but otherwise he looked well.

"Happy to see you, Cap'n! 'Til you got here, we weren't sure we could hold dem off."

Soot joined them, leaning his smoking pistol against his shoulder. "Nice o' ye to join us, Cap'n!" He grinned.

"Seems you two—" Cadan glanced over the rest of his crew on the deck, many of whom had slumped due to exhaustion. "And all of you were doing great without me. We've won our ship back, men! Huzzah!"

"Huzzah!" they all shouted in unison.

"Those scumfaced princocks!" Kipp spat to the side. "We showed 'em, Cap'n!"

"Kipp!" Cadan stared at the man who'd been injured on shore. A blood-stained bandage wrapped around his waist. "I see you are well and back on board."

"We 'eard the fightin', Cap'n, and couldna stay away." Olin emerged from the crowd, a wide grin on his soot-smudged face.

"And Hawk?" Cadan asked about his other injured pirate.

"Below, restin'," Kipp answered, glancing at Moses.

Cadan nodded. "My finest rum for everyone!"

More cheers swirled in the salty air.

Moses scoured the deck with his gaze. "Where's Omphile? An' the lady?"

Swallowing down a lump of dread, Cadan faced the carpenter. "Captured by Allard."

The man's face seemed to fold up in pain. His nostrils flared.

Cadan gripped his meaty arm. "We'll get them back. You have my word."

For a moment, he wondered if this man had reached the limit of his loyalty to Cadan, for he said naught, just stared at him as if he'd gladly toss him overboard.

Then, taking a deep breath, he nodded.

"Durwin." Cadan faced the first mate. "Check the men. Send all the wounded with Moses below, then bundle the dead in sailcloth." He would send Allard's dead back to him, while his own, if any, he'd give a proper burial at sea. He scanned the area for Smity, intending to set the man to task.

Where was the wily bosun anyway? Cadan had not seen him fight, had not seen him since he'd climbed from the cockboat. Dread squeezed his heart and he dashed to the railing and peered over.

Smity had returned to the boat and was rowing away. With Matthew in the box.

God must really hate her. There was no other explanation Gabrielle could come up with for finding herself back on this ship from Hades, back in the devil's cabin, back as a slave, where memories rose to terrorize her.

Her only consolation was Omphile, who sat in the chair beside her, gripping her hand and doing her best to reassure her God was still with them.

Perhaps He was, but that didn't mean He didn't hate her. *Aye, He does hate you. Accept it.*

Shaking away the slippery voice, she still could not deny the single ray of hope shining through this dark nightmare. Matthew was safe with Cadan. A fearful chuckle rose in her throat at the thought. When had she considered anything or anyone safe with the man who had kidnapped her, caused all this pain? Still, against every ounce of sense within her, she hoped he would take proper care of her babe. Tears burned her eyes once again, for she had no idea what he would do with her child. Who would care for him? Who would feed him? Watch over him? The captain had made his loathing for the babe quite plain.

Even now, her breasts were near bursting with milk, longing to feed him. Would she ever see him again?

Footsteps pounded above, along with shouts and commands, and the ship heaved slightly to starboard as sails thundered in the wind. Allard had set sail.

"Now cease your crying, Child. It'll be all right. You'll see." Omphile's large dark eyes glistened with hope as she offered Gabrielle a slight smile.

Either the woman had gone utterly mad, or she had no idea the monster under whose thumb they now found themselves.

"I'm so sorry you got mixed up in this, Omphile." Gabrielle's whimper stuck in her throat.

"Not your fault, Miss. God has a plan."

"I want my babe," Gabrielle cried, tears pouring down her cheeks.

"I know, Child. I knows. But he's safe. Rest in dat. You'll see him again."

Gabrielle batted her tears away. "At least Damien will not have him."

"Aye. You did a brave thing. Never saw the likes of it! You saved your child." She squeezed her hand.

In truth, 'twas all Gabrielle could think to do. She'd assessed the situation and knew Cadan had been defeated. She took a chance, a *wild* chance, that he would save her child. She'd spent enough time with him to know that he possessed a speck of kindness within his darkened heart. She gambled that 'twas enough to not watch an innocent babe drown.

She'd been right.

Bootsteps thundered down the companionway, and Gabrielle's heart seized. Quickly, she dried her eyes and swung back her shoulders, not wanting to satisfy Allard's lust for power and control.

The door swung open and the monster himself strode in, halted, and stared at them.

Gabrielle drew a breath and raised her chin. "Damien, there is no need to keep this woman here. I insist you send her back to the *Resolute* at once."

He chuckled and sauntered to the round mahogany table where he kept his maps and instruments. "You insist, do you?"

Moving past the desk, he approached a bookcase, opened the glass case, and grabbed a bottle of French Brandy.

"I do," Gabrielle said, hoping he could not hear the tremor in her voice.

Damien carefully poured the liquor into a glass, then sat upon the stern window ledge and studied them with eyes full of avarice and deceit.

And to think she'd once seen love in his gaze. Once, she'd found him to be extraordinarily handsome and charming. With his light hair pulled back cavalier style, his strong chin and jaw, his aquiline nose and piercing blue eyes, what woman wouldn't be lured into his snare? In addition, he was well built along strong muscular lines, always impeccably dressed in silver and lace, and always with a single ruby drop earring in one ear.

In truth, his cabin was immaculate, everything in its place, from the teakwood trunk to the bookcases filled with tomes ranging from mathematics to novels, the mahogany sideboard, the silver tea set and candlesticks, the elegant tapestries lining the wall, and the heavy dark-blue brocade curtains that hung down each side of the stern lights. It seemed more the room of a king, not the cabin of a pirate.

The opposite of Cadan. Gabrielle couldn't help but smile.

"Something amuses you, *ma douce*?"

"Just that you haven't changed a bit."

He smiled. "I shall take that as a compliment."

Gabrielle gestured toward Omphile beside her, though the woman defiantly shook her head. "Now, about the woman."

Damien sipped his drink. "*Non*. She stays. If only to keep you compliant."

Gabrielle squeezed Omphile's hand. "I will never be compliant. Not ever again."

"We shall see. But for now, I'll have her placed comfortably in a cabin. Nate!" His sudden shout started Gabrielle.

Instantly, the door swung open, and a pirate with a purple sash tied about his bald head marched in.

"Take the woman to Sanders' cabin and lock her inside."

Nate's leering grin landed on Omphile.

"And do her no harm, or you'll answer to me."

The man frowned but grabbed Omphile by the arm and hoisted her from the seat, ripping their hands apart.

"Nay!" Gabrielle leapt to her feet. "Please no. Let her go, Damien!"

"Tsk-tsk, *ma cherie*. You have my word she will not be harmed."

"Your word means naught to me!" She took hold of Omphile's arm and tugged on it, but the beast continued to drag her away.

Damien's arms surrounded her and yanked her back. The scent of his lavender musk cologne made her want to vomit.

Naught but peace filled Omphile's eyes. "It will be all right, Miss." She attempted a smile before the pirate hauled her out the door and slammed it with a heart-rending thud.

Pushing from Damien's embrace, Gabrielle slumped to the floor and sobbed.

Arms lifted her from behind. More fury than fear flooded her, and she shoved her elbows into his chest and flailed her legs. If this man would attempt to ravish her again, she'd make it neither easy nor pleasant.

He gave a sordid chuckle. "Ah, my little kitten has become a wildcat." He shoved her into a chair.

Her back slammed against the hard wood, and she gripped the arms and glared up at him.

Clearly surprised by her actions, he retrieved his drink and sipped it. "So you bore my child?" he said almost nonchalantly as he waved jeweled fingers through the air.

Gabrielle said naught, merely stared out the stern windows.

"I must say, my sweet, I was not so pleased when you tossed him into the sea."

She lifted her chin, attempting to still the trembling coursing through her. "I would do it again if only to save him from you."

"From his own father?" He cocked his head, a nondescript emotion scrambling across his blue eyes. "You wound me to think I would do him harm."

"I do not wish him to grow up and become like you."

A pinch of pain creased his face for but a moment before he swung his arms around the cabin. "Like me? Wealthy, powerful, successful?" He finished his drink and slammed down the glass. "So you wish him to be like Cadan Hayes, uneducated traitor, prisoner, thief, and all around failure?"

The man did have a point. Though Cadan had misused her and put her and her child in danger, there was something about him, a goodness she sensed. Whereas, with this man, she doubted a single ray of light existed in his black heart.

She glanced over at the four-poster bed against the bulkhead and shivered. "What do you want with me, Damien?"

The tight lines on his face softened. "You are the mother of my child. When I get him back, we will raise him together."

"I will do no such thing."

He charged her. "I will silence that vicious tongue, woman!"

Backing against the chair, Gabrielle let out a squeal of terror as he grabbed her shoulders, heaved her up, and shoved her against the bulkhead.

Pain spiraled down her back. Her breath came fast. His wild furious eyes shifted between hers as the smell of his brandy and cologne filled her nose.

He glanced toward the bed, and for a moment she thought he'd force her onto it.

Memories came hard and fast, sending ice through her veins and terror through her heart.

A knock rapped on the door. "Cap'n?"

He pushed from her. "What is it?" Anger burned in his voice.

A pirate entered, water dripping from his trousers. "We lost the *Resolute*."

Marching across the cabin, Damien uttered a roar that would wake the dead.

Gabrielle dared not move. Neither did the pirate.

"Captain Hayes returned?" Damien finally asked.

"Aye."

"Where stands she?"

"She still anchors in the harbor, Cap'n."

Damien gripped the hilt of his rapier, staring out the stern windows, fury fuming off him in waves. Would he attempt another attack? Surely not with Cadan back on board.

"Raise all canvas to the wind. Set sail immediately!" He barked, then waved at Gabrielle. "And lock this woman in with her mulatto."

Chapter 21

Leaping on the bulwarks, Cadan dove into the turquoise water. The liquid swept over his body, cooling the heat of battle, but not cooling his anger at Smity's betrayal. Images and memories swamped him of the man's words and movements of late, further infuriating Cadan. How had he been so blind? Lady Fox had been right all along.

He reached the boat within minutes. Grabbing one of the oars Smity was furiously slapping into the water, he shoved the handle into the traitor's gut. Moaning, Smity slumped over, giving Cadan enough time to climb aboard and slam the hilt-end of his knife onto the cullion's head, knocking him out. Then clutching both oars, he rowed back to the *Resolute,* draped Smity over his shoulder, and climbed up the rope ladder.

Moses leaned over the railing to help him over the side, where Cadan tossed the unconscious man to the deck. Then grabbing a nearby bucket of slop, he poured it on him.

Smity coughed, gasped, shook his head, and finally opened his eyes. Terror streaked across them, terror and a fury Cadan had not seen before in the man.

"Moses, bring up the babe in the box and secure the boat."

"Aye." The large man leapt over the railing with more grace than one would expect from him.

Smity struggled to rise, rubbing the back of his head. Blood stained his hand.

The other pirates surrounded him, loathing twisting their expressions. A few spat on him.

"How much did he pay you?" Cadan asked, his soaked breeches dripping onto the deck.

Smity glanced over his fellow pirates, once his friends. His jaw tightened. "I don't know what yer sayin', Cap'n."

"To spy on me!" Cadan barked, stepping toward the man. "To tell him about my trap."

Smity's bad eye drifted to the left as he rubbed the rippled skin on his face. The fear of only a moment before transformed into fury. "Ye ruined me life. Look at me! I'm a monster. No woman will come close t' me. People run when they see me. All because o' yer stupidity, yer foolishness. What do ye expect? Me t' bow down an' serve ye every day?" He spat onto the deck by Cadan's feet.

Cadan swallowed, shocked at the flaming arrows of hatred firing from the man he'd considered his friend. And each arrow hit its mark, straight in Cadan's heart. He plowed a hand through his wet hair. What a fool he'd been. He'd been blind to the man's hatred and need for revenge.

And now this revenge, this loathing oozing from Smity, disgusted him with its darkness. 'Twas like an evil spirit had been unleashed on the ship, pouring an inky film of despair and hatred over the deck.

"Lock him up below," Cadan ordered two of his men, sorrow weighing down his own heart. Anger too, aye, but also sorrow.

Grabbing Smity, Rawlins and Barnett dragged him off, curses trailing in his wake.

Moses crawled over the railing and handed the box to Cadan. Placing it gently atop a barrel, he opened it. Little Matthew was sound asleep, oblivious to the dangerous world around him, a vision of purity and innocence among so much evil.

He couldn't help but smile.

"Scope." He held out his hand to Pell, who gave him the spyglass. Then marching to the railing, he pressed it to his eye and swept it in the *Nightblood*'s last location. The ship was gone. Moving the spyglass to his left, he spotted her mountains of snowy canvas spread to the morning breeze, heading out to sea.

"Scads!" Gently picking up the box, he took the ladder in two leaps and marched across the quarterdeck, Pell close behind him.

"Olin!" His shout brought the man's gaze up to him. "You are promoted to bosun."

The man's thin brows shot up as excitement sped across his wrinkled face. "Aye, Cap'n!"

"Stand by to raise all sail!" Cadan shouted.

Parading across the main deck like a peacock, Olin began braying commands that sent topmen into the ratlines to unfurl sail.

Moses appeared beside Cadan, one meaty hand rubbing the brand on his neck beneath his scarf. "What did he want wit' Omphile?"

Cadan noted the rare fear in his carpenter's eyes. "To aid the lady with the babe. Now, go tend the injured." He wanted to apologize, to do his best to ease Moses' fears, but to do so would show weakness, something he could not afford at the moment.

"Let go the halyard, sheets, and braces," Cadan shouted. "Make all!"

"Where to, Captain?" Pell asked.

"Follow Allard!"

Wailing emerged from the wooden chest still in his arms, and Cadan spun about and headed below.

A vision of a blonde beauty with turquoise eyes circled in his mind, fear clenching his gut for what she must be enduring. Yet…she had trusted him with her son.

The thought both warmed and terrified him.

The ship bucked like a wild stallion. Matthew let out another ear-piercing wail. Amazing how such a tiny thing could scream louder than a storm. With the babe tightly in his arms, Cadan rocked him back and forth as he paced across his cabin.

The sea crashed against the hull, pounding the stern like a mighty leviathan desperate to enact tribute from all who dared cross these waters. Wind howled, joining young Matthew. Thunder rumbled, shaking the timbers as footsteps pounded the deck above and harried shouts flung through the air.

Aye, he should be with his men, not down here nursing an infant. Not that he had anything to give the poor child. Moses had crushed sodden bread into a soupy paste and dribbled it into Matthew's mouth nigh an hour ago. The child had gobbled it up and finally settled into a peaceful sleep in a bed Cadan had made in his teakwood chest. Hence, he'd left him and gone above.

That's when the storm rose. Black clouds tumbled across the eastern sky quicker than a cannon blast. And before the *Resolute* could flee for safety, the waves leapt and foamed like a boiling cauldron while the wind pelted them with stinging rain.

Cadan had been through many such storms. They often left as quickly as they came. Hence, he had stood on the quarterdeck, shouting orders to his crew to lower all sail, raise storm staysails, and secure the guns.

Olin took over the position as bosun with more efficiency than Cadan would have thought from the elder pirate, and soon the *Resolute* rode out the storm as best she could, scudding before the wind.

The ship pitched over a mighty wave and swept down into the trough, angry squalls sweeping back over the deck. Wind struck Cadan, pushing him back as he balanced on the heaving timbers. His pirates scrambled over the main deck below, lashed to masts, lest they get swept overboard. Thunder growled. Lightning flashed, casting everything in silver before gray swallowed up the light again.

'Twas not the worst storm Cadan had endured, and it was soon coming to an end, for he could see a hint of blue sky in the distance.

Nay, the worst thing about the tempest? They had lost Allard.

When things began to settle, Cadan's thoughts had drifted to young Matthew, and he hoped the infant was doing well down below. He should entrust the babe's care to one of his crew. He was the captain! Trouble was, he didn't trust any of them, save Pell, and he needed the quartermaster on the tiller.

Hence, Cadan had returned to his cabin to find Matthew howling and quivering with fear in his trunk. He'd quickly scooped him up, yet now, after what seemed like hours but was surely only minutes, the child would not be comforted. Cadan's shoulder ached, and the sword wound on his leg throbbed with each step.

The deck slanted to larboard, and it took all Cadan's strength to keep from tumbling over.

Lightning streaked across the steel gray sky outside his stern windows as if bidding him goodbye, for as quickly as the squall had come, the seas began to settle, the wind eased, and the ship took to rocking instead of bucking.

Indeed, the storm had ceased outside the ship, but not the storm in his heart.

He should have seen Smity's hatred, should not have trusted the man. And now, Lady Fox and Omphile were in a dire situation.

He should go above and check on things, but poor Matthew still screamed, his little hand shivering with each wail.

Finally, a ray of sunlight broke through the clouds and drifted into the cabin, scattering the shadows as the rumble of thunder faded in the distance.

Pell entered, water dripping from his breeches and pasting his shirt to his chest. Durwin, Soot, and Barnett on his heels.

"Barnett, go tell Moses the child is hungry again," Cadan ordered, sending the man skittering away.

"How stands the ship? Damage?"

Pell cringed as Matthew let out another wail. "No damage, Captain. I ordered Olin to lower storm sails and unfurl main."

Nodding, Cadan continued pacing and jostling the babe in his arms.

Durwin approached and wrinkled his nose. "What be that stench?"

Cadan sniffed near the child's rear, then jerked back. He handed him to Pell. "Fix him."

Pell chuckled, holding the babe away from his wet shirt. Matthew howled, flailing his tiny arms and legs. "Fix him?"

"Clean him." Cadan waved him away.

"Thought you raised a bunch of siblings, Captain."

"Thought you had a son," Cadan returned, regretting it instantly when Pell's expression soured, and he heaved a sigh.

"Do you have a clean cloth somewhere?" he asked.

Cadan stormed toward his chest and pulled out one of the shirts he'd used to bundle the babe. "Use this."

Pell's face scrunched.

"I'll do it." Soot stepped forward and took the child from Pell. "Ye'd think it were a slitherin' snake 'stead o' a babe." Then grabbing the shirt, he plucked a few others from the floor and laid Matthew on Cadan's bed.

Within minutes, he had the child cleaned and Cadan's shirt wrapped tightly around his bottom.

Cadan gaped at him. "Where did you…?"

"I 'ad a younger brother. Me mom were sick a lot."

Moses entered, a bowl in his hand. His eyes landed on the babe in Soot's arms, and his brows shot up in surprise. "I added some coconut milk dis time, Cap'n."

"Good." At least Cadan hoped it was good. From what he remembered, infants were only supposed to drink their mother's milk for a time after birth. But what did he know?

Zada finally poked his head out from under Cadan's bed, stared at them all, then dove back into hiding. Cowardly lizard.

Moses took the babe from Soot and sat down to feed him. At least the child was quiet for now. Cadan shook his head, trying to evict the incessant ringing.

"Where to now, Captain?" Pell asked.

"Ye have the clue t' Dempster's treasure." Durwin rubbed his hands together. "I says we go find it!"

Cadan circled his desk and stared at the map. He had checked the clue already and found it still legible even after he dove into the water. He'd not thought of it at that moment. All he could think about was saving Matthew. But thank God, he'd tucked it deep in the pocket of his leather waistcoat or the entire trip would have been for naught.

"Nay," Pell said adamantly. "Surely you know you must go rescue the women."

"Aye!" Moses added as he dribbled slop into the babe's mouth.

Cadan drew a deep breath and glanced over his men. "The treasure will remain. The women's safety will not. We go after them first."

The only trouble was, he had no idea where they were.

Chapter 22

Gabrielle sat huddled in the corner of the cabin. Thankfully Omphile had finally fallen asleep on the single cot in the room. They'd spent a frightful morning clinging to each other *and* to the bedpost during a violent storm that felt as though it would split the ship in two. Lightning flashed across the porthole, giving them brief glimpses of angry foam-topped waves curling above the ship. During one such flash, Gabrielle could have sworn she'd seen the pirate Cadan had ordered to watch over her standing in the cabin. But how could that be? No doubt the *Resolute* was far away, even farther now due to the tossing of the sea, for even if Cadan had thought to follow them, he'd have lost them by now.

A shiver snaked through her. Her gown, damp from the rain coming through the window, clung to her uncomfortably. Her breasts ached with milk, her stomach begged for food, and her broken heart yearned for her son.

She stared across the tiny cabin, numb from sorrow, numb from pain, and numb from a hopelessness that drained her of the will to go on. For what was the purpose?

God had granted her a beautiful son—a blessing in the midst of so much horror and pain.

And then He had taken him away.

She'd cry if she had any tears left.

Omphile stirred, moaned, then pushed to sit up on the bed. Blinking, her gaze finally found Gabrielle.

"Oh, Child. I's so sorry to have fallen asleep on de bed." Quickly sweeping her feet over the edge, a look of true horror marred her lovely features.

Gabrielle shook her head. "I was unable to sleep anyway. I'm glad you got some rest."

The woman looked at her as if she'd told her she was a mermaid. "You are not like most noble white women."

Gabrielle smiled. She supposed not, having been raised on a pirate ship among all colors and ranks of people and where all were treated equally.

Footsteps clomped on the deck above, along with shouts to lay aloft and loose all sail. The mighty crash of water against the hull had finally faded to a swish as the ship ceased its violent rocking.

"We should pray, Miss." Omphile patted a spot next to her for Gabrielle to sit.

"To what end?" she snapped back.

Omphile's brows collided. "To ask for de Laud's help, o' course. To thank Him for His blessings."

"Blessings?" Gabrielle spat, then stood and brushed off her damp gown. "We are both prisoners of a madman, and I've lost my son." The last words came out with a whimper as tears burned in her eyes. "I see no blessings!" she sobbed out.

Instead of cringing at the anger in Gabrielle's tone, Omphile merely stared at her with more peace than the woman should have. "We are alive, Miss. Unharmed thus far, an' Matthew is in a safe place."

"Bah! On a pirate ship with a captain who used him as bait to get his revenge. I hardly call that safe."

"You don't know de captain like I's do. He'll do no harm to de babe, you'll see."

Too tired to argue, Gabrielle sat beside Omphile. "You can pray if you want, but God and I are not on speaking terms at the moment."

"Ah, but He still has His eye on you." Omphile smiled.

Gabrielle dropped her head in her hands, sorting through her thoughts. "I spent my entire life serving God. My parents were missionaries, and we spent much of our time preaching the Gospel and helping the poor."

Omphile gripped her arm. "What a wonderful childhood. You are blessed, Child."

Blessed? Perhaps back then. Sitting up, she attempted to run fingers through her tangled hair. "I suppose in a way, yes. I had loving parents, a safe home, and all my needs met." She cast Omphile a look of contrition. "I know I must sound ungrateful to someone who grew up with so little."

"You do." Omphile chuckled. "But I's learned not to compare myself wit' others. God places each of us in different places for different purposes."

"Then my purpose must have been to follow in my parents' footsteps, preach the Gospel, help the poor. Which is what I wanted to do! I wanted to get married, you see, raise Godly children, and take in orphans. That was the desire God put on my heart."

"A worthwhile one, Miss."

"I thought so." Memories paraded through her thoughts, stopping on a particular one. *Jonas.* "I was engaged once. To a wonderful man, or so I thought. A physician aboard my brother's ship. I was so in love."

Sails thundered above, then caught the wind in a jaunty snap. The ship veered to larboard and Gabrielle clung to the bed for support.

Omphile said naught, merely took Gabrielle's hand in hers.

"He left me at the altar. Ran off with another woman." Pain sliced through her heart, opening wounds that had never healed. "I was unwanted, unloved, discarded like so much bilge water." Tears poured down her cheeks, dripping onto her gown as the horrors of that day returned.

Omphile squeezed Gabrielle's hand. "I'm so sorry, Miss."

"Everyone looked at me with pity, even my family." Anger burned. She welcomed it, for it burned away the pain. "Tell me now about this God of yours! The one I served for years. All I ever asked of Him, all I ever wanted was to get married, have children, and continue His work. Instead, He tore everything away and left me naked and ashamed, not even worthy to be any man's wife."

"Oh, Child. I knows dat's not true."

Tearing from her grip, Gabrielle stood and took up a pace—a short pace for the cabin was no bigger than three steps. "Since then, I've been captured—twice—ravished, and my son stolen. Hence, you tell me how God loves me and answers my prayers!"

Omphile frowned but made no reply.

"Just as I thought." Gabrielle shot back.

"I's don't have answers for you, Miss, but you knows my story. Life isn't always fair."

"I do remember your story. What I don't understand is why you still bother to pray? Why you trust a God who would allow you to suffer so much?"

"Ah, Miss. Dis life is not all there be. Ders so much more beyond what we see. We may not understand why things happen, but if we truly follow the Laud, He turns all out for our good."

Gabrielle huffed. "I would settle for *anything* turning out good."

"Den be thankful you are alive and well an' Matthew is too."

"Perhaps that is more curse than blessing, for what is my life worth now…"—a sob caught in her throat—"without my son?"

"Do you really know de Laud?"

Gabrielle halted and stared at Omphile. "What do you mean?"

"It's jist, Miss, that de way you talk, seems to me you don't know Jesus at all. Did you ever know Him or did you jist follow what your parents believed?"

Gabrielle couldn't stop thinking about Omphile's question. It plagued her the rest of the day, taunted her, defied her every attempt to shove it aside. It didn't help that they were confined to the tiny cabin with nothing but their own thoughts and fears.

Fears mainly on Gabrielle's part, for Omphile spent the day either praying or humming as if she hadn't a care in the world.

When a pirate brought them a tray of food—if one could call it that—the mulatto thanked him, eliciting a strange look from the man, followed by a curse. Regardless, she thanked God for the food before they both gobbled it up.

Though Omphile attempted further conversation about God, Gabrielle insisted they change the subject. She was too hurt, too afraid, her emotions too raw to discuss a God who appeared to be more enemy than friend.

Yet one thought kept nagging her. Either Omphile was mad or the God she prayed to was as real to her as Gabrielle was. Which reminded her of her parents, of course, for they had showed the same zeal, same devotion to God as this woman did.

No matter. Gabrielle waved her hand over her neck, attempting to cool herself. 'Twas far too hot to even think. In truth, it took all her strength to keep from continually sobbing for Matthew.

By the time the sun touched the horizon, a glorious sight of red and orange ribbons out the tiny porthole, Gabrielle thought she'd go mad with fear.

The lock jangled, and the door opened to a pirate with a pointed beard, hair that stuck out like a porcupine, and a gold ring dangling from his left ear. His lascivious gaze wandered over them both, and he licked his lips in delight before tossing a gown toward Gabrielle. "Cap'n requests yer presence fer dinner."

Gabrielle swallowed, fear hiking up her throat.

The pirate slammed the door and locked it.

She exchanged a glance with Omphile, an understanding passing between them, though neither said a word.

She knew the gown. 'Twas one she'd worn before on this ship of horrors. However, this time, it fit a bit too snugly on her new figure. She thought to simply discard it, but no sense in infuriating Damien more than necessary.

After helping her get dressed, Omphile gripped her shoulders and said a prayer over Gabrielle before she left. But as she walked the hallway leading to the captain's cabin, she felt like a condemned prisoner being led to the gallows. Memories surged like billows in a storm, crashing over her one by one, stealing her breath, her reason, her hope. Hence, by the time she was shoved inside and the door slammed behind her, she felt like she might swoon.

Gripping the back of a chair, she gathered her breath *and* her wits. She'd learned long ago that Damien fed on fear, and she must never grant him that power over her again.

There he stood, looking handsome in his doublet of Murry taffeta with high wings to the shoulders and embroidered sleeves. Trousers of fine cambric were stuffed into leather boots, while a cravat stitched in silver was tied about his neck. A rapier with a jeweled hilt hung at his side. Light hair, slightly lower than his shoulders had been slicked back and tied, revealing a strong jaw, noble nose, and piercing blue eyes. Lantern light glistened over the ruby eardrop hanging from his ear.

No wonder she'd so easily been caught in his web. Little had she known that a snake lurked behind the peacock. A fact she would never forget.

He grinned and gestured for her to sit at a small candlelit table set for two.

China plates, silverware, and glasses glimmered in the light while the scent of roasted fish filled Gabrielle's nose.

"What need have you to put on such pleasantries, Damien? I am fully aware of your darkened heart."

He placed a hand over his chest. "You cut me, my sweet."

She'd like to do more cutting than that. Gaining her strength, she forced back her shoulders. "What do you want?"

"Merely to offer you a meal. You must be famished after giving birth to our son."

Our. The word sent a wave of nausea through her stomach. "I fear I have no appetite."

"Tsk-tsk. A tragedy, for my cook is quite proficient."

As she remembered. Her glance took in the bed against the bulkhead, and an unavoidable tremor skittered down her spine.

He followed her gaze. "I have no need to take what is already mine."

"You cannot claim that which you stole, Damien." She regretted the curt reply immediately for his face contorted with a fury she well knew.

Damien ground his teeth and forced down his anger at the woman's impertinence. He'd not brought her here to argue, to castigate, nor to ravish—though the idea was not without its merits. In truth, he'd wanted a pleasant evening with the woman who had consumed his thoughts for the past six months. A yearning that was only reinforced after seeing her on that island with Cadan and discovering she was with child—*his* child. She'd been a tasty treat to be sure, but no woman had ever carried his seed within her. This may just be a woman he should keep close to nurture their child, for he well knew what life without a mother could do to a young boy.

"Let us put the past behind us, shall we?" He pulled out a chair for her. "Our dinner grows cold."

Not as cold as the look she gave him. "If you are so interested in spending time with me, why did you leave me in prison on Nassau?"

"I did not know where you were, *ma douce*." In the thick of a battle with a French merchantman, the royal navy had come upon them so fast, Damien had no idea where most of his crew had been hauled off to. "I myself was escorted to Jamaica to stand trial for piracy, but as fate would have it, I was finally able to prove that I held a Letter of Marque from the British. I am half British, after all."

Grabbing the flask of brandy, he poured two glasses, then picked up one and glanced out the stern windows, where a scattering of stars flickered in and out of view with the sway of the ship.

"Privateering, is it?" Her curt tone brought his gaze back to her. "Do you not also have papers from the French?" she added. "And did I not witness you blowing up British munitions? Pray tell, which side of this war are you on, Damien?" She huffed in disgust.

He shrugged. "I am on my side."

"You are a liar and a thief."

Though Allard schooled his expression, the barb hit its mark. He sipped his drink, relishing its power to numb his pain, then took his seat at the table.

"What is it between you and Captain Hayes?" Gabrielle asked as the deck tilted slightly.

"Sit, eat, and I will tell you." He gestured toward the chair opposite his, then watched as she moved across the room toward him.

She truly was a lovely woman, all softness and curves with hair any goddess would envy. Tonight, she wore a portion of it pinned back, allowing the rest to cascade down her back. His gaze dropped to a figure that had changed for the better since he'd seen her last, fuller, rounder. Creamy skin and brazen alluring blue eyes completed the exquisite picture.

She eased onto the chair, casting him a look of disdain. Candlelight flickered over her lustrous skin, and he longed to touch it, to feel its softness once again.

"Drink." He pushed her glass closer, but she shook her head.

"I have learned to keep my wits about me in your presence."

He cocked his head. "Your tongue has sharpened since we last saw each other."

She lifted her chin. "I have endured much and have little left to lose."

"Ah, a dangerous predicament, that." But one he well understood.

Lifting the silver lid from a platter, he smiled, inhaling the scent of salted cod, garlic, and onions. Cook had done well. He scooped a portion onto the lady's plate.

She stared at it, gripping her stomach.

"What ails you, *ma douce*. Surely you are famished."

She snapped angry eyes his way. "What ails me? You have imprisoned me once again aboard your ship."

"Imprisoned is such an unpleasant term." He waved his hand through the air. "I prefer temporarily unwilling guest."

He had wanted to make her smile as she used to do when they'd first met, when she trusted him, when perhaps she was beginning to love him.

Instead, she frowned. "What happened to you, Damien, to make you so cruel? Were you beaten as a child? Tossed onto the streets? Had your heart broken?"

Water sloshed against the hull as the ship tilted to starboard, sending its timbers creaking, the sound grinding on his nerves.

He stared at her, fingering his glass. *Non*, he'd had every privilege growing up in a noble home in Lyon. Every privilege, except the one thing he craved, the one thing he craved even still. Love and belonging.

He gestured toward her food. "Eat. Before it gets cold." He took another sip of brandy.

The lady finally drew a fork full of fish into her mouth, pleasing him when she seemed to enjoy it.

"Where are your parents now?" she asked him in between bites, making him wonder what possible interest she could have. Perhaps, like him, she realized that it was best to know one's enemy in order to defeat him. The thought did not settle well in his gut.

"My father is no doubt seducing a new courtier somewhere and my mother is dead."

She stopped chewing and looked up at him. Good. He could play this game as well. He could use his past to garner her sympathy, for women's hearts were so tender and weak.

"I am sorry," was all she said as she set down the fork and raised her glass for a sip of grog.

Damien downed the rest of his brandy and poured more. "My mother hailed from British nobility. Hence, I have no real loyalty to either country."

This did not seem to surprise her as she studied him. "You promised to tell me what tragedy has made enemies of you and Cadan."

Cadan. He hated the sound of his given name on her lips. He gulped his drink, needing its numbing power to dredge up a past he'd rather forget. "Aside from my mother, did I ever tell you of my noble connections?"

"You mentioned something about a cousin."

"My father's cousin is Hugh de Dreux, viscount of Gimois." He studied her, waiting for some indication of admiration, but the lady seemed bored. "Surely Cadan told you of his wife?"

Candlelight sparkled in her lustrous eyes as she sat back in her chair and laid a hand on her stomach. "Not much. Just that she was associated with you, and she's dead now."

Damien rubbed his chin, hiding the unusual ache in his heart. "Elyna Browning, his wife, was Hugh de Dreux's granddaughter."

She blinked. "You are related to her?"

"Distantly. First cousins far removed or something." He waved a jeweled hand through the air. "It matters not. The point is Elyna's mother married a British man, a captain in the royal navy." He huffed. "It was such an affront to her family, they disowned her. But her father, Hugh de Dreux never stopped loving his daughter, so when she had a daughter of her own, Elyna, he kept track of her with the hope of someday persuading her to come back to France and rejoin the family."

"Hmm. Might I guess that Hugh was not pleased when she married Cadan?"

"Precisely. Hence, I was sent to seduce her away from him."

The lady's quick intake of air was the only indication she found the story shocking.

He smiled, fingering his chin, finally enjoying the lady's full attention. "Cadan had joined the navy, but on an unexpected leave, he returned home and found us in bed."

Chapter 23

Gabrielle pushed from the table, disgusted by Damien's story. "How horrible. Must you ruin everyone's life?"

"I was only doing my dear cousin's bidding. You see we French value family, especially nobility, for blood lines are of vital import to us."

"Family is important to us all," she retorted, a longing for her own family weighing down her heart. "So, what did Cadan do?"

"He fought me, of course, but I bested him." Grinning, he touched his right ear. "Sliced part of his earlobe if I remember."

Gabrielle nodded. So that was why Cadan gripped it whenever he spoke of Damien. Yet she knew that was not the end of the story. "Then what happened?"

"The woman ran off with me, and Cadan vowed revenge. But I couldn't very well have him chasing me around the world, messing up my plans, so Elyna and I worked up a scheme to trap him and have him branded a traitor. By then, her father was well connected in the royal navy, you see, and he had never approved of Cadan, being lowborn as he was." Grinning, Damien shrugged. "We planted evidence, paid off witnesses, and he was sent to Barbados as a prisoner. I thought I was rid of him." Huffing, he flattened his lips. "How he escaped I have no idea."

Gabrielle stared at him, horrified. "How could you do that to an innocent man?"

"Innocent!" He uttered a foul curse, narrowing his eyes. "He's a pirate. Why do you defend him?"

"Whatever he is now matters not. He didn't deserve imprisonment for defending his wife's honor."

Damien laughed. "Honor? The woman practically begged me to bed her."

"As I'm sure you think all women do." She glanced at the bed, fish souring in her stomach.

A flash of pain…or was it sorrow? crossed Damien's brandy-glazed eyes.

No matter. Gabrielle could well understand the reason for Cadan's revenge. This man, this mongrel before her, had not only stolen his wife, but his life and his freedom. No wonder he hated him so. No wonder he had turned to piracy when he finally escaped. Gabrielle well knew the feeling of desperation a person faced when everything they relied upon, everything and everyone they loved, was stripped away.

Damien poured more brandy, a sultry grin lifting his thin mustache. "All except you, *ma douce.* You were not so easily lured into my bed."

Panic soured in Gabrielle's mouth as the mighty crash of the sea swept against the hull. Candlelight shifted over Damien's face, casting more shadows than light. Why had she not seen what a devil he was? "Hence, you forced me instead."

He raised a brow and adjusted the lace at his cuffs. "An action I regret." Yet no remorse tainted his tone.

She sliced him with her gaze. "Regret? You ruined me. I trusted you. I thought you cared for me."

"But I do…I came to love you." He rose, stumbled a bit, and for a moment the hard veneer over his eyes lifted like a gauze curtain swept aside, offering a moment's glimpse. And in that glimpse she saw a whirlwind of pain and loneliness.

"You do not know the meaning of love." Turning, she stepped away from him. She must change the subject. And quickly. Lest, in his besotted state, he'd drag her back to bed. Yet…that same condition also loosened his tongue, giving her a rare opportunity to discover his plans.

"Your son is still out there, Damien. Do you plan to retrieve him?" Just saying the word *your* made her blood turn to ice, but she'd do anything to get Matthew back.

"Ah, no need to go after the babe when Cadan will come to us."

She faced him. "Why would he do that?"

"Because I have *you,* my sweet." One side of his lips curved.

"What makes you think Cadan cares enough to come after me?" She gave a ladylike huff. "He used me as bait to trap you."

Damien ran two fingers down the side of his mouth and eyed her with suspicion. "Ah, *ma douce,* you deceive yourself. I saw the look in his eyes when he came to your rescue. How gallant!" He snapped his fingers. "The hero coming for his lady love."

Look? What look could Cadan possibly have had aside from anger that he'd been bested by his enemy. "I assure you, he only cares to get his revenge on you."

"And now." Damien's eyes brimmed with joy. "I have stolen yet another woman from him."

"I am not his woman!" Gabrielle stomped her foot. "Besides, he has your son. 'Tis enough to satisfy his revenge for now."

The truth of that statement rang loud within her. Perhaps doing harm to Matthew or selling him as a slave would be enough to satisfy Cadan's vengeance.

"You do not know him that well." Damien fingered the jewel on his finger. "He will come after you. Of that I have no doubt."

Gabrielle frowned, frustration rising. Part of her wanted Cadan to come to her rescue, part of her wanted him to stay far away where Matthew would be safe.

Gripping her hands together to stop their sudden tremble, she met Damien's gaze head on. "So, you will set a trap for him?"

Cadan stared out the stern windows facing the island of Saint Thomas oscillating in his vision with each rock of the ship.

Rays from a setting sun turned sand into gold and the wooden buildings of the town of Charlotte Amalie into amber as men, women, servants, and slaves strode across the busy streets. An occasional carriage or horse drawn wagon parted the mass of humanity as they went about their work, shopping or doing the bidding of their masters. Muscled slaves hoisted crates from docked ships onto the wharf before loading them into wagons. Hawkers sold their wares as chickens clucked about unhindered. Doxies draped over upper balconies of punch houses called to lusty sailors below.

If his intuition was right, this port would be the most likely place for Allard to stop after the storm for either repairs or supplies, perhaps both. Hence, he'd sent Durwin and Pell into town to inquire at the various rum houses if anyone had seen the deviant Frenchman.

Cadan's gaze landed on a tavern he frequented, and he licked his lips. He could use a night of revelry, a night to forget his troubles and drown himself in rum and women. Well, perhaps just rum. He'd lost interest in women since Lady Fox had come into his life. Muddle, for the effect she had on his mind and, more importantly, his heart. He had to find her, rescue her from that madman.

And give her back her babe. He hated children, never wanted any of his own, and now here he was caring for one, a demon babe at that!

The child had done naught but scream and wail and soil all over Cadan's shirts, enough to torture a confession out of the bravest of men. So much so, he'd had to hand him over to Soot for a few hours of peace.

He had to think. Had to plan.

Had to appease a crew who voiced rather vehemently their demand to go after the treasure and leave the ladies to their fate. All save Pell and Moses.

He ground his fists together. His power to usurp them only came in battle. On any other matter, the majority ruled.

Yet how could he abandon the ladies now?

Who is she to you? She spurned you at every turn.

True words, though where had those thoughts come from?

He rubbed his eyes. He must be going mad.

Rubbing the back of his neck, he glanced at his bed where his coverlets and quilts remained in a tangled heap. He'd spent another restless night, only this time the nightmares returned. He'd been strapped to a wooden post, his bare back to the wind. He could still smell the musky scent of the wood, the sweat of his fellow prisoners in shackles standing to the side, and oddly a salty breeze that brought the scent of flowers.

Slap! Pain tore across his back, spiraling down his legs. He ground his teeth, vowing to not scream out and give the guards the pleasure they sought. *Slap*! Worse this time. Heat seared across his skin. The prisoners moaned. One of them cheered. The distant bell of a church rang. *Snap*! Agony wrenched what was left of Cadan's will. He slumped to his knees, his cheek grinding against the wooden post. The guards laughed. *Snap*! Rays from a hot sun scorched his raw open wounds. Blood trickled onto his breeches.

Cadan had woken with a start, breath huffing and sweat covering his chest. That fateful day when he'd been hanging onto the post for dear life, suffering the most torturous pain any man should feel, he'd vowed to get his revenge on Allard.

The sound of a baby wailing grew louder, snapping him from his memories. His first inclination was to hide and pretend he was not in. Crazy notion! He'd commanded men in battle, boarded and captured over a dozen merchantmen, defeated both captain and crew with blade and musket. He would not be disarmed by an infant. Especially not Allard's brat.

Someone rapped on his door.

"Enter!" Cadan shouted over the din, and in marched Soot, a screaming Matthew in his arms and a look of abject horror on his reddened face. "Cap'n, I can't. I can't. I can't stop 'em from screaming."

"Did Moses feed him?"

"Aye, and we changed his nappy, tried rockin' him. Nothin'." He extended the babe to Cadan and, with great reluctance, he took the stinky, howling bundle. After Cadan's mother died, he'd been forced to care for five younger siblings, and he seemed to recall they needed burping after a meal. Hoisting the child upright, he leaned him against his shoulder and gently patted his back.

Soot remained, relief loosening the lines on his face, though his right eye continued twitching.

A burp as loud as cannon fire emerged from the babe.

Followed by something warm and damp soaking through Cadan's shirt down his back.

"Uhhh!" Cadan held out the infant, vomit dripping from the child's mouth. A putrid stench saturated the air.

The babe gurgled in delight, quite pleased with himself, but when his eyes met Cadan's, he began to wail again.

"Here, take him for a moment." He handed him back to Soot, but the man backed away, eyes filled with more terror than Cadan had seen cross them during battle.

"Sorry, Cap'n. I got t' check the guns." And before Cadan could issue an order, the master gunner bolted from the cabin.

Traitor.

Ignoring the sour liquid running down his back, Cadan drew Matthew close, cradling him in his arms. Though he made every attempt to hate the babe, in truth, he found it hard to do so. 'Twas Lady Fox's face so full of love for her child that forced down his animosity.

And for the first time in four days, the babe quieted and stared up at Cadan, cooing softly.

"You're just like your mother." Cadan couldn't help but grin. "Driving me mad one minute, and charming me with your winsome smile the next."

Bootsteps brought his gaze up to see Durwin and Pell enter beside a slovenly looking man with a shock of greasy black hair atop a head as round as a cannonball.

Their eyes landed on Matthew. Pell grinned. Durwin's face scrunched, and the other man merely stared dumbfounded.

Pell thumbed toward the stranger. "This man says he knows where Captain Allard is heading."

"Out with it, man," Cadan shouted a bit too loudly.

Matthew let out a whimper.

The sailor ran a hand beneath his nose as if he smelled something foul. "Cap'n Allard an' some o' 'is men came ashore two days ago. 'E came into the Smelly Goat fer a drink an' bragged about gettin' the best of ye, Captain Hayes. Aye, he did, but I knew it weren't true." His gaze landed on the baby again and he cringed.

Matthew took up a howl, and Cadan began jostling him in his arms. "Did he say where he was heading?"

"To Martinique. That's wha' 'e said."

Pell frowned. "A French port."

Cadan studied the sailor, wondering if the information was trustworthy. "Are you quite sure?"

"As sure as a sailor loves 'is rum." He tugged the blue scarf tied around his thick neck. "Said 'e were goin' t' a celebration or ceremony, I can't remember."

Cadan gestured for Pell to pay him, and he reached in his pocket and handed him a silver coin.

The man gave a toothless grin. "Thank ye, Cap'n. An' if ye ever need anythin', ole Mack Friggens be yer man."

"Take him back to shore," Cadan ordered Durwin, and with a tap to his hat, the first mate turned and escorted the man out.

"I think he likes you, Captain." Pell gestured toward Matthew in Cadan's arms. The child had fallen sound asleep, looking like an angel rather than the screaming demon he was.

Approaching, Pell held a hand to his nose and winced, gesturing toward Cadan's shoulder. "Ah, there's the reason for the stench. His tummy has settled."

"Aye, all over me." Moving toward the makeshift cradle he'd made in his teakwood chest, Cadan carefully laid the infant within. Then yanking his soiled shirt over his head, he tossed it onto the deck.

Pell handed him a clean cloth, and he swiped the vomit off his shoulder and back.

All the while Pell watched him, grinning.

"Something amuses you?"

"I never saw this side of you, Captain. The nurturing father."

Anger suddenly welled, quickly banishing any nurturing sentiments. "I am not the boy's father," he shouted a bit too sternly to his friend. Allard was. Which was another reason to steer clear of the lad. But who else could he trust to care for him?

Huffing, he headed for the sideboard and poured himself a drink.

Pell shifted his stance. "You're going after Allard?"

"Aye."

"To get the woman back."

"And to destroy him."

"In a French port? When we are at war with France?"

"He has gone there to hide like the coward he is." Cadan sipped his rum. "Which is why 'twill be the perfect opportunity for me to get to him. He will not expect it."

Pell nodded and fingered the cross hanging around his neck, a look of concern creasing his brow. "The crew voted to go after the treasure, Captain, now that you have all the clues. While I agree the fate of the women is of the utmost importance, I fear if you do not oblige them, you may be facing a mutiny."

Chapter 24

Cadan stood on the quarterdeck, feet spread against the heaving deck, arms crossed over his chest, scanning his crew that had assembled below him on the main deck. They were a bedraggled mob from all ranks and races, wearing all manner of colorful attire they'd pilfered off their many victims, the shining satin and lace so at odds with their grime-covered skin. Some had no hair, others had braids down their back. Some were rotund, others stick-like, some with long beards, others with barely a whisper sprouting on their chins. All strapped with blades and pistols, gazing up at him with suspicion.

"I promise you all a share of Captain Demster's treasure, and I will keep that promise!"

Huzzahs and shouts saturated the air while some of the men stared him down, skepticism written on their faces.

"But first, we stop at Martinique to repay a debt."

Boos, threatening growls, and curses fired at Cadan like grapeshot.

"We already voted t' go straight t' the treasure, Cap'n. Not go after yer lady," one pirate shouted.

Cadan gripped the hilt of his blade. "I've filled your pockets with more gold coins than most captains, have I not? I've not heard complaints from any of you. I've kept you safe in battle and made you wealthy men."

Nods and "ayes" filtered through the crowd.

"We make this one stop, and then you have my word I will drown you in silver and gold like I promised. Anyone who doesn't agree, I'll drop off at the nearest port. Anyone who defies me will find his bed in the hold." With that, he turned around, nodded at Pell by the tiller, and dropped down the companionway.

Grunts and curses haunted him all the way to his cabin. He shut them out with a slam to his door.

It couldn't be helped. Time was of the essence. He must rescue Lady Fox and Omphile when Allard least expected it, and that was when he felt safe at a French-held port.

Matthew began to howl. "Blast it all!" Why had he slammed the door? He scooped him up and began bouncing him.

"'T'will be beyond risky, Captain." Pell's voice brought his gaze up. He hadn't heard the door open. "Dangerous even for you. We may not come out alive."

"We? I won't risk you."

"I's going wit' you." Moses' large frame filled the doorway.

"This is my battle, gentlemen. I need you to remain with the ship, keep the crew in line, and protect her against being sighted by the French."

"I's goin' wit' you," Moses repeated, eyes like flint, meaty arms crossed over his chest.

Omphile. How could Cadan have forgot his carpenter's attachment to the woman? "I will allow it, Moses, but only you."

"And your job," he nodded toward Pell. "Keep the men happy and watch over this little one." The babe had settled and reached a hand to touch Cadan's chin.

Pell snorted. "I'm suited for neither task."

"Soot will help you with Matthew. And as far as the crew is concerned, you're a preacher. Use your exquisite oratory skill to convince them that going against me would not be to their advantage."

Pell laughed. "You trust a man whose *oratory skill,* as you put it, garnered him not a single convert?"

"I trust *you,* my friend."

Unable to sleep yet again, Cadan held the lantern above his head and scanned the hold of the *Resolute.* Crates filled with flour sacks, barrels full of salted meat, and other foodstuffs lined the bulkheads. Extra sailcloth, along with ropes, were stored neatly to the side. A copper-plated shot locker held gunpowder, cannon balls, and coal. Water sloshed in the well hole, competing with the mad rush of water against the hull. The scent of sodden wood, moldy food, and human excrement curled his nose.

He rarely came down here. With a crew to do the dirty work, there was no need. But tonight, no man could take his place. Tonight, he needed to settle the confusion doing flips in his mind. He needed to hear Smity's own words, for his pride could not fathom how wrong he'd been about the man.

Weaving around several crates, the pitter-patter of rats echoed in the dank air, running from the light like the vermin they were. The ship canted over a wave. Water sloshed over his boots. Cadan gripped a nearby stack of barrels tied with ropes for balance until the ship righted itself again.

The bars came into view, then Smity, lying on a cot. Cadan hooked the lantern above him and approached the cage.

"Come t' gloat, Cap'n." Smity sat and faced Cadan, running fingers through his beard.

"Nay. Just to ask why."

"Why what?" He spat to the side and stood, staring at Cadan with pinpoint eyes full of hatred.

"Why risk everything because of a mere accident?"

Huffing, Smity ran a thumb down the rippled skin on his face. "As I said, 'twere yer incompetence, yer bad decision that left me lookin' like a monster."

Cadan drew a deep breath, fisting hands at his waist. "It could have happened to anyone. A risk we all take as pirates."

"Yet I'm the only one whats got burned that day."

Like a rabid animal, seething hatred fumed off the man as he bared his teeth and uttered a savage growl. If there were no bars between them, Cadan had no doubt Smity would be more than happy to maul him to death.

"For a year now, you've been my bosun. Acted like all was well."

"Bidin' me time, that's all. Bidin' me time t' get revenge on ye." He huffed, grimacing. "Ye got yer pretty face, Cap'n. Women fallin' all over ye. What would ye know of how I feel?"

He was right. Cadan wouldn't know. In truth, he hadn't even tried to understand. "You sought revenge on me from the moment it happened? I'll grant you, you are as good a liar as any."

Smity made no reply. Instead, he gripped the iron bars and shook them with all his might. The rattle and squeak of iron carved a trail of remorse through Cadan.

And suddenly, the hatred, the loathing, the mad drive for revenge appeared evil, dark, as if a force outside of Smity had taken him over and blackened his heart into charred soot.

"Your revenge got you nowhere, Smity, save in this hold." The ship bucked, and Cadan balanced his boots over the deck.

Releasing the bars, Smity turned aside. "How long ye goin' t' keep me 'ere?"

"As long as necessary." Cadan would have to make an example of the traitor or chaos would rule his ship. Yet deep inside, he understood the man's hatred and need for revenge. Turning, he grabbed the lantern and started away.

"I'll get me revenge, Cap'n. One way or another!"

A shipload of foul curses and insulting names followed Cadan all the way to his cabin, where he made a straight line for his rum. Though the encounter with Smity had cleared up his confusion, it had replaced it with a new perspective on the evils of revenge, how it consumed a man, stole what's left of any light in his heart.

He needed a drink.

Grabbing the decanter, he started to pour a glass when a slight whimper met his ears, followed in seconds by a roaring wail.

Scads! Setting down the rum, Cadan strode to the chest and picked up Matthew. This was why he never wanted children of his own. They were nuisances, demanding, selfish, and time-consuming. You couldn't reason with them or even threaten them, for they were silly and nonsensical. You couldn't even lock them in the hold or send them out on their own, for they couldn't fend for themselves. Besides, they smelled bad. He sniffed and shrank back from the foul odor.

He should call for Moses, but 'twas late. Besides, Cadan could do it, a decision he quickly regretted, for he'd never seen or smelled such a putrid discharge from man or beast. Good thing he hadn't eaten much for dinner, or he'd surely have tossed it by now.

To make matters worse, the babe kicked the entire time, flinging his mess over the deck and onto Cadan's coverlet in little splats of yuk.

Finally, he had the child wiped clean and with a new nappy Moses had made from old, discarded clothes. Yet Matthew was not impressed. Though his wail had lessoned, he continued to fuss and moan just like Cadan's pirates had the last time he'd seen them.

He jostled the babe up and down, up and down, but to no avail. Paced back and forth across his cabin. Nothing worked. Food. Babies were hungry all the time, right? He moved to his desk and saw that Moses had left some crushed coconut meat soaked in milk. Wonderful man. Soaking the edge of the rolled cloth in the liquid, he dribbled it into Matthew's mouth and the babe ceased his whimpering and gobbled it up. This was going to take a while, for the cloth could not hold much liquid.

Dragging a chair over to the desk, Cadan sat and continued to feed the boy until finally he seemed satisfied. "You are a big eater for one so little." He ran a thumb over the babe's cheek, amazed at the softness.

Matthew smiled. At least Cadan thought it was a smile. Ever so slight. Yet his blue eyes stared up at Cadan with the most innocent, dependent look. Did the child know the precarious situation he was in? On a pirate ship and hunted by a vicious man, albeit his father? Nay. All Cadan saw in those eyes were wonder and…*trust.*

Trust him? He didn't deserve that, especially not from this child.

Cadan rubbed his eyes. He needed a drink and then sleep, but the babe had wrapped his tiny hand around Cadan's finger in a death grip. The Kraken didn't have so strong a grasp!

No matter. Rising, he laid him gently back in the chest.

When a scream blared that would wake the urchins at the bottom of the sea.

Growling, Cadan raked back his hair and picked up the lad once again, then sat down on his bed, cuddling him close. "Very well, you little tyrant."

When Pell's light rap on Cadan's door received no response, he gently opened it and froze at the sight that met his eyes. A stream of morning sunlight swayed over the captain, fully dressed, sound asleep on his bed with the babe snuggled tight against his chest. Little Matthew, however, was wide awake, cooing and gurgling and grabbing Cadan's chin with his chubby little hands.

Entering, Pell closed the door ever so softly and simply stood, admiring the scene. Emotions clogged his throat. Not only at the shock of seeing the fierce Captain Hayes cuddling a babe, but at the memories that tore his heart wide open. How often had he slept beside his own son, Michael, when he was a baby? How often had he nestled him close, fed him, comforted him, until they both had fallen asleep? Even as the child grew, they'd all slept together as a family—his wife, Miranda, himself, and Michael. Visions flooded his mind of Michael's first steps, his first bite of solid food, first tooth, and first word, *Nay*.

Pell smiled even as tears burned in his eyes. His son had grown into a curious, happy young boy, full of life and love, a miraculous gift from God, or so Pell had thought.

The ship tilted, and Pell caught his balance as a tear escaped his eye. He swiped it away. Michael had not deserved his fate—

drowned in the sea. Though it had been deemed an accident, both Pell and his wife knew foul play was afoot. Michael had been well trained to stay away from the shore, and even then, he'd been taught to swim. Something the lieutenant governor of Antigua had no way of knowing.

Pell ground his fists together, his heart thumping so loudly, he could hear it above the groan of the ship's timbers. He should have heeded the man's warning to leave the island, to stop his proselytizing.

But he'd trusted in God to protect them. His wife died of fever shortly afterward, but he knew she'd really died from sorrow.

The babe continued to play with Cadan's scratchy chin as if it were a new toy.

Pell squeezed his eyes shut and rubbed away the tears.

A vision appeared. As real as if it were right in front of him.

His wife Miranda stood in a field of flowers, her dark hair blowing in the breeze. Their son, Michael was beside her, holding her hand. He was older, at least nine now. Behind them, a city of gold glimmered on a hill. They both smiled his way—smiles of complete joy and peace. Miranda nodded as she used to do when she was telling him something important.

"We are well, my love. Don't give up." Her whisper floated on the wind.

Pell could hardly believe his eyes. His breath heightened, and he reached out toward his family, desperate to touch them, hold them, stay with them!

But they disappeared.

He snapped his eyes open and searched the cabin. Only a dream. Or was it? He was fully awake. A vision, then? But it had seemed so real.

Trust me.

Pell fell to his knees, sobbing. *Trust You? You took everything from me!*

Silence responded. In its place a litany of recent answered prayers paraded across his mind, requests he'd lifted up to God, not fully expecting them to be answered. He'd prayed they'd rescue Matthew. They did. He'd prayed they'd stave off Allard's attack. They had. He'd prayed they'd find Allard. They had.

Was God finally answering his prayers? But why now and not when he'd so desperately prayed to save his family?

Chapter 25

"Must I attend Damien's ridiculous ball?" Gabrielle tossed the gown onto the four-poster mahogany bed and moved to look out the window. Tropical gardens glistened in the setting sun—an array of every colored flower imaginable. Stone paths circled a fountain where birds gathered to drink. Beyond the garden, sugarcane stretched as far as the eye could see. And beyond them, a strip of blue was all she could see of the Caribbean.

She glanced down the five stories to the dirt below and huffed. "If only I could jump."

"Nows you don't mean dat, Child." Omphile appeared beside her. "What good would dat do your son?"

"My son." Gabrielle swallowed and forced back tears. "I'll never see him again."

Omphile gripped her hand and squeezed it. "No, Miss. The Laud told me you'll see him real soon."

Suppressing her anger at the woman's incessant positive prognostications, Gabrielle offered a tiny smile. She meant well, no doubt only trying to comfort Gabrielle. But hearing from the Lord? Even if He did talk to people, why would He bother with such a trivial matter when He had the world to run?

She bit her lip. Of course, her parents had insisted they heard often from God. Gabrielle had always thought they were exaggerating, for she had never received a single word from the Almighty.

Tugging from the woman's hand, she moved to the table and fingered the ruby necklace and bracelet, along with the jeweled mask Allard's steward had left. All trinkets she was expected to wear tonight. "I don't see how, Omphile. We are at

Fort Royal, an enemy port on an enemy island. And worse, in the governor's palace. Cadan would never be able to sail a mile within this place."

"Nothing is impossible wit' de Laud." Omphile eased a hand over the gown on the bed and whistled. "Feels like silk, Miss. An' it's so pretty. You're gonna look like a princess in dis."

Gabrielle shook her head. Though it was the most beautiful gown and jewels she'd seen, she had no intention of honoring Damien with her presence. "I'm not going."

"I don't sees how you have a choice. 'Sides." Omphile shrugged. "What harm could it do?"

Gabrielle sank into a stuffed chair and glanced around the opulent room they'd been escorted to upon landing. Elaborately carved oak and walnut furniture spread across the large space—a bed, chest of drawers, writing desk, and two chairs. Plush red cushions filled the chairs with matching pillows spread over the embroidered counterpane on the bed. Tapestries and paintings decorated the walls, depicting scenes of the French countryside. And in the corner a clawfoot porcelain tub beckoned to her for a bath she'd not had in months.

She'd not seen Damien since their dinner, and she had to admit that after two more days inside that tiny cabin on the *Nightblood*, she'd been thrilled to feel the wind in her hair and the sun on her face once again. But the crewmen who'd escorted her and Omphile off the ship, onto the docks, and into a carriage, had not answered a single of their questions as to where they were going and why they were there.

Gabrielle did not recognize the city that passed outside the carriage windows, nor the elaborate mansion they stopped in front of. Apparently, Damien had higher connections than she'd thought. They'd only seen a small portion of the estate as they were escorted through the front door and up a series of stairs, but 'twas enough to see the ivory statues, crystal chandeliers, marble floors, and bevy of servants skittering about.

After locking them in the bed chamber, Damien's steward, Louis, brought them a tasty repast and extended Damien's invitation to a costume ball that evening. 'Twas Louis who finally answered her question as to their location—the island of Martinique. An hour later, he brought up the costume she was to wear and informed her that maids would soon arrive with hot water to bathe.

She would admit to being excited about the bath. After spending most of her time on a ship the past month, plus giving birth, she could use a good soak.

"I just don't understand," she said with a huff. "Why does he want me to attend a ball? Does he plan to shackle me in front of everyone, for surely he knows I'll take every opportunity to escape." She glanced at Omphile, who stared in awe at a stunning painting of a ship at sea on the wall. "Not that I would leave without you," Gabrielle added.

"Oh, no, Child." Omphile's brow tightened as she swept her concerned gaze to Gabrielle. "If you see a chance to escape, don't you worry 'bout me. Jist go!"

Gabrielle shook her head. "I could never leave you here." She sighed and set down the ruby necklace she'd been caressing. "Which is most likely his plan, after all."

"Don't be frettin' so, Miss. You must go to dis ball. I sense it. 'Sides, you knows he will force you anyway, an' it might be interesting." Her glance took in the gown. "I'd take any chance I got to wear sich a gown."

Gabrielle smiled. "You always give me hope, even in the worst situations."

"Then I's doin' de job de good Laud gave me."

An hour later, as announced, four maids entered, carrying buckets of steaming water. After two trips each, the tub was nearly full, and Gabrielle couldn't wait to get in. The warm sudsy water cloaked her in a comfort she didn't feel within. Yet, if she shut her eyes, 'twas easy to believe she was back home on Jamaica bathing in the tub in her bedchamber. In truth, Omphile's constant humming and praising of God reminded her so much of Charlisse, her mother, making the vision easier to imagine. But soon the water cooled, along with her dreams, and Gabrielle had to face the reality of her situation. She had lost her son and was once again the prisoner of a madman.

By the time the final rays of the sun withdrew from the window, Gabrielle, with Omphile's help, had donned her undergarments and gown and put the jewels around her neck and wrists. A knock on the door was followed by the entrance of a lady's maid, who took great pains to style Gabrielle's hair in an upsweep of curls.

Finally, she grabbed her mask and spun around.

"Good Laud, Child." Omphile exclaimed, clapping her hands together, eyes wide. "You look stunning. Like the princess you are."

"I'm no princess," Gabrielle returned, frowning.

"Ah, but yes you are. We all are daughters of de King." She pointed upward, and Gabrielle knew she spoke of God. Odd, but Gabrielle had never thought of herself as God's daughter.

Drawing a deep breath, she swallowed down a burst of nerves. She didn't know what this night would bring, but it couldn't be anything good. Nevertheless, she would attempt to get Damien deep in his cups, and if so, she might have a chance to slip away, get Omphile, and make their way to the docks. How they would barter their way on board a ship in a French port, she had no idea, but she had to try. What did she have to lose?

Lud. She sounded as adventurous as the rest of her family. She? Who'd always been as scared as a ship's mouse. She'd laugh if her situation weren't so dire.

Damien stood near the front entrance to the governor's ballroom, sipping his brandy, and feeling as nervous as a schoolboy with his first infatuation.

"She must be a special lady, Damien, for you've not taken your eyes off the door since we entered an hour past," Nicolas de Gabaret, Governor of Martinique, said from beside him.

"She is." Damien smiled, surprising himself by the immediate declaration.

"Then congratulations are in order, Captain, for it is rare to find such a wife. Most marriages are arranged for money, power, or land." Scowling, he glanced at his wife, Marie-Anne, across the ballroom, cackling with a group of women. "But for *l'amour*? Well done."

Damien shifted his stance and scanned the large gallery. Was it love he felt? He had no idea, for he'd never experienced such a sensation before. In truth, it felt more like a longing, a desire for something he was desperately missing in his life.

Candlelight glittered down upon the crowd from chandeliers of wrought silver hung high from a beamed ceiling. Elegantly carved crown molding circled the room, matching four white posts on either end that held up arched doorways. Gold-gilded mirrors lined the walls, making the room look larger than it was, while sideboards crafted in island mahogany held all manner of dainties and drinks. Chairs with stuffed velvet cushions were perched against the walls beside hangings of silk brocade that were pulled back from open doors leading to an outside veranda.

The governor's guests drifted over an exquisitely patterned tropical wood floor, dressed in the finest silk, velveteen, and satin in all colors and styles, each one hiding their faces behind gaudy bejeweled and feathered masks while displaying themselves like peacocks in a bizarre mating ceremony.

At the far end of the gallery, an orchestra fine-tuned their instruments atop a dais.

"My lord." A man halted before the governor. "Monsieur Bastien wishes to inform you that the priest is ready, and the ceremony will take place in the salon after the ball commences. It is up to you"—he glanced at Damien—"to get Lady Hyde there."

Damien nodded. "I'll have her there."

"A noble lady?" The governor raised his brows.

"*Oui*, the daughter of an earl. Perhaps you've heard of him? Captain Edmund Merrick Hyde, Lord Clarendon."

"*Mon Dieu*! Who hasn't? He's been the plague of France for years! Well done, Damien. Well done. A regular Romeo and Juliet, I'd say. If we weren't already at war, this union might well be the catalyst." He chuckled, shaking his portly belly, and then clapped Damien on the back. "She must truly be smitten to betray both her family and nation."

Damien smiled. He'd not tell the man that he intended to slip some opium into the woman's drink, make her confused, sleepy, and unaware of what was happening, and then whisk her off to get married before she sobered. *Non*, he'd let the man believe she actually loved him.

The thought sent a pang through his heart. What would it feel like to be loved, *truly* loved by a woman like Gabrielle? For her to want to be with him, for *any* woman to want to be with him for more than to pad her pockets?

Damien adjusted his mask, glad it hid the moisture in his eyes as the governor begged off to speak to a guest. Once he wed Gabrielle, he would set a trap for Cadan and retrieve their son. Then they would be a family—the family he'd never had.

A stirring at the entryway drew his gaze, along with several others in the room.

An angel glided through the open doors on the arm of his steward, Louis.

A gown of purple silk, fringed in gold lace fell elegantly to her feet. Ruffled bell sleeves emerged from a jeweled stomacher bedecked with pink ribbons, while a low décolletage pressed against her creamy breasts. Her golden hair was expertly coiffed in delicate layers atop her head, allowing a few spirals to dangle about her neck. Pearls shone from the pink filigree mask she wore over her eyes.

His heart leapt even as his blood heated. Why had he ever let her go?

Yet no smile graced her lips as Louis spotted him and headed his way. The lady halted beside him, her skirts swishing about her and the scent of roses flooding his nose and alerting every sense.

Louis bowed and left, leaving them alone for a moment, though Damien spotted several people making their way over for introductions.

"I am here, Damien, as ordered. Now what?" Her curt tone cut hard.

"Now you enjoy yourself, *ma douce*."

"If that is what you wish, then 'twould be my greatest pleasure if you would set me and Omphile free at once."

He chuckled. "Perhaps after the ball, provided you behave yourself." Of course, he had no intention of doing so, but a speck of hope might keep her more pliable for the night's events.

The right side of her lips quirked, and though he could not see her full expression, the light in her blue eyes revealed his plan had worked.

Unfortunately, conversation halted as Monsieur Longuess arrived, along with at least a dozen guests, anxious to meet Gabrielle. None knew of their impending nuptials, only that Damien had brought the daughter of a British earl as his intended. Besides, on the tiny island, anyone new became an immediate fascination.

After introductions were made and idle conversation endured—all the while Gabrielle behaved with more civility than he'd expected—the guests excused themselves and left. Damien extended his arm. "Allow me to escort you to get a drink, *ma douce*."

Frowning, she refused his arm, but followed him nonetheless to the other side of the gallery where a long buffet table held every kind of pastry and drink one could imagine.

He waved an arm over the chicken, pigeon, and fish topped with lemon and a parsley butter sauce. "I'm told this is delicious. Shall I prepare a plate for you?" He gestured toward the end of the table. "I hear the mango sorbet and candied plantains are not to be missed."

"I'm not hungry," she responded, glancing over the room as if bored.

"A drink, then?" Damien poured two glasses of claret. Then, after ensuring Gabrielle's attention was elsewhere, he plucked a vial from his pocket, uncorked it, and poured it into her drink. Picking up the glasses, he handed her one.

Much to his chagrin, she shook her head. "As I have said, I prefer to keep my wits when around you."

"The wine is not overly potent. Perhaps it will settle your nerves?" He extended it again, but she held up a hand.

"Perhaps 'tis your nerves that need settling, Damien, for you are as jittery as a puppet on a string."

"Am I?" He silently cursed. His jaw tightened. Grabbing his wine, he sipped it at first, then finished it off with a gulp.

"Have another." She smiled sweetly, a hint of chicanery in her tone that gave him pause.

The orchestra began playing a tune, and couples started for the center of the gallery.

"Will you honor me with a dance if I do?" He gave her his most charming grin.

Though her lips pursed tight, she nodded.

He scanned the table for his favorite port and refilled his glass. The sweet pungent brandy wine instantly sent a wave of warmth through him. Perhaps he *had* needed a drink, after all. "Now your turn. A sip before our dance?"

She huffed, her cute nose wrinkling, but finally she picked up her glass and took a sip. Not enough for the opium to work, but it was a start. He refilled his glass and then took both their drinks to the other side of the room where he placed them on a private side table. No sense in having someone else inadvertently drink the lady's wine.

"Shall we?" He extended his arm and was pleased when she took it and allowed him to lead her out onto the floor.

Chapter 26

Gabrielle would rather boil in oil than dance with Damien Allard, but at the moment, it couldn't be helped. She needed him to continue drinking, and the only way to do that was to be as pleasant as she could stomach. Yet from the vile brew bubbling in her belly, she'd already reached her limit.

In truth, Damien looked quite the posh gentleman in his gold-embroidered doublet, lined with colorful ribbons, and black breeches trimmed with Flemish lace. A foam of Mechlin bubbled from beneath his chin, and he had slicked back his light hair with lavender scented pomade.

However, behind his gold mask, there was something in the monster's eyes, something she'd not seen before, a vulnerability, a longing that unnerved her. What was the man up to? Another thing she must discover as the night went on.

People stared at her from behind their masks as Damien led her onto the floor. A minuet was just beginning, and Gabrielle took her spot beside him and curtsied as he bowed. It had been quite a while since she'd danced, and she hoped she didn't make a fool of herself, though what did it really matter? However, this would be the perfect opportunity to lure information out of Damien as they proceeded through the steps of the dance.

Gabrielle took two steps forward, meeting Damien in the center.

"You look lovely this evening, my sweet," Damien whispered in her ear.

Retreating two steps, she circled the lady to her right.

"We did not finish our conversation from the other night," Gabrielle said as they passed one another.

Hopping, Damien joined hands with the lady to his left and spun around.

"Did we not?" he said when they met again.

"Nay, you did not tell me what happened to your mother."

He frowned, turned away, and circled around a rather corpulent lady to his right.

They met in the center again, grabbed hands and spun around. "She did not die," he offered, "but rather ran away, abandoning her only son."

Releasing his hand, Gabrielle swallowed at the deep sorrow in his voice and took two steps back. "Who raised you, then?"

"Nurses, tutors, one after the other. Not many could live up to my father's demands."

Gabrielle spun around and wove in between the couple to her right. Damien had never known the love of a mother or a father. How terribly sad. And yet so telling of how he came to be so heartless and cruel.

She met him in the center again. "Is that why you hate women so? Because of your mother?"

"Enough!" His sharp tone brought the gazes of those around them. He pasted on a smile, grabbed Gabrielle's arm, and led her to the side where he'd place their drinks.

A figure caught Gabrielle's gaze. She glanced to see the seaman whom on occasion seemed to be guarding her on board the *Resolute*. Oddly, he remained in his sailor's garb, brown trousers and checkered shirt. No mask, no damask waistcoat graced his figure, and yet no one in the room seemed to notice. He merely stood near the entryway, his eyes on her. Upon noticing her gaze upon him, a gentle smile curved his lips....

And then he was gone.

Blinking, Gabrielle continued to stare at the spot, unnerved, unsure of what was happening. Perhaps she'd finally faced her limit of fear, and her mind was slowly drifting out to sea.

"Are you unwell, my sweet?" Damien peered at her quizzically.

"Why have you brought me here?" she snapped back at him.

Instead of answering, Damien picked up her glass of wine and handed it to her.

She took a sip. True, the wine was not potent at all, and it tasted rather good.

"You are the mother of my son." Damien smiled. "I wish to honor you."

Honor? She wanted to laugh, to scream. How could the man speak of honor when he had imprisoned her, ravished her?

She took his glass and handed it to him. "Then let us toast to Matthew. Shall we?"

Surprise flitted across his blue eyes before a smile lifted his lips. "Indeed."

They clinked glasses and Damien gulped down his port while Gabrielle pretended to sip her wine.

A servant passed by, and he set down his glass on an empty tray. "Drink up, my sweet." He gestured toward her wine, but she simply smiled and set down her nearly full glass.

"I'm afraid it does not settle well this night."

Scowling, he fingered the lace fringing his cravat. "Perhaps another dance will make you thirsty?"

Another dance might cause her to toss what little she had in her stomach, but still, she allowed him to lead her onto the floor once again.

She was not oblivious to the glances of the men in the room. Though her mother had told her she was beautiful, she had never felt so. She'd always lived in the shadows of her gorgeous mother and vivacious sister. And although the attention she was getting should make her feel special, she only felt self-conscious. Even the women were pointing at her as if they knew a dark secret about her, the likes of which she could only guess.

She endured a gavotte and sarabande, avoiding all discussion this time, and instead searched the gallery for the best doorway through which to escape. She settled on the servant's entryway tucked in the corner, but in the meantime, she must get Damien well into his cups.

Finally, the monster led her off the floor, seemingly more unnerved than he'd been earlier in the evening. He was up to something, though for the life of her, she could not figure out what.

More guests crowded around them, anxious to hear of Damien's exploits at sea as well as meet his betrothed. *Betrothed*? Blood raced from Gabrielle's heart. So, that was his plan.

Breaking free from the guests, he led her to a cushioned seat. He fingered the ruby drop in his ear, then tugged upon his cravat, repeating the actions over and over, clearly distressed. She stared at her unfinished wine, and suspicion crept up her spine like a poisonous spider.

She smiled at him. "Why don't you get another drink, Damien, you seem parched."

"Only if you finish your wine, my sweet." He spread two fingers down his thin mustache and glanced anxiously around over the gallery as if expecting someone.

Against every impulse within her, she grabbed her glass with one hand, slipped the other into his, and stood. "I will but let us refresh yours first. Besides, I believe I'll try one of those candied plantains."

The intimate gesture had the intended impact as he flinched slightly before he smiled and led her to the buffet table.

Once there, Damien quickly filled his glass and raised it to her before gulping it down. She pretended to drink from hers when fortunately, a man standing on Damien's other side drew his attention.

"Heard you've been quite successful as a French privateer, Captain Allard," the man began.

Before Damien could answer, Gabrielle glanced around to make sure no one was looking, then poured the remainder of her drink into his glass.

Excellent. Gabrielle had finally finished her drink. Faith, but the woman was stubborn. Smiling, Damien grabbed the decanter of wine and refilled her glass. The potion should take no longer than twenty minutes to affect her mood, remove all inhibitions and make her more compliant. He handed her the glass and grabbed his own. The evening was going splendidly and yet would be even more enjoyable after they were wed. Especially in the wedding bedchamber the governor had arranged for them.

He extended his arm and was once again thrilled when she placed her gloved hand in the crook of his elbow—another sign that the ice around her heart was melting. Leading her through the throng, ignoring the greetings and smiles, he gestured for her to sit in one of the stuffed high back chairs against the wall.

"You must be tired, *ma douce*. Rest awhile." He grinned. *And wait for the potion to take effect.*

Meanwhile, Damien turned to watch the couples dancing a loure, admiring the beautiful women who gave coquettish glances his way. He was handsome. Handsome, successful, from a noble family, and soon to be wed to British nobility. Despite his father's predictions that he would amount to nothing but a churlish wastrel, he was on his way to great success. *And* fortune, if he could trap Cadan and find Demster's treasure. He sipped his wine. *Oui*, things were going his way.

Gulping the rest of his drink, he set down his glass and was about to take a seat beside Gabrielle when he heard gasps from some of the ladies standing nearby. In fact, as he glanced around the ballroom, all eyes—even those engaged in dance—drifted toward the entryway.

Gabrielle was more interested in watching to see what happened to Damien after he finished his drink than she was in whatever or *whoever* caused a commotion in the room, particularly among the women.

Yet when Damien's entire body stiffened, and his eyes narrowed behind his mask, she couldn't help but rise to her feet and follow his glance toward the entryway.

A man had entered. Not any man. Nay, this man moved with the grace and authority of a god. A man whose very presence had drawn all female eyes his way, including several male's.

He wore a suit of black velvet with silver lace, the trousers of which were stuffed into tall Hessian boots. A crimson damask waistcoat provided the only color on his person, save for a matching plume on his cocked hat. Dark hair was tied behind him cavalier style, and a brazen rapier was strapped to his hip. A black silk mask hid the top half of his face, and he strode into the ballroom as if he were the French king himself.

A slight curl to his lips was the only indication he was aware of the attention he garnered. He had an authority, yet a wildness about him, a confidence, a power that permeated every inch of the room.

Unbidden, Gabrielle's heart began to beat faster. Her breath caught.

Several women offered him flirtatious glances above fluttering fans. One poor lady seemed to swoon as she slid onto the seat behind her.

"Who is that?" Damien said with spite.

The mysterious man's eyes scanned the room, quickly glancing across the buffet table, the crowds lining both sides of the room, the groups of chattering people around the dance floor, and finally they landed on her….

And remained.

There was something…*familiar* in that gaze. But no, it couldn't be! He wouldn't be so bold…so foolish! Gabrielle's heart thrashed against her ribs.

Damien blinked, rubbed his eyes, and touched a column beside him for support. "What is happening?" he slurred.

The enigmatic man in black headed toward Gabrielle. One glance toward Damien told her that her suspicions about the drink had been right. He wobbled on his feet and began to hum some nonsensical tune.

Every female eye followed the dark man until he halted before Gabrielle and bowed, sweeping his hat out before her. "May I have this dance, my lady?"

That voice! Those eyes! *Cadan.*

Damien's mumbled protest faded away as Cadan swept Gabrielle out onto the floor. The orchestra started an allemande, and with more elegance than she thought he possessed, Cadan executed the steps with precision and grace.

She leaned into him. "Are you quite mad?"

"Entirely," he responded, twirling her around.

"You'll be caught and shot."

"Unlikely." Grinning, he kissed her gloved hand and gazed up at her, a twinkle crossing his hazel eyes.

Heat flushed her. "What are you doing here?"

"Why, isn't it obvious? I'm rescuing you!"

She wanted to laugh, to cry, to scream in terror, to shout for joy. This man, this wonderful, crazy, brave man had come for her. Not only had merely come, but the two of them were dancing in the French governor's ballroom, the envy of all there!

He nodded toward Damien, who had slunk onto a seat and was holding his head in his hands. "What happened to him?"

Gabrielle smiled. "Let us just say I gave him a bit of his own medicine."

"That's my girl," Cadan replied, and the endearing term warmed every inch of her. He smelled of salt and spice, the familiar scent bringing every cell in her body to life.

"Matthew?" she asked the next time they drew close.

"Safe and well, Lady Fox."

They parted then came back together. "I could kiss you, you know."

His eyes glistened behind his mask, and a sensuous curve raised his lips. "I'll take that kiss when we are back on the *Resolute.*"

A blush rose on her cheeks, and she hoped it wasn't visible. He spun her around. His hand pressed protectively on her back. 'Twas like a dream. The music, the candlelight, the people in their finery, and all eyes on her and Cadan as they glided over the dance floor. She wanted to remember every moment, every sound. The curve of his handsome lips, the way he looked at her with such…. love. *Love*? From this man who had kidnapped her, used her son as bait? Yet here he was, risking everything for her.

When had she begun to feel these strange sensations, for her heart nearly burst. She'd never felt such excitement, such passion, never even knew she could feel this way.

The music halted and the dancers parted.

A hefty man with a long gray mustache headed their way, two French soldiers following behind.

The spell broke. Gabrielle's fear returned. "How are we to escape?"

Cadan scratched his chin. "Hmm. I had not actually planned that far in advance."

Chapter 27

Cadan glanced at Governor Nicolas de Gabaret heading their way and quickly grabbed Gabrielle's arm, hurrying her into the middle of the throng of dancers leaving the floor. She trembled beneath his grip. How could he reassure her of their safety if he wasn't sure of it himself? Aye, he had a plan, but a madcap one. One that both Pell and Moses, upon hearing it, had declared him out of his wits. Neither advised him to proceed, but there was no other alternative. He would not, *could not* leave Lady Fox and Omphile in Damien's evil clutches. If he were a praying man, he'd appeal to the Almighty, but he'd leave that up to Pell for now.

Hunching over, he nudged aside the mass of humanity, finally emerging near the side door where the servants came and went.

"*Arrêtez-les!*" the governor shouted behind him just as they slipped through the door and fled down a flight of stairs to what surely was the larder, kitchen, storerooms and servants' quarters. On the way, they knocked over several liveried men, sending their trays clanking to the steps and flinging food and curses everywhere.

"Apologies!" Cadan shouted as they continued downward into a galley filled with long tables laden with all manner of food and drink.

Cooks, slaves, and servants alike stared at the couple as they sped past, Gabrielle clutching her skirts and Cadan gripping the hilt of his rapier.

French curses and bootsteps thundered down the steps behind them.

"In here!" Cadan shouldered a thick oak door, crashing it open, and tugged Gabrielle inside, down a long hallway, up another flight of stairs and into a parlor. Tapestries and paintings lined the wainscoted wall, while polished walnut furniture perched atop Turkish rugs.

"Where are we go—?" Gabrielle started to ask.

Shouts echoed through the hall behind them. "Follow them!"

Cadan ducked through another door, past the servants' quarters, down another hall, and slid into a small room filled with brooms, mops, buckets, and rags. He shut the door and swung about, groping for the candle he'd left. Then striking flint to steel, he lit it and proceeded to toss rags from a shelf onto the floor. Reaching behind, he prayed the sack was still there.

It was. Thank God.

Gabrielle bent over, heavy breath rasping.

Reaching into the bag, he pulled out two pairs of trousers and canvas shirts, a leather vest, and two hats.

He handed her the smaller set. "Put these on."

Even in the flickering light of a single candle, he saw the incredulous look in her eye. "What?"

"Sorry, Lady Fox. 'Tis the only way."

"But these are men's clothes."

"Precisely." Cadan eased out of his waistcoat and began unbuttoning his shirt.

Her gaze shifted from the clothes in her hand to him and understanding swept over her face. "I need help with the buttons." Lifting the curls that had fallen down her back, she spun around.

Cadan was not without experience at removing women's clothing, but the buttons on this elaborate gown were cumbersome at best. And it was taking too long. He could hear footsteps growing nearer and shouts to search this room and that. It wouldn't be long before they found them. Finally, he gripped both sides and tore the back of the gown open, eliciting a gasp from the lady. Yet to her credit, she did not complain, merely asked him to avert his eyes.

He grinned but complied. However, listening to the swish of her gown and petticoat, her laborious moans and sighs as she undressed and inhaling her sweet fragrance was driving him utterly mad! He'd love nothing more than to steal a glimpse, to touch her silky bare skin, to take her in his arms. But nay! This woman, this lady, deserved more than sordid glances and lusty gropes. She deserved respect.

Removing his boots, he jumped into the dirty trousers and tore the silk shirt over his head.

"Hurry, my lady. We haven't much time."

"I'm never going to pass for a boy," she said. "Look at me."

He needed no further invitation to turn around, his eyes immediately landing on the swell of her breasts beneath the canvas shirt. Huffing, he handed her the leather waistcoat, the smallest he could find. "Here, put this on and button it up."

While she did so, he examined the rest of her, from her slender feminine toes to the rounded curve of her hips to the glorious billow of her chest.

Shouts and curses thundered down the hallway outside the door.

"I can't." Gabrielle's fingers trembled.

Pushing her hands away, Cadan quickly buttoned up the vest. 'Twas not as tight as he'd hoped. "It'll have to do," he said. "Now, bunch your hair beneath this hat." He handed her the largest floppy hat he had found on his ship, then turned to find his canvas shirt.

A gentle touch caressed his back, instantly spinning him to face her.

Gabrielle didn't mean to stare, but when the candlelight flickered over the long ribbons of pink rippled skin on Cadan's back, her heart nearly stopped. How many whippings had this man endured? How many lashes had been dealt from the hand of a cruel taskmaster? And all for a false imprisonment. Unbidden tears pooled in her eyes as she eased her fingers over the bands of pain, as if she could not only erase them but the memories they contained.

Cadan spun around and grabbed her wrist. "What are you—"

"I'm so sorry Cadan. You've suffered so much. Unjustly suffered."

His eyes shifted between hers as if searching for her sincerity. He must have seen her tears, for confusion crumpled his expression, followed by a moist sheen covering his own eyes.

Turning aside, he found his shirt and tossed it over his head. Then blowing out the candle, he took her hand and gave it a squeeze. "Keep your head down. Act like a servant and stay close behind me."

She gripped his arm. "Omphile. We have to get her!"

"Moses will. Now come."

Nodding, Gabrielle expelled a nervous breath.

"Never fear, my lady. I'm with you," he added. Then, opening the door, he led her out into the dark hall.

Gabrielle could not feel her feet. She knew she walked barefoot over wood and stone, but no sensations of either reached her mind—a mind numb with terror. Cadan was either the bravest man she knew or the most foolhardy. She'd been in many a precarious situation before, but as he led her up a set of stairs into the clamor above, she could not remember a time when so much was at stake. Not merely her life but the life of Cadan and, most importantly, that of her son.

At the top of the stairs, Cadan turned right as if he knew where he was going. With his head down, he shuffled forward, behaving like a servant who wished to be anywhere but here. She mimicked him, sinking her chin toward her chest lest anyone see her face. Oddly, none of the other servants took much note of them as Cadan slipped into a storeroom and picked up a crate from a table. He handed it to her and took another for himself before heading toward a door at the back of the room.

With difficulty Gabrielle hefted the crate and pressed it against her chest in an attempt to hide her curves. She had no idea what was in it, but the contents tumbled back and forth as she followed Cadan out the door onto a wide platform abuzz with servants carrying boxes, crates, and barrels into the mansion from several parked wagons.

The hint of a crescent moon shone through the fronds of two large palms, adding to the flickering light of several lanterns hung on posts.

She broke out in a cold sweat. Her mind buzzed in terror. They were but steps away from circling those wagons and slipping into the dark gardens beyond…*mere steps.*

Her vision blurred and she blinked. 'Twas but a blink, but in that moment, she bumped into something massive and warm. Stumbling, she gripped her crate and lost her footing.

Down she went, landing on her knees. The crate slammed against the wooden platform with a loud *SMACK.*

The large black man Gabrielle had bumped into shouted at her in French, something about her being a stupid boy. She grabbed the crate and attempted to stand, all while keeping her head down and chest covered.

Halting, Cadan moved to stand between her and the man, uttering a flurry of French that surprised her with its eloquence. Then kneeling, he gave Gabrielle a look of reassurance and helped her lift the crate.

The man spit onto the ground and uttered another sentence about a worthless boy who couldn't carry his own chamber pot.

"What's the trouble here? Get back to work!" Bootsteps thundered over the platform toward them, shaking the wooden planks. The overseer no doubt.

Gabrielle stiffened. Her pulse roared in her ears. Her hands trembled as Cadan placed them onto the crate and stood, hoisting the bulk of the weight until she had a solid grip.

Turning toward the overseer, he avoided eye contact and once again, spoke fluent French to him in an apologetic tone.

The man snorted in disgust, but his gaze focused on Gabrielle. Only then did she notice a curl had escaped her hat and dangled about her neck.

"What's this?" Before she could stop him, the man removed her hat, releasing her hair in a waterfall of golden waves.

Moses had memorized every word the traitorous servant had told him and Cadan, every door, every hallway, every stair and turn that would lead him to where Omphile was imprisoned. Yet everything looked different than he pictured in his mind. Shifting shadows leapt at him from each corner, while lanterns spread circles of eerie light over the polished wooden floor. Eyes from long-dead French noblemen followed him from paintings lining the walls. He wasn't one to believe in such things, but he could sense the presence of restless ghosts in this place.

Footsteps echoed down the hallway. Glancing this way and that, Moses opened the closest door and eased inside just as two servants hurried past. Darkness permeated the bedchamber, cloaking it in shadows, except for a shaft of light piercing the window and landing on a small writing desk toward the back of the room. Curious, Moses moved toward it, examining the words written across the parchment. He wouldn't have bothered to care except he saw the word Allard, so he read further, interested only because some of the words were in English.

A noise outside the door jarred him and drew him back to task. He must find Omphile!

Slipping out the door, he glanced both ways and continued on his way to the room the servant had said the women had been escorted to. He'd been paid well for the information, and Moses could only pray he'd been telling the truth. But he felt the good Lord with him, despite the evil sensations swirling around him.

Down the hall, up another set of stairs, he stopped at the second door on the left and breathed out a prayer. A padlock chained the door handle to a hook on the wall. This had to be the place.

Plucking his ax from his belt, Moses looked both ways and, after hearing no one coming, he slammed the ax blade against the lock. It split with a loud *clank*, but he caught it along with the chain before they fell to the floor and made more noise. Hopefully, the loud party below had muffled the sound.

Excitement buzzed through him as he opened the door. Omphile stared up at him from her seat by the bed, beautiful as always, eyes wide with shock, then twinkling with delight.

"Why, Moses, what on God's green Earth are you doin' here?" Pushing against the chair, she slowly rose, wobbling on her feet.

Dashing forward, he took her in his arms as he'd been longing to do ever since he'd first laid eyes on her. Heaven. Her soft curves and sweet scent was better than he'd imagined. He could stand there with her pressed so close to him for hours. But they didn't have hours. Not if they were going to get out of this alive.

Chapter 28

$\mathcal{E}$veryone on the platform stopped and gaped at Gabrielle. Whistles pierced her ears. An authoritative voice shouted in the distance. "Capture them at once!"

Cadan grabbed her hand and tore off so fast down the platform, she nearly fell. He leapt down the steps and dove toward a copse of trees. Pistol shots pummeled the night air behind them. The eerie *whine* of a shot whizzed by Gabrielle's head and struck a tree to her right.

She couldn't think. Couldn't breathe. All she could do was follow Cadan as he zigged and zagged through a web of trees, pushing aside branches and vines as he went. They emerged onto a large moonlit field of sugarcane standing nearly as tall as Cadan.

"Get them! This way!" Voices blared behind them.

Cadan yanked Gabrielle into the cane and hurried down a narrow row between stalks. Spindly arms reached out, scratching her skin as they dashed by.

She welcomed the pain. It kept her alert, moving, and not folding into a ball of agonizing terror. Terror that now only increased when her thoughts once again sped to Omphile. How was Moses going to find her in the mansion? Even if he did, how would he escape with her unnoticed?

She yanked on Cadan's arm, once, twice, until finally halting him. "We must go help Moses. I know where Omphile is!" She heaved out between breaths.

"So does Moses. Trust me, my lady. Now hurry!" Squeezing her hand tightly, he tugged her behind him once again.

Trust him? But what choice did she have?

Within minutes they left the sugarcane behind and raced down a dirt road to the edge of town. Darkened storerooms and warehouses rose on both sides of the path like sentinels of the night. Oddly the warm mud felt good on her bare feet, now cut and bruised from their run.

Perspiration trickled down her back and moistened her neck and forehead as the scent of fish, horse dung, and spirits filled her nose.

Yet they continued. Slower this time.

"Wish you had that hat," Cadan commented, glancing at her loose hair. "We'll have to stick to the shadows behind town. It will hurt your feet." He frowned.

"There, I see them!" a man shouted.

Clutching Gabrielle's arm, Cadan pulled her between two buildings. Then facing her, he pressed his arms on either side of her and cloaked her with his body.

His hot breath whooshed over her. The warmth of him leached through every bone. His masculine scent of leather and nutmeg saturated every pore of her skin. He covered her like a shield…a breathing, pulsating shield. And for the first time in her life, she felt truly protected and cherished by a man.

The French troops marched past. Cadan looked up and, without saying a word, took her hand once again and led her behind the building.

They kept to the shadows, hiding amongst trees and brush behind shops, taverns, and punch houses. Though 'twas nearly midnight, a few people still milled about, but mostly 'twas sailors, pirates, and lonely men drifting from one brothel or alehouse to another. Gabrielle caught glimpses between buildings of the silver-streaked wavelets in the harbor where ships rocked to and fro.

Surely the *Resolute* was not among them. But where was Cadan going? She didn't ask. For some reason, she trusted him. He'd come for her. Risked everything. He could have gotten his revenge on Damien at the ball when the man was incapacitated, yet he'd chosen to save her instead. Why, she could not fathom.

Soldiers flooded the town, some on horseback, others in groups with pistols and blades drawn. Angry French words ricocheted off buildings and trees.

"What are they saying?" she dared ask Cadan.

"They are asking if anyone has seen us." He stopped behind a small building and drew her close, listening. His breath came heavy. He stood nigh inches from her, the tip of her head only reaching his chin.

"They are everywhere, Cadan." Gabrielle hated the tremor in her voice.

Even in the shadows, she thought she saw him grin. "Not everywhere, my love."

His endearment warmed her down to her toes. What was wrong with her? Was she falling for this man, this pirate who had used her and her son as bait? Could she not at least fall for a decent man?

They continued onward, soon leaving the town behind and entering a mangrove swamp. Hesitant, Gabrielle finally followed Cadan through knee high water, doing her best not to think about the creatures that lived there—frogs, lizards…snakes! Her feet sank into soft silt one minute and then balanced over a tangled mass of thick tree roots the next. Her sodden trousers weighed her down with each painful step. Fish nibbled at her feet, and she prayed there were no lethal predators about like the crocodiles she'd heard of. Yet thoughts of seeing Matthew again, even if that hope was small, kept her moving forward.

After what seemed like hours, swamp gave way to sand, and the smell of the sea filled her nose even before she heard the lap of waves on the shore.

The shadow of a large man came into view, standing beside a boat. A woman eased out from behind him at the sound of their approach.

Gabrielle squealed. "Omphile!" She ran toward the woman, immediately swallowing her up in her arms.

Moses clasped hands with Cadan. "Good t' see you, Cap'n."

"And you."

Leaves rustled, sand shifted, and a voice behind them shouted. "Halt there!"

Gabrielle looked up to see three men pointing rapiers straight at Cadan's heart.

"Take the women and go!" he shouted to Moses, drawing his blade.

"Nay!" Gabrielle shouted as Moses turned and gestured for them to get into the boat. "I will not leave you!"

"Neither will I," Omphile added, gripping her hand.

Growling, Moses plucked a knife from his belt and turned to face the attackers.

Cadan charged the first man. The clang of swords echoed through the night sky. Dipping his rapier this way and that, he forced the poor Frenchman backward into the brush, then kicked him in the gut.

Clinging to Omphile, Gabrielle squinted to see in the darkness. Beside her, Omphile whispered a prayer.

Moses swept his knife up to block a man's blade, then barreled into him, knocking him backward. The third man, rapier held aloft, swept it down on Moses and would have struck him if Cadan had not rushed and met his attack with his own blade. He shoved the man aside and drove his rapier toward him, slicing him. Blood trickled down the Frenchman's arm and marred his shirt. With a wail of pain, he stumbled off into the darkness.

Cadan glanced at Moses who had flung his opponent's rapier into the brush and was now pounding him into the sand.

Turning to face the final soldier, Cadan spun his rapier before him. "Your turn."

The poor French soldier hesitated for a moment, then dropped his blade, turned, and bolted into the brush.

Cadan didn't hesitate. "Come, Moses! Into the boat!"

Gabrielle pulled Omphile into the surf and helped her into the wobbling boat just as Moses approached, sweat gleaming off his ebony skin.

Leaping in the craft, Cadan sat at the bow whilst Moses gave it a shove and jumped into the middle. The boat wobbled and nearly overturned under the man's weight, but soon, with oars in hand, Cadan and Moses maneuvered the skiff out of the small cove and around the bend.

Gabrielle pressed a hand to her chest to still her thrashing heart. Would they never be out of danger? A brisk wind swept over them, cooling her perspiration and bringing with it the scent of brine and…freedom. The familiar scent, along with the splash of oars, helped calm her down as they rowed around the edge of a sharp peninsula. Moonlight flung silver ribbons atop waves as stars twinkled from a velvety sky. But her eyes were on the dark outline of a ship anchored near the coast. The *Resolute! My son is on that ship!*

She sought out Cadan in the darkness, wanting to thank him, to hug him even. The man's audacity…to anchor beside an enemy island. Yet there his ship was, her distinct elegant lines forming in the shadows, sails limp upon her mighty masts.

Soon they thudded against the hull, and a ladder rope was tossed over. Moses climbed up first, then helped Omphile and Gabrielle.

Something wasn't right. Pirates clogged the main deck. A few stood up on the quarterdeck, but most kept to the shadows. A chill skittered over Gabrielle. Where were Durwin or Pell? Shouldn't someone be there to greet them?

Lastly, Cadan appeared over the railing, his eyes instantly narrowing, his face turning to steel. He marched toward the center of his men just as Smity, a cocksure grin on his scraggly face, emerged from the crowd.

Gabrielle flung a hand to her mouth.

"What is the meaning of this?" Cadan fisted hands on his waist.

"The meanin' is, I'm takin' o'er the ship, Cap'n." He turned toward the men behind him. "Digby, Jugg, lock them in the hold."

Gabrielle could hardly believe her eyes *or* her ears. Had they just gone from one prison to another? From one dire predicament to an even worse one? If she had any doubt God was with her, it blew away in the chilled night breeze.

Smity ordered another of the pirates, a skinny man named Rawlins who bore an oily grin, to escort her and Omphile below deck. She exchanged a glance with Cadan and saw naught but fury flaming in his eyes, his hair wild about him, and his jaw about to burst. A flicker of understanding passed between them before the pirates pushed him and Moses down the hatch.

Matthew! Was her baby here? Who had been taking care of him during the mutiny? Would she find him dead of hunger and neglect? She scanned the throng of pirates, seeking her son, but none carried a bundle. Wait. Was that her pirate guard walking behind the mob, casting glances her way? But nay, she must be seeing things.

"My babe!" She shouted back at Smity as Rawlins gestured for her and Omphile to climb down the companionway.

Smity merely scowled in reply. "What's it to me, wench?"

Her heart shriveled in her chest. Tears filled her eyes, her only thought to escape the pirate's clutches and search the ship for her son.

But then Durwin slid next to Smity and said something to the man, gesturing toward her, and finally Smity ordered another pirate to "fetch the brat and bring it to its mother."

Relief flooded her. Omphile squeezed her hand, and soon they found themselves back in the tiny cabin Gabrielle had been imprisoned in before. Thankfully, Rawlins left the lantern, granting them a little light in the ever-increasing darkness.

"Oh my, this is all my fault." Gabrielle sank to the cot and dropped her head in her hands. "The mutiny, Cadan and Moses and you locked up. None of this would have happened if Damien hadn't kidnapped us and Cadan hadn't come to our rescue."

"Now, now, Child. You can't be blamed for de evil actions o' others." She slid beside her. "Remember God's in control."

In control? Bah. He's nowhere to be found.

The sinister voice rattled what remained of Gabrielle's hope, and she batted a tear from her eye and stared at the door. "Where's my son? Oh, my, do you think he is…?

"No, Child. I told you de Laud said you'll hold him agin soon."

Gabrielle huffed, her fears growing. She was about to respond unkindly when the sound of a baby crying reached her ears.

Flinging hands to her mouth, she dared to hope, not willing to take her eyes off the door.

The crying grew louder, and finally the lock clinked, the door opened, and a screaming white bundle was shoved into her arms.

Cussing, the pirate slammed the door, but Gabrielle didn't care.

She stared down at her son, his face red from screaming and little tears streaming down his puffy cheeks.

"Matthew, oh Matthew, I've missed you so."

At the sound of her voice, he stopped crying and looked up at her as if he, too, had missed her. But that wasn't possible. He was too young for that.

Omphile moved to glance down at him. "He looks healthy an' sound, Miss. All is well. I told you."

Smiling, Gabrielle kissed her son on the forehead and drew him close. At least in all this madness, God had blessed her with one tiny miracle.

Cadan had only been this furious once before, and that was when Elyna and Damien had conspired to have him convicted of treason and sent to Barbados as a slave. And just like back then, he had not expected this mutiny. What a fool! He'd thought he'd engendered a smidgen of loyalty amongst his crew. But they were pirates, after all.

Digby, a man big of head and less of brains, shoved him down the ladder to the gun deck.

"Didn't I line your pockets with enough coins, Digby?" Cadan growled. "That you turn on me so quickly?"

"Nothin' personal, Cap'n," Jud said, pressing the barrel of his flintlock at Moses' back. "Smity offered us a fortune if we sided wit' 'im. That's all."

Cadan laughed. "And you trust that feckless ingrate?"

Which earned him another shove.

"Down below wit' ye, an' shut yer trap."

One glance over his shoulder revealed Moses, rage tightening all his features, and a fire in his eyes Cadan had not seen before.

"Don't be thinkin' it, Cap'n. Ye try anythin', and yer Negro friend 'ere gets gutted."

Cadan ground his teeth, but continued onward, climbing down the ladder into the dark moist stink of the hold. Hadn't he just been down here talking to Smity? How had the man escaped? No doubt he'd bribed one of the pirates by saying he'd go after Demster's treasure. Not that he knew where it was. Cadan grinned.

Another smile stretched his lips at the sight of Pell and Soot inside the cage. At least they had remained loyal to him, though he was not happy to see them thus.

Digby unlocked the gate, shoved Cadan and Moses inside, then slammed the door with a mighty clank that echoed through the hold.

Jud spat to the side then left, chuckling all the way up the ladder, Digby lumbering behind him.

Darkness as thick as the grave encompassed them.

"I did my best, Captain." Pell's voice joined the creak and groan of the ship's timbers.

"You were outnumbered." Crossing arms over his chest, Cadan leaned against the bars. "I should have listened to you."

"Aye."

Moses must have found the cot and sat, for it creaked beneath his weight.

"Durwin?" Cadan had thought he'd seen his first mate above, but he couldn't be sure.

"Joined them. Smity can be very convincing."

Cadan nodded, another sting to his heart from a man he'd considered a friend. But thinking back, Durwin's passion had always been riches. And since Cadan had delayed finding Dempster's treasure, 'twas no wonder the man's loyalty shifted to someone who would.

"And the ladies?" Pell asked.

"We got dem," Moses said. "De captain's plan worked perfectly."

"Well, not entirely perfectly," Cadan said with a huff. "We had to fight off three Frenchmen at the end."

Pell chuckled. "'Twas a mad plan, but if anyone could carry it out, you could."

"Lot of good it did me."

"At least you rescued them from Allard," Pell said. "They are safe for now."

"Aye." Cadan would never forget the look on Lady Fox's face as Smity ordered one of the pirates to lock her and Omphile back in their cabin. He only hoped the cur would allow her to have her son.

"What of the babe?" he asked Pell.

"He's well last I saw him."

Gripping the bars, Cadan shook them until his fingers ached. "If he dares hurt her or the babe, he'll wish he'd never been born!"

"He'll answer t' me too, Captain," Moses interjected.

Shouts bounced over the deck above, followed by the flap of sails. Smity was preparing to set sail.

Pell blew out a sigh. "He's a malicious cockroach, but to kill an innocent babe?"

Cadan plowed back his damp hair, his mind searching for a means of escape. "You have too much faith in mankind."

"Perhaps. But I'm starting to put my faith where it ought to be. With God."

Cadan snorted. "Then start praying my friend. Start praying."

Chapter 29

Lazy-eyed Smity marched into the captain's cabin, head held high and spirits even higher. With Cadan, Pell, Moses, and Soot locked below and the crew on his side, he'd singlehandedly taken over the *Resolute* and all that came with her without a single shot. From being imprisoned in the hold as a traitor to the captain's cabin in just one day! Captain Avery would be proud. He'd learned a lot from that master pirate, but the most important lesson was that power shifted easily by discontent. A man merely waited for an opportune moment when the crew was unhappy with the current leadership and then he promised to make all their dreams come true.

Never again would he be ordered about. Not a man of his keen intellect and skill. Nay, he should be the leader of men, and he'd prove it by finding the treasure every pirate sought most of all, the infamous treasure of Captain Edward Dempster. He ran a thumb down the right side of his face. And in the process, he'd have his revenge on the man who disfigured him. Besides, the riches would do much to attract women who would otherwise shun him.

Aye, his life finally sailed down a course of success, power, wealth, and women. What else did a man need? A knock on the door jarred him from his pleasant thoughts, and he gave the order to enter.

Kipp and Durwin lumbered inside. "Kane wants t' know where t' point the tiller, Smi…I mean, Cap'n," Durwin said.

The first gray of dawn cast an eerie glow over the cabin, scattering the dusty mist.

Smity scratched his beard and made his way to the desk where light from a lantern above swayed back and forth over Cadan's map.

The half-witted fuddler had kept Smity from seeing the map or hearing anything about the treasure, though, as bosun, he'd had a right to do so. "Durwin. Show me what ye know."

The first mate approached and studied the map. "Wells, Cap'n Hayes knew the treasure were right in this string o' islands. He jist didn't know which one till he got a clue when we anchored at Nevis. He gestured toward the center island. "It be this one."

"Where Dempster buried his treasure?"

"Aye. That be the one."

"And?" Smity tapped his fingers on the desk. "Where on the island? I can hardly dig up the entire place."

Durwin began searching through the parchments on Cadan's desk. "He got the final clue in that church. I saw it in 'is hand. Got t' be 'ere somewhere."

The infernal iguana skittered across the desk, scattering parchment and knocking over a half glass of rum onto the map.

Uttering a foul curse, Smity raised his fist to crush the disease-encrusted pest, but the lizard darted away and disappeared under the bed.

"Blasted filthy vermin!" Smity shouted, righting the glass. Then grabbing one of Cadan's shirts from the floor, he attempted to soak up the alcohol, but to no avail, for the ink on that corner blurred into nonsensical smudges.

"It don't matter, Smity." Durwin shrugged. "We's know which island. I jist need t' find the last clue."

Smity growled. "Cap'n Smity to ye, Durwin."

"Sorry, Cap'n." Durwin sifted through the papers and notes on the deck, then rummaged through drawers, emptying their contents onto the deck. But no note or clue appeared.

With each passing minute, Smity's fury rose.

Finally, Durwin shook his head and rubbed the back of his hand beneath his hawk nose. "Not 'ere."

Smity let out an ominous growl. "I want this entire cabin searched from every crack in the deck below to every hole above, every nook and cranny, chest, table, and chair!" He gestured toward Durwin and Kipp. "Tear the pages out of every book if you have to."

An hour later, with no clue found, Smity strapped on his cutlass and headed down to the hold.

"Forget something, Smity?" Cadan squinted against the light blaring from the lantern in the traitor's hand, but he could still make out the snake standing beside it, along with Durwin and five pirates behind him.

"That be Cap'n Smity t' ye."

"Captain, is it?" Cadan glanced at Pell and the others, and they all shared a chuckle. "You couldn't captain a sea turtle in a swamp."

Scowling, Smity charged the cage, then halted, pasting a smile on his face. "Yet ye are the one in the hold, and I be in the captain's cabin."

"For now." Cadan's gaze shifted to Durwin, cowering behind Smity. "You too, Durwin?"

To the man's credit, he lowered his gaze, unable to meet Cadan's eyes.

"I took you on my ship, nursed you back to good health, gave you a job."

The sea crashed against the hull as the *Resolute* veered slightly to larboard. A rat skittered across the deck.

Durwin shifted his boots. "He offered me a king's ransom, Cap'n. Sorry."

Cursing, Smity slapped Durwin upside the head. "What's wrong wit' ye? Don't say sorry t' the likes of 'im." He hooked the lantern above.

Durwin stepped back.

Soot approached the bars, eyes bulging at Durwin, rage strangling his voice. "Ye thievin', cur! Expected this from Smity, but ye?"

Durwin stepped further into the shadows.

"What is it you want, Smity?" Pell asked with his usual calm composure.

"That be easy." Smity fingered the pearl in his right earlobe. "I need the final clue t' Dempster's treasure."

Cadan smiled. "Is that so?"

"Tell me where it be, an' I'll let ye an' yer friends live."

"Don't tell him, Cap'n," Moses said from behind him.

"Aye. Don't give this scabrous mouse anythin'," Soot hissed. "We'd rather die than see him win."

Cadan crossed arms over his chest. "I guess you have your answer, then." He longed to ask the man about Lady Fox and Omphile but dared not give him the ammunition.

An evil grin lifted one side of the traitor's lips, and he unclipped a key from his belt. "Pistols at the ready, men. Shoot any o' them who moves." Then unlocking the door, he gestured for Cadan to come out.

Cadan glanced at the six pistols pointed their way. Even if he and his men charged, they'd not get far before they'd all be shot dead. "I believe I'll stay here with my men."

"Lawks! But ye be a stubborn hen." Smity shook his head. "I'll shoot yer men one by one if'n ye don't step out right now."

Heaving a sigh, Cadan complied.

Shoving him aside, Smity slammed the door and locked it once again.

"Now, up t' the deck wit' ye!" Drawing a knife, he poked Cadan in the back.

Though everything in him longed to turn and beat Smity until every last breath left his body, he knew it would do no good and would only hurt the chances that his friends might survive.

Hence, he followed Durwin up the ladder to the gundeck and up another ladder to the main deck where a blast of wind swept away the stink of the hold clinging to every inch of him.

The rising sun spread a blanket of gold and orange lace over the horizon, transforming the sea into a shifting rainbow. He drew in a deep breath of salty air, happy to be free of the hold…until he spotted Gabrielle, Matthew in her arms, standing by the starboard railing, terror screaming from her beautiful face.

Her turquoise eyes brimmed with a silent appeal to help her, to rescue her from this madman.

Ah, how he longed to do so, would gladly risk his life to set her free! His glance took in the sails above billowing in the morning breeze, sailors speeding up ratlines to their tasks. Up on the quarterdeck, Kane had taken Pell's place as quartermaster.

Casting him spurious glances, his traitorous crew lulled about on the main deck, whether to protect Smity from him or to gloat at his misfortune, he couldn't tell, for their eyes followed his every move.

He returned their gazes with a look of steel, of authority, for he was still their captain.

Smity shoved him toward the railing where Gabrielle stood, and it took all his strength not to take her in his arms and tell her all would be well. Her eyes flitted between his and a tiny smile graced her lips. Perhaps she was as glad to see him alive as he was her.

Smity marched to the lady, and before Cadan could react, he snatched little Matthew from her arms and held the babe over the railing. "Give me the final clue or I'll toss the brat."

Uttering a scream that would wake the Kraken, Gabrielle pounded Smity's back, but two pirates caught her arms and held them behind her. Still, she struggled, her tear-filled eyes shifting from Matthew to Cadan.

Fury raged through every vein. Was there no limit to the man's wicked heart?

"Please, Cadan, please!" Gabrielle cried.

The hatred from Smity's one good eye seared into Cadan. "What'll it be?"

Cadan had no choice. He could pretend he cared not a whit for the boy or his mother, but the fiend might very well drop the babe anyway.

"Very well. I'll take you to the treasure. Just give the boy back to his mother."

Gabrielle had not let go of her son, not once since Smity had returned him to her after his threat to throw him overboard. Returned rather reluctantly, from the expression on his vile face. In truth, after the terrifying incident, she'd had nightmares the past two nights filled with visions of little Matthew wailing over a raging sea, reaching out to her with his chubby arms, face red and tears spilling from his cheeks. Though she tried with all her might, she couldn't move, couldn't rescue him, bound by what felt like iron shackles. Then he plunged into the billowing waves, his scream instantly silenced by the waters as he disappeared into the deep.

Both nights, she'd leapt up in bed, heart thundering, sweat streaming, only to find her babe safely tucked in the coverlet beside her.

Poor Omphile touched her from her other side, uttering sleepy, but reassuring words, until she lay back down and nestled Matthew close.

The soothing sounds of water against the hull slowed and shouts and footsteps above jarred Gabrielle awake from yet another restless night. Gathering Matthew, she eased off the coverlet and swept her legs over the side of the cot. Rays of morning light drifted through the tiny window, along with other sounds—the sweet warble of birds amid more shouts from on deck. Finally, the crank and rattle of the anchor chain rang loud and clear, followed by a mighty splash as the anchor landed in the water.

The *Resolute* jerked to a stop, nearly sending Gabrielle onto the floor. Omphile moaned from the far end of the tiny cot, and

Gabrielle glanced at the woman who had become a much-needed friend.

Matthew began to fuss, and Gabrielle quickly unbuttoned her gown and started to feed him, thankful Omphile had taught her to keep her milk flowing when they'd been separated. She was also grateful that Omphile had stuffed an old gown in a drawer from their previous time in the cabin, or Gabrielle would still be wearing men's canvas breeches and shirt.

Crawling past her, Omphile stood and stretched. Then dragging the chair over to the porthole, she stood atop and peered out. "Land. An island is my guess."

The treasure. Cadan had told Smity he'd lead him to it. All to save her. "It does not bode well for us, Omphile," she said. "As soon as Smity gets what he wants, he'll have no further need of us. Or Cadan."

"Oh, you do fret so, Child." The woman waved a hand at her and smiled, stepping down from the chair.

"When I have no reason to hope, aye, I do." Gabrielle returned more sharply than she intended.

Omphile sat on a chair, grabbed a brush from the table, and began brushing her long black hair. "But we do have hope. Our Father owns de cattle on a thousand hills, an' He loves you. The Good Book says all things work together for good for dem who love God."

Gabrielle sighed, shifting Matthew to her other side. Did *she* love God? Did she even know Him?

"Hasn't He saved us dis far?" Omphile continued. "Isn't your babe back in your arms as He told me?"

Matthew gazed up at Gabrielle as he suckled, eyes full of life, love, and innocence. True. God had answered her prayers…or…. "'Twas your prayers He answered."

"Mebbe 'cause you didn't ask Him yourself." One brow raised.

Gabrielle stared at the woman, that ever-present peaceful smile on her face.

Nay, Gabrielle had not asked, had not prayed, not *really* prayed in a long time. "Do you truly hear from God, Omphile?"

Her smile couldn't be brighter. "Most every day, Miss. Inside here." She pressed a hand over her heart. "An' in His Word."

Frowning, Gabrielle stared down at her precious son. "I guess if I admit it, I've never honestly heard from Him, though my parents are like you, speaking to Him all the time. Or so they say."

Omphile inched to the edge of her seat. "Mebbe, Miss, you have not known Him. Like I said, you jist believed 'cause your parents did. But you never had dat relationship wit' Him yourself."

Matthew stopped sucking. His little eyes shut as he drifted off to sleep. Wiping his mouth with his blanket, she cuddled him close, pondering Omphile's words. "You may be right, Omphile. I guess I believed because my parents did. I mean, I believe in God. I believe Jesus is His Son. Isn't that enough? I grew up hearing tales of God's miracles and deliverances—all things that happened to my family. But never to me."

"'Cause you needs to have your own walk wit' Him, Child. It is not 'bout believing in here"—she pointed at her head—"but about knowing Him in here." She laid a hand over her heart again.

"Knowing God? Talking to Him as if He were here? And hearing Him answer?" Gabrielle could not fathom such a thing. "Why would the Creator of all things want to have that kind of intimacy with each of His children….with her?"

Omphile's face lit. "That's why He died for us so's we can know Him now an' live wit' Him forever in eternity."

Gabrielle couldn't help but smile at the woman's exuberance, the same passion she'd often seen in her parents' eyes. Still, she began to wonder whether she knew God at all or if she'd just been going through the motions to please her parents.

The sound of the lock clinking jarred her from her thoughts. Shooting to her feet, Gabrielle spun around for modesty's sake just as the door blasted open and a gust of wind blew in from the companionway.

"Shame on you, Kipp." Omphile moved to stand between her and the pirate whose footsteps she heard entering. "Barging in on a lady unannounced!"

The man chuckled. "Ain't no ladies 'ere. Cap'n wants the wench an' 'er brat up on deck."

"What for?"

"To go treasure hunting."

Chapter 30

Ｉf ye don't lead me t' the treasure, if ye make one mistake, if ye try anythin'," Smity said to Cadan as they waited for Gabrielle to come above deck. "I'll gut 'er an' the babe as quickly as I can look their way."

Swallowing his fury, Cadan nodded, yanking against the ropes that bound his hands before him. He knew the man's threat was real. He only regretted that Smity was smart enough to bring the lady along to ensure he behaved. Or as surely as Cadan had an ounce of breath in his lungs, he would have *tried something*—as in killed Smity with his bare hands. No matter the consequences.

His hatred of this insolent, mutineering dog was only surpassed by his hatred for Allard. And his need to see both of them in hell only grew by the minute.

At least the man had agreed to Cadan's demand that he be the one to take him to the treasure. He'd lied when he'd said he lost the clue, lied when he'd said the location would be too hard to explain. Perhaps he had only bought himself another day of life, but a better day it would be on the lush greenery of an island rather than locked in the hold, where he'd spent the last eight days.

Eight miserable days in their journey to Eleuthera, one of the tiny islands in the Bahamas. Eight miserable days in which Cadan had far too much time to think, to ponder, to regret his past mistakes and dwell on his hopeless future. Eight days in which his fear for Gabrielle and Matthew grew until it began to gnaw at his soul.

Finally, she appeared from the companionway, and he mouthed an *I'm sorry* as she approached. But before she could respond, a pirate shoved her toward the rope ladder, took Matthew against her protests, and assisted her into the boat below before handing him back. Men with shovels and pick axes already filled the wobbling craft by the time Cadan clambered in with difficulty due to his restraints. Smity leapt in behind him.

Rays of the sun pierced the morning mist hovering over the island. Gentle waves from a turquoise bay lapped upon the shore as if nothing at all were wrong with the world. Birds danced from limb to limb through a web of trees that led up to green rolling hills. 'Twas a beautiful place to bury one's treasure, Cadan supposed. But not so beautiful were it to become his grave.

Gabrielle's eyes sought him out. Terror screamed from within them, yet he saw no hatred, none of the accusation he deserved, for he alone was to blame for her present circumstance. He'd made mistakes. He'd played loosely with innocent lives, and now, they all faced certain death.

All for what? Revenge, Money? He wondered if it was worth it.

They rowed ashore within minutes. Once on the sand, Cadan attempted to slip beside Gabrielle to offer her some comfort, but Smity pushed him toward the jungle. "Which way?"

Drawing a deep breath, he glanced over the palms, sea grapes, and fig trees lining the shore, then back at the *Resolute*, hidden in the bay, looking as majestic as ever as she rolled with the incoming waves. *His* ship. He thought of Pell, Moses, and Soot still locked in the filthy hold, and he fisted his hands.

Somehow, he'd have to free them. But first he had to free himself.

God, if you're listening, please help. 'Twas the first prayer he'd uttered in twenty years, ever since his mother had died and left him to care for his siblings.

He glanced down shore, uttered a "This way," and started walking toward the jungle, his bare feet flinging sand in the air. The final clue described a circular outcropping of rocks in the shape of a half-moon. Dempster had hidden the treasure in a locked chest at the bottom of a cave in the center of that moon. Or so the clue had said. But first they had to cross a section of the jungle to get to the other side of the small island. Aye, he could have led Smity to anchor there, where they'd only have a few yards of jungle to traverse before arriving at the treasure. But Cadan wanted to prolong his last minutes alive, and a trip through tangled brush may grant him an opportunity to escape with Lady Fox. Though now as he glanced over the four pirates Smity had brought with him—four of the meanest of Cadan's crew—his hope for that chance faded. Leaving but one final shred of hope. He'd told Pell the exact location of the treasure should fate smile on them, and Pell could somehow escape.

Batting aside a large fern, he entered the jungle, the leaves of the forest floor cooling his feet from the hot sand. Dempster's treasure! He'd been longing for this moment for two years, ever since he'd discovered the map in a secret compartment of the old pirate's desk. He'd been the one to find the map, he'd been the one to follow the clues. The treasure was his! The wealth he'd gain would grant him land and power, and never again would men like Allard and Smity be able to squash him beneath their rapacious thumbs.

But now as he walked the same path Captain Dempster must have walked, he found no excitement, no pleasure in it. In truth, he was more concerned for the lady and her babe than he was at losing the treasure. Treasure he could always get back. But not Gabrielle. There was no woman like her.

"How much further?" Smity whined as Cadan circled around the large trunk of a tree. What kind he didn't know, but its roots spread out like a web over the sandy soil. Halting, he glanced up at the canopy of lush green leaves and wiped the sweat from his brow.

"Not much," he finally said, glancing back at Gabrielle.

Kipp held her tight in his clutches, dragging her beside him. Struggling to keep Matthew secure, she stumbled over an exposed root, and the pirate uttered a curse and shoved her forward.

Rage stormed through Cadan. Grimacing, he faced Smity. "If that bloated crock harms her, or *anyone* harms her, I'll take the location of the treasure to my grave."

Dipping a cloth into the cool water of a tiny creek, Gabrielle dribbled it over Matthew's mouth. Waving his chubby arms through the air, he made gurgling sounds as he welcomed the refreshment. She brushed a lock of his hair from his forehead and kissed him gently. She had not known 'twas possible to love someone as much as she loved her son. She would gladly die, be tortured, *die on a cross*, if only to save him. Lifting her head, she glanced over the labyrinth of greenery around her. Where had the thought, *die on a cross*, come from, for she'd not been thinking of Jesus.

Movement drew her gaze to the right. A figure dressed in brown breeches and a checkered shirt passed between two trees and disappeared into the brush. The pirate Cadan oft assigned to guard her? Shaking her head, she glanced down at her son. Nothing made sense anymore.

Dipping the cloth into the water again, she brought it to Matthew's mouth, hoping 'twould be enough to sustain him until she could feed him properly. One glance behind her revealed Smity tipping a flask to his mouth, surrounded by four of his men, while Cadan stood to the right tied to a tree. Their eyes met briefly, and though they were separated by several yards, she saw both fury and longing within them. A purple bruise formed near his right eye where Smity had struck him after Cadan had announced he'd not lead them to the treasure if any harm came to her.

Her knight in shining armor! Who would have guessed this pirate, who once had been willing to toss her to the sharks to satisfy his revenge, would now be willing to risk his life for her?

When had he changed? When had her own heart become so tethered to his?

Still, she was grateful when Smity agreed to stop for a rest, "if only to silence the brat's constant screaming," he had said.

"Tend t' yer brat, wench," he'd ordered. "An' make sure he's quiet from now on, or I'll silence him meself!"

Ignoring the fear curdling in her belly, she'd found a spot by the creek where she could change Matthew's nappy and give him some water. For now, he seemed satisfied.

Birds sang a pleasant tune above her, and she glanced up at a particular one whose multi-colored feathers would put any nobleman to shame. God's creation was so incredible. Just like the wee one in her arms.

Matthew gurgled again. His blue eyes scanned the canopy with the wonder of sweet innocence, flailing his arms out as if he could touch and explore this new world around him.

Lord, please rescue us. Please save Cadan and me and this precious child you've given me.

He never answers your prayers.

The silent voice stabbed her, haunting in its malevolence, torturing in its truth.

She sighed. Perhaps 'twas true of late, but Omphile's words still rang in her mind *and* her heart. *You jist believed 'cause your parents did. But you never had dat relationship wit' Him yourself.*

Looking back on her life, as one did when approaching certain death, all Gabrielle saw was a young girl who'd idolized her parents, who believed whatever they told her, who followed all the rules, and obeyed God's commands, the perfect daughter, the perfect Christian. But why? Had she done it for them or for God? Or perhaps she'd done it to stroke her own ego, feed her own insecurities, make herself out to be a saint that others could admire. 'Twas no wonder then, that when things didn't go her way, she blamed God. Didn't He owe her a good life after all her sacrifices?

Perspiration slid down her back, and huffing, she eased a finger over Matthew's cheek, relishing the softness. In truth, now that she pondered it, she'd never really known God, never had a relationship with Him at all.

Lord, I'm so sorry. I thought I was doing everything right. I thought I was pleasing You, pleasing my parents, but I did it for all the wrong reasons. Not out of a love for You, but out of an obligation, out of pride.

Matthew grinned up at her and brushed his hand over her chin. She wouldn't want Matthew to grow up, do everything she asked of him, but never speak to her, never spend time with her, never get to know her. Never *love* her. She'd much rather have a close relationship with him than have him be perfect.

Understanding blossomed within her like a rose long since closed for a long winter. Omphile had been right. Gabrielle had never taken the time to know Jesus, to spend time with Him, to love Him. And if He loved her half as much as she loved Matthew, then she was in good hands, mighty, loving hands!

Lord, forgive me. She closed her eyes. *I've been so foolish. I want to know You. I want to grow to love You. I've spent my life trying to be perfect, but all you ever wanted was me, my love. Help me now, Lord.*

Precious daughter.

The words brought tears to her eyes. *Daughter?* Was she really God's daughter? A breeze fluttered leaves and swept over her, cooling her skin and drying her tears. Love like she'd never experienced filled her heart to near bursting. She let out a giggle that caused Matthew to grin and kick his feet excitedly. "Thank you, Jesus!" she whispered.

So this was what her parents had been talking about, the incredible presence of God, the love, joy, and peace that filled her heart, her soul, her very being! She never knew it could be like this.

And it was only the beginning.

"Get up, wench!" Smity's churlish command blared over her, slicing through her newfound joy.

Tucking away the cloth, she drew Matthew close and struggled to her feet. Alas, perhaps 'twas only the beginning of the end. Yet not the end. She knew that now. Life here on Earth was only the beginning.

Twigs snapped, drawing her gaze to her pirate guard standing on the other side of the small creek, smiling at her. And at that moment, that precious moment, she knew without knowing that he was no pirate assigned by Cadan to guard her.

He must surely be an angel sent by God Almighty to keep her safe.

At the top of the rocky ledge, Cadan glanced down and smiled. Beneath him, just like the clue had described, a cliff formed a half-circle around a foamy pool of water coming in from the sea. At the center of the circle, a small dark opening sat just above water level.

"There." He pointed to the cave entrance. "A man can only get inside during low tide."

"Guess where yer goin', then." Smity chuckled and shoved him onward. Sharp rocks bit his feet. Pain carved up his legs as he navigated across the ledge to what looked like the easiest way to climb down. At the bottom, he jumped into the pool of water. Waves sloshed to his knees, and he glanced up at Gabrielle above him on the top of the cliff. One pirate remained with her while the others headed down with shovels and pickaxes. Matthew wailed, and she attempted to comfort him. Oddly, he longed to hold the babe in his arms again. Just one more time.

Keep her safe, Lord. Please.

"Best get in afore the tide rises." Smity pointed with his pistol toward the opening, and Cadan did the only thing he could do. He took one last glance at a sun he might never see again and dove inside the dark opening.

Darkness stole his sight. Water soaked his breeches. Blinking, he waited for his eyes to adjust to the few rays of sunlight filtering in through slits in the rock ceiling. He slowly rose as lantern light followed behind him, along with two of his crew, *his* crew. He wouldn't give them the dignity of speaking to them. Or to Smity, who crawled in after them. Instead, he splashed through the few inches of water at the bottom of the cave toward the back where the clue said the skull of a man marked the spot where the treasure chest lay.

And indeed, there it was, perched atop a pile of rocks, the large empty eyes and grinning teeth smirking at Cadan for his foolhardy quest. To whom had it belonged? Cadan had no idea, but no doubt the man had attempted to steal Dempster's treasure and met his just reward.

"There." He gestured to the skull. "Beneath those rocks."

Shouting with glee, the pirates tossed their implements aside, along with the poor man's skull and began digging like ravenous dogs for a bone.

"There she be!" one of them screeched. "Look Cap'n, I mean Hayes. Jist like ye said."

Cadan crossed arms over his chest. "Too bad you turned on me. You think Ole Smity's going to share with you?"

Something hard slammed across his skull. Pain scorched a trail from his head to his toes as his vision blurred and he stumbled.

"Enough out o' ye!" Smity stood over him, the handle-end of his pistol tight in his grip.

The pirates grabbed hold of the chest handles, and with much groaning and heaving, brought it out of the hole at the bottom of the cave.

Smity's grin couldn't be wider, nor the evil gleam in his single eye brighter. "What ye waitin' fer. Haul 'er out."

The two pirates pushed the chest through the water toward the entrance. A gush of the sea rushed in through the hole, stopping them momentarily, but as soon as it withdrew, they managed to get out with the chest, Smity right behind them.

Cadan followed, happy to be free of the close confines of the cave. Also happy because the tide was slowly coming in and soon the cave would be flooded.

Smity ordered another pirate to assist in carrying the chest up the rocky cliff, his full attention on the treasure. Cadan stared at the water rising in the pool, sending white foam swirling around rocks. It wouldn't take but a few seconds to jump in, dive behind one of those boulders, and make his way out of the outcropping. He was a good swimmer and could easily make it to another part of the island.

He locked eyes with Gabrielle, and she nodded as if she understood his plan.

But nay! How could he leave her now? Smity might kill her just for spite.

The moment—and the chance—passed as Smity turned, pistol leveled at Cadan's head.

"Say goodbye, Cap'n." He ran his other thumb down his wrinkled face.

"Nay! Nay!" Gabrielle screamed and struggled in the pirate's grasp. Matthew's cries bounced off the rocks, spearing Cadan's heart. Still, he stood his ground, staring at his adversary. He would not go down like a coward. He would face his death with honor. His only regret, as he stole one more glance at Gabrielle, was that he wouldn't see her again, couldn't protect her and love her as she was worthy of being loved.

The sound of at least a dozen pistols cocked, along with the chime of swords being released from scabbards.

"Time for *you* to say goodbye, Smity."

A reprieve? A rescue? Nay, not from the sound of *that* voice.

Cadan knew before he looked up who he would see standing on the top of the cliff with that cocksure grin on his face.

Damien Allard.

Chapter 31

Gabrielle's shock at seeing Damien was only matched by the look of horror on Cadan's face. At least he was still alive! Her heart barely had a chance to settle when Damien glanced her way with a lascivious grin. "We meet again, *ma douce.*"

At least a dozen of his pirates surrounded them, and without much resistance, Cadan's crew dropped their weapons. All four were quickly subdued and forced to the ground, ropes tied about their wrists, while Damien ordered two of his men to climb down the cliff.

"You dare betray me?" Damien turned to Smity. "Hoping to abscond with the treasure without me?"

"I...I..." Smity blubbered, his tone spiked with fear.

Then, without even blinking, Damien ordered the man beside him to shoot him.

Horror widened Smity's eye. Horror and panic. A shot rang out. Blood spurted from his chest, and he fell backward into the pool with a mighty splash and sank in the murky water.

Lowering her gaze, Gabrielle clung tightly to Matthew. Her blood turned to ice. What would be her fate now?

She hadn't long to find out.

After ordering his men to grab Cadan, who still had not taken the chance to escape, Damien turned to her. "Come with me, my sweet. You will be my wife, and we will raise our child together." He extended his hand, the lace at his cuffs fluttering in the breeze, his lavender perfume stinging her nose, and an almost desperate pleading in his tone.

Shuddering, she glanced at Cadan.

Damien followed her gaze and scowled. "If you come with me, I will let him live."

But she knew Damien, knew that tone. He would never allow Cadan to live.

"I will never go willingly with you," she spat back, clinging tighter to Matthew. "Nor will I ever be your wife."

A few of his men chuckled, earning a searing glance from him.

He slid his fingers over his thinly-coifed mustache, a storm clouding his blue eyes. "Very well. As you wish." He turned to one of his men. "Hugo, grab the child. Francois, escort the lady to her lover below."

Horror screamed through every inch of Gabrielle. "Nay!" She started to run, but the pirate caught her and plucked Matthew from her arms as easily as one would a sack of rice. Desperate, she clung to him tightly, tugging and pulling with all her might. "Let him go! Let him go!" But to no avail. She finally released him, for the man's powerful wrenching would no doubt hurt her precious babe. Matthew screamed, flailing his chubby arms through the air.

Gabrielle's heart plummeted to the rocks below, and she sank to her knees, sobbing.

The other pirate yanked her to her feet and violently pulled her down the cliff into the pool where Cadan remained, his expression mimicking her own horror. Her feet hurt, her legs ached, bruises and cuts marred her arms, but the greatest pain of all? Her broken heart.

"Now," Damien said with a smirk and a wave of his jeweled fingers. "Into the cave you go. Both of you."

"It will soon flood, Allard," Cadan said. "You can't be that heartless."

"Oh, you have no idea, *mon ami*. Now inside, or I'll be forced to shoot the lady." He snapped his fingers, and a pirate next to him leveled his pistol at Gabrielle.

Matthew's mournful howls joined the crash of the incoming tide as all hope fled her, leaving a numbness in its wake.

One of the pirates shoved his pistol in Cadan's back. "In wit' ye, ye bloated milksop."

Bubbling water swirled around Gabrielle's gown. Just a few feet away, the waves slammed Smity's lifeless body against a boulder. She tore her gaze from the horrid sight.

Cadan grabbed her hand and gave her a nod as if to say, *let's do what they say*. Was he serious? She'd rather be shot than slowly drown. But Matthew's cries ripped holes in her heart. If there was a chance, even a small one they could survive…. *Lord*? Hadn't she just felt the Almighty's presence? Scanning the top of the cliff, she searched for her angel.

There he was, looking down on her with confidence, sparking her hope. Yet…perhaps he merely waited to escort her to heaven.

Facing Cadan, she nodded back, turned, dropped to her knees, and crawled, sloshing through the water, into the dark cave.

Cadan splashed in after her.

Moments later, grunts and groans sounded from outside, and a boulder was shoved over the opening, covering it by half.

A darkness as thick and malevolent as the water clawing up their thighs surrounded them. All save for a shaft of light coming from a narrow opening at the top.

Squatting in the water, Cadan shouldered the massive boulder covering the opening. It didn't move. Turning, he sat, raised his legs and kicked it with all his might. Nothing. Then, finally, he attempted to squeeze through the remaining opening. But to no avail.

'Twas too small even for a child.

Rising, he splashed back toward her and took her in his arms. She welcomed his embrace and leaned her head against his sodden shirt, listening to the beat of his heart.

More water gushed in through the opening.

"We are going to die, aren't we?"

Pell leaned back against the cold iron bars of the tiny cage that had been his prison for over a week. He'd grown accustomed to the darkness as thick as tar and the stench that could wake the dead. He'd grown accustomed to the sound of Moses' deep breathing and Soot's nasally whine. He'd even grown accustomed to the rats that frequented their cell, skittering about their feet seeking scraps of food.

What he hadn't grown accustomed to was the deep well of despair that had taken over his soul. Having been a man of God, a preacher, a missionary, he'd always embraced hope, for wasn't hope a central theme of the Holy Scriptures? Hope, even in the direst of circumstances, hope in a faithful God who protected, provided, answered prayers, and who loved His children. Hope that there was an eternity beyond this world, a place where all would be made right, every justice resolved, every pain healed, every tear wiped away. A hope that enabled a man to face whatever came, whether poverty or riches, sickness or health, injustice or fairness, persecution or providence, all to be endured with perseverance, knowing that this life was but a vapor compared to the eternal bliss that awaited him. That hope came from belief in a Savior who gave up everything to die for mankind, thus opening the pathway to God and that blissful eternity.

A rat began to nibble on his boot, and he kicked it away. When had he lost that hope? Surely after his son died—a burst of raw pain clumped in his throat—it had begun to dwindle. Then after his wife succumbed to her grief, more had been burned away. But now, locked in this hold for days, his life in the hands of a vindictive madman, the last shred of hope had dissipated in the rank air.

Or had it?

I have never left you.

That voice, that tender, loving, yet powerful voice! Pell had once known that voice well, had heard it often, had relished the wisdom and love flowing through its words.

Moisture burned in his eyes. *Why, Lord, why?*

My plans are not your plans. All things work together for good.

Good? What good could come out of him losing his family? But then he remembered the vision he'd had of his wife and son in…*heaven*, was it? And her words, *we are well, my love. Don't give up,* eased over him.

The timbers creaked as the ship rode a wavelet. They'd made anchor somewhere that morning, or was it evening? Pell couldn't tell. The cockboat had been lowered, oars had slashed the water. Then all had grown silent. He had no clue what was transpiring. No clue how Cadan, Gabrielle, and Omphile fared or whether they were even still alive. No clue if anyone would bother to feed them in this cell, or if their emaciated bodies would be found weeks later.

But he knew the One who had a clue, the One who knew everything.

Sliding down the bars, he squatted and dropped his head into his hands. *Father, I've been a fool. I blamed you for the deaths of my family. I blamed you for my pain. Yet I now see that Miranda and Michael are with You, happy and at peace.* Perhaps God had taken them home early to spare them undue pain that He saw coming in their future. Pell had never considered that. He'd only felt the agony of their loss.

He gripped the cross around his neck. He should have known better! He was a preacher! *I'm so sorry, Father. Please help me. Please be with my friends. Please deliver us from this prison.*

He drew a deep sigh and rose to his feet, suddenly feeling like an anchor had been removed from his shoulders. The peaceful presence of the Almighty surrounded him, that familiar sensation of love and hope, of belonging and purpose. Oh, how he had missed it! *Thank you, Father.*

Still the darkness remained, crowding around him.

Yet somehow it didn't seem so threatening, after all.

Two hours later, a shaft of light appeared in the distance, spiraling down the ladder from the hatch above. Moses, Soot, and Pell rose to their feet and approached the bars, yet none of them uttered a word. Without water, their throats were far too dry to speak. Another few days without a drink and they'd all be dead. Pell had resigned himself to whatever the Lord wanted. If he should die, he'd be with his family. If not, then God had more for him to do here on Earth.

But the light….it renewed his hope for the latter.

Soot gasped, and Pell stared back at the ladder where Hellfire leapt down each tread, making a clanging sound with every bounce.

The hatch closed. The light disappeared, but the clanging continued.

"Come 'ere Hellfire!" Soot managed to squeak out. "Over 'ere!"

The strange jangling grew louder. Pell heard Soot kneeling.

"There ye are, Helly!" Soot exclaimed, and the jingling ceased.

Pell scratched the stubble on his chin. Why would anyone send down Soot's rabbit?

A screech of delight answered him.

"She's got the key round 'er neck!"

Before Pell could process those words, the clank of a lock snapped, and the screech of the door echoed through the hold.

"We's free!" Soot exclaimed. "Come on!"

"Huzzah!" Moses added.

"Wait!" Pell reached into the darkness and grabbed Soot's shirt. "The ship is not ours. Not yet. But we have at least one man on our side."

And God.

More than enough.

Chapter 32

Gabrielle clung to Cadan, her tears mingling with the sea water soaking his shirt. How could this have happened? Hadn't she finally come to know the Lord herself? Hadn't she finally submitted to the One who had died for her? Hadn't she heard Him say *precious daughter*?

Then why had things gotten worse? Worse than worse. She'd lost Matthew again, and now she would die a slow, painful death in this cave.

The only consolation was that she'd be with Cadan, but even as the thought drifted through her mind, she chastised herself for her selfishness, for she didn't wish him to die. She didn't wish this on anyone.

She felt his body tense before he nudged her back. His face was all shadows and steel. "Nay! We will not die here!" He waded through the water, now at their waists, and moved hands over the jagged rock walls, pushing, pulling…cursing. "There must be a way out. There must be!"

Gabrielle joined him, starting on the other side.

The ocean gushed through the hole, sending foam bubbling across the surface. Moisture dripped from the craggy ceiling onto her face.

Panicking, she drew in as big a breath as she could, over and over…relishing in the feel of air in her lungs—lungs that would soon be filled with water. Her shoes sank into the soft silt beneath her.

Lord? Where are you? She pressed against the jagged walls, ignoring the pain in her hands as the sharp rock cut and sliced. Still nothing moved, nothing budged, no loose rocks, no holes to be found. The only openings were a few narrow slits at the top of the cave through which rays of sunlight drifted, too small to squeeze through and too high to provide air.

Cadan's curses grew louder and more frequent, an indication he was having no more luck than she was.

The sea gushed through the opening again.

Salt and brine mixed with fear and terror filled Gabrielle's nose as finally, Cadan waded over to her. He grabbed her hands from the rock walls and brought them to his lips.

"'Tis no use, my love. We are trapped." He gazed above at the rock ceiling nigh two feet above them and then down at the water.

"How long?"

His eyes met hers. "Perhaps an hour…I don't know. Only God can save us now."

"True." And perhaps He would. Either way, Gabrielle must trust Him. Then why was her heart shriveling in her chest?

"Oh, Cadan." She fell against him. "What will become of Matthew?"

His chest rose and fell with a huge sigh, but he said naught. They stood there for several minutes, clinging to each other as more water burst in with each wave. She moved back to gaze up at him, wanting to remember his strong features, the life and intensity in his hazel eyes. His hair dripped onto his shoulder. His jaw was heavily stubbled from days without a shave. She ran her fingers over it, relishing the feel of him.

He brushed a strand of wet hair from her forehead and smiled.

And before she knew it, his lips were on hers.

Madness! Pure Madness! She should push him back. They were about to drown together in this dark place, her own terror and sorrow reaching its peak. And instead, she allowed his kiss! Allowed? Nay, she enjoyed it. Immensely. An unintended moan of pleasure burst in her throat as he deepened the kiss and drew her closer, cupping her jaw with his hand.

So this is what a kiss should feel like? All wonder and power and thrill, all warmth and hope and daring. Her body would never be the same. Neither would her heart.

He pulled back, breathless, and ran his thumb over her cheek. "You enchant me, my lady. Now that we are to die, I must tell you that I am completely and utterly smitten."

She smiled, every inch of her leaping at his declaration. "Smitten, is it?" She would offer some sarcastic retort if not for the seriousness of their situation. Instead, she replied. "If 'tis a disease, then I fear I too have been stricken as well."

He kissed her on the forehead and drew her close again, wrapping his arms around her tightly.

The sea rushed through the hole once again, this time rising to their waists.

"How did you ever end up with Damien?" Cadan finally asked her the question that had been driving him mad for days. Ever since her true nature—that of a good, honest, honorable woman—had come to light.

She withdrew from him and hugged herself, and he regretted the question immediately. If he were to die this day, he'd rather enter eternity in her arms.

She gave a sad smile and glanced into the dark, dripping cave. "I was left at the altar, jilted. His name was Jonas, a ship's surgeon, and a wonderful, Godly man"—she swallowed—"or so I thought."

Cadan wanted to tell her the man was an absolute fool, but he longed to hear the rest of her tale.

"I was quite ashamed, you see. Everyone knew, all of Kingston, my family, our friends, and they all cast spurious glances my way wherever I went. I was a woman scorned, a castaway, tossed out like so much refuse."

He reached for her, but she backed away, stirring the water around her. "He ran off with another woman." Pain seared in her eyes. "Then I met Damien. He attended a party in Kingston." She shook her head. "He had a slight French accent, which I found quite charming, but he had British Letters of Marque, so I assumed he was on our side." She uttered a sigh and bit her lip. "He was handsome, charming, mannerly, kind, and educated. Everything I wanted." She shrugged. "We began to court, though against my parents' wishes. They saw something in him and warned me. I should have listened." She wiped a tear spilling down her cheek. "But I was heartbroken, angry, and bitter, at them and at God. So, I allowed, even encouraged, his intentions."

Water surged through the opening again, gurgling and crashing and billowing nigh up to her chest.

"One day, he asked if I would like a tour of his ship, the *Nightblood*, so I foolishly went aboard without benefit of escort." She finally met Cadan's gaze, pain leeching from her face. "He kidnapped me, and before I knew it, we were out to sea. Then he…" Tears flooded her eyes, and she batted the air. "You know."

Now Cadan *did* reach for her and wrapped his arms around her. "I'm so sorry. No woman should have to endure that."

"I was so foolish, Cadan," she sobbed. "I was running from my parents, from God. I wasn't listening to Him. I didn't even know Him. I was so desperate to run my own life, to fulfill my own dreams of getting married and having a family, I never consulted the One who made me, who loves me. I made a muck of things. And now I am here about to die."

Cadan's heart crumbled at her story. And to think he'd accused her of being a trollop when he'd first met her. After all she'd suffered. "Nay, my love. We are here because of my foolish actions, not yours. I was so intent on getting my revenge, I didn't care who I hurt in the process." He cursed. "Now Allard will win. He will finally put an end to me and most likely get my ship as well."

She squeezed him tighter. "Allard told me your story. How he seduced your wife for his uncle, how together they conspired to have you branded a traitor and sent away."

"Did he tell you my wife killed herself later when he rejected her?"

Gasping, she pushed from him. "Nay. 'Tis no wonder you hate him so."

Cadan huffed, drawing in a deep breath of the moist, salty air. "But where has it gotten me?"

Another swell of water rushed through the opening, sending sudsy froth swirling around Lady Fox's shoulders.

"I'm sorry I've gotten you in this mess, Gabrielle."

"'Tis not your fault, Cadan. My own actions have led me here."

Reaching for her waist, he drew her up into his arms if only to give her a few more minutes of air.

Cadan balanced against the incoming tide, clinging tightly to her, their faces but inches from each other.

Still, they said naught, for what else was there to say? He should be pondering the pain he was about to suffer, the terror as his lungs filled with water. But all he could think about was the lady in his arms, desperate to save her from that fate.

The water was up to their chins now.

"I love you, Cadan Hayes."

He stared at her, thrilled, amazed, yet filled with such deep anguish.

"I love you too, Gabrielle."

Then drawing a deep breath, Cadan waited as the sea rose above his nose and onto his forehead.

Chapter 33

Gabrielle drew one last breath as the sea covered her head. Though the salt water stung her eyes, she could make out Cadan's blurry face beside her. His arms were still wrapped around her like iron bands of strength.

Lord, I'm ready to come home if that is your will. All I ask is that you care for Matthew all the days of his life.

Her lungs began to ache. Her thoughts swirled in terror.

Cadan yanked her downward. What? Grabbing her waist, he drew her to his side and swam toward the opening.

Was he mad? He couldn't budge the boulder before, why was he even trying now?

Wait.

Someone was ahead of him—a figure, a person. He disappeared through an opening that was no longer blocked.

Cadan shoved her ahead of him through the hole. Rough hands grabbed her arms and heaved her upward into the light.

She couldn't think, couldn't move. All she could do was gasp for air, her lungs clawing and clutching for every precious breath.

"You all right, my lady?" Pell's dripping face appeared in her vision.

She gripped his arm and snapped her gaze to the cave entrance. *Cadan.* But there he was, rising from the water like a hero of old, sodden shirt and breeches, water dripping from his hair and face, tilting his head to the sun and drawing in breath after breath of air.

"Aye, thank you, Mr. Pell," she finally managed to respond, still having a hard time believing they were alive. "Am I dreaming?"

"Nay, Miss." Moses, standing waist deep in the water, smiled her way, then clapped Cadan on the back. "Looks like we got here jist in time."

A squeal brought Gabrielle's gaze upward to where Omphile stood on top of the cliff. "God be praised!" she said, clapping her hands.

Gabrielle returned her grin with an "Amen." Indeed, 'twas hard to believe, but God had rescued them. *Thank you, Lord.* She drew in another breath of beloved air and glanced around the pool that was now filled with water. Smity was nowhere in sight. No doubt his body had been swept out to sea.

Chest still heaving, Cadan glanced her way, and the look of understanding and love he gave her sent a warm tingle to her toes. He'd been so brave and caring in the cave. He'd not once panicked, not once abandoned her. He'd even declared his love! Tearing his gaze from her, he approached Pell and clasped his arm. "Thank you, my friend."

"'Twere me and Moses who moved the boulder!" Soot waded forward, his hair a tangled mass of sodden red strands, but his face aglow with joy. He cast a quick wink at Gabrielle.

Cadan nodded toward him. "Good work, Soot. All of you." He glanced over Moses, Soot, and Pell. "I thought we were done for." Then moving toward Gabrielle, he took her hand in his, causing Pell to raise a brow.

"The ship?" Cadan asked.

"Ours, Captain," Pell answered. "But we must hurry. Allard may be close."

Nodding, Cadan led Gabrielle to the edge of the pool, and together they climbed up to the top of the cliff.

Once there, Gabrielle flew into Omphile's open arms. "I'm so glad you're well!"

"An' you, Child!" She chuckled and squeezed her tight, not caring that Gabrielle's clothes were dripping wet.

Movement caught Gabrielle's eye, and she released Omphile and backed away. Durwin emerged from the greenery.

In a move too swift to see, Cadan plucked the cutlass from Soot's scabbard and leveled it at his mutinous first mate. "What is he doing here?"

Cadan stormed into his cabin, immediately yanking his wet shirt over his head and tossing it in the corner. Pell, Soot, Moses, and that rat Durwin entered after him. Omphile had taken Gabrielle to the cabin to change out of her wet attire. He should do the same, but he had too many questions and not enough answers.

Sails snapped above as they caught the wind, and the *Resolute* jerked forward, the hiss of the sea against her hull growing louder.

Though night had fallen, he'd ordered the topmen aloft to set every rag of canvas on her yards and Barnett to man the tiller and sail quickly away from the island. Cadan would take no chances that Allard was still lurking about. He hated leaving the quarterdeck in the hands of mutineers, but Pell had assured him Barnett was to be trusted.

Grabbing a bottle, Cadan poured a glass and gulped it down before pouring another. Outside the stern windows, stars winked at him from a charcoal sky as a moonlit sea came in and out of view. He faced his men. All returned his gaze with confidence, all save Durwin, who, with hat in hand, stared at the deck, shuffling his feet.

Pell raised a palm. "To allay your fears, Captain, you should know that most of your crew remain loyal to you."

Soot, rabbit in his arms, nodded. "Aye, Cap'n 'twere only 'bout twenty of 'em who were wit' Smity. The rest jist went along 'cause that double-dealin' parasite convinced 'em ye weren't goin' fer the treasure."

Moses tugged upon the red scarf around his neck. "An' wit' Smity gone, it didna take much convincin' to set dem straight."

"In truth, Captain." Pell glanced at Durwin. "'Twas Durwin who set us free. Put the key to the lock round Hellfire's neck and sent him down to us."

Laughing, Soot, scratched the rabbit between the ears. "Came right t' me, Cap'n."

Cadan's brows rose at the strange tale, his anger slowly abating.

"Then"—Pell continued, fingering the cross around his neck—"When we came above, Durwin armed us and informed us who of the crew remained loyal and who did not."

Moses gave a rare smile. "We took back de ship wit'out a single shot an' put dem mutineers ashore."

The deck canted to larboard, and Cadan spread his bare feet out for balance. "You set them on the island?"

"Aye." Soot's eyes flashed. "Wit' no food or water, the plaguey dogs."

Gulping down the rest of his rum, Cadan set down the glass. "And the rest of the crew are loyal to me?"

Snorting, Pell quirked his lips. "As loyal as any pirate crew, Captain."

Indeed. Cadan rubbed his earlobe. "And where is Allard? Why had he not taken the *Resolute* when he had a chance?"

Pell's face lit with a rare excitement. "Our lookout spotted him coming around the bend of the island, no doubt seeking your ship. So we set sail and circled around the other side, at the ready should he follow."

"But he didn't." Moses crossed beefy arms over his chest. "So's we dropped anchor an' came t' find you."

The lantern hooked above them swayed with the ship, oscillating globes of light over the deck.

Overcome, Cadan spun to face the stern, not wanting his men to see him weak. Still, he couldn't help the surge of joy and pride filling him at his friends' loyalty and willingness to risk their lives for him. 'Twas not the pirate way. Any of them could have easily taken over the ship and sailed away.

Steeling his expression, he faced them again. "Good. Very good." His stern gaze landed on Durwin, who had not once looked his way.

"And you, Durwin. What have you to say for yourself?"

The skinny man stepped forward but still did not look up. "'Twas me greed, Cap'n. It got the best of me. I wanted the treasure, an' Smity promised me a large share. It were wrong of me. I knows it now."

A lust for wealth was something Cadan could understand, but not disloyalty, not after he had nursed the man back to health and given him a powerful position on the ship. "And what should I do with you now?"

All eyes swerved to Durwin. He shifted his feet over the deck. "I deserve t' be keelhauled, Cap'n. I deserve whatever punishment ye think best. But I want ye to know"—he finally looked up at Cadan, both fear and pleading in his gaze—"I changed me mind. Because of me, ye 'ave yer ship back, an' I realized treasure ain't the most important thing in life."

Cadan studied the man. "And what is?"

The swish of skirts sounded, and Gabrielle swept into the room, her eyes on Cadan. "Love."

His heart leapt at the sight of her. Spirals of damp golden hair tumbled over her shoulders to her waist, waving over her light blue skirt and an embroidered stomacher that restrained her alluring curves. Cadan swallowed.

Omphile entered behind her and shared a glance with Moses.

Attempting to hide his joy at seeing her, Cadan stiffened his jaw. "Indeed, my lady. But I should like to hear Durwin's answer." For even Cadan himself was not entirely convinced that anything but wealth could make him happy, save perhaps this lady who now moved to stand beside him.

Zada finally made an appearance, making such a fuss skittering about the lady's skirts that she finally picked him up.

Shaking his head, he faced Durwin again.

The wrinkles between the man's eyes folded even tighter as his glance took in the men standing beside him. "Friendship," he finally said. "An' loyalty t' those who 'elp me in this life."

Cadan almost believed him. Almost. Could a man change his ways? Could a *pirate*? Could friendship ever provide the power he needed to live life the way he wanted, on his own terms?

"Regardless," he said in his fiercest captain voice. "You will be confined to your cabin until I can determine your loyalty."

Durwin nodded and almost seemed relieved he'd not be punished more severely.

Pell started to say something, then stopped and smiled.

Moses and Omphile had inched closer to each other, stealing glances, and Soot continued to pet his infernal rabbit.

"Dismissed. The lot of you," Cadan ordered, reaching for his rum.

"Where to?" Pell asked.

Setting Zada down on his desk, Gabrielle bit her lip, and he knew what she was thinking. The same thing he'd been thinking since they'd been rescued.

They had to get Matthew back.

"We find Allard." Cadan poured another drink.

Pell quirked a brow. "And where might he be?"

Alas, there was the critical question. Cadan glanced at Gabrielle, her expression now twisting in fear. In truth, he had no idea where to search for that demon.

"I think I's know where he might be." The voice was Moses's, the words spun confusion in Cadan's mind.

He faced the large black man.

Moses looked lovingly at Omphile. "When I was searchin' for Omphile in dat governor's mansion, I came into what must 'ave been Allard's chamber an' I saw parchment wit' writin' on it."

"Writing?" Cadan cocked his head. "But you can't read."

Moses smiled and gripped Omphile's hand in his. "Omphile's been teachin' me, Cap'n."

"Indeed." Cadan didn't know whether to hug the woman or chastise her for her secrecy. But what did it matter now? "Out with it, then."

"It was jist a name, but it caught my eye. It said Saint-Domingue."

Gabrielle gasped, drawing all eyes her way.

Her breath grew fast. "I remember Damien mentioned that place. Once, well in his cups, he told me he had an estate there."

Grinning, Cadan raked back his wet hair. "Then that is where we are heading."

Soot finally looked up from his rabbit. "But that be a well-armed French post, Cap'n."

"Which is why we must find Allard before he gets there."

Would the man please put on a shirt! Gabrielle shifted her gaze away from Cadan *yet again* as he ordered Moses to lock up Durwin and dismissed his crew with their orders. Pell smiled at her as he left. Was she imagining things, or was there a new light in the preacher's eyes that had not been there before?

Cadan reached for his bottle of rum, but she quickly moved to stay his hand. Their eyes met. "Perhaps you've had enough?" And when defiance began to fill them, she added, "I need you sober, Cadan. We must find Matthew." Tears burned her eyes, and she turned away.

He grabbed her arm and brought her back. "You're right. I'm sorry. I miss him too."

"You do?" She gazed at him curiously as Zada scrambled over his desk and perched at the end, one dark eye fixed upon her.

Cadan laughed. "Seems Zada's been doing some missing too. But aye, who do you think cared for the babe when you were Allard's captive?"

Honestly, she'd assumed it had been Moses, but now that she studied Cadan, she could see affection for the babe in his eyes. "I never…" she huffed. "I guess I never thought."

Muscles rolled across his chest and rounded his arms. Breeches hanging low on his hips clung to his thick thighs. His right eye swelled and darkened with a bruise, and cuts sliced across his waist and arms. Even devoid of belts, baldric, and blades, he exuded a power and confidence that made her knees wobble.

He lifted her hand for a kiss. Damp strands of his hair fell across his stubbled jaw as his masculine scent rose to taunt her with memories of their kiss in the cave. Like none other. Yet…

Were his declarations of love merely a result of their impending deaths? Doubts suddenly assailed her. She'd been horribly betrayed by two men she thought loved her. In truth, she had more than proven herself a complete fool when it came to men. Perhaps she was so desperate for marriage and children, she clung to any promises of affection tossed her way.

And this man before her, this handsome, enigmatic man, who made every inch of her feel things she'd never felt before…this man was a pirate, and hence a thief and liar. Hadn't he made his goals quite plain? Revenge and treasure. Marriage and children were not a part of his future. In fact, he had expressed his loathing of both.

Withdrawing her hand, she backed away from him. She would not be played a fool. Neither would she allow her heart to be crushed again. Especially not from this man, for her feelings for him far surpassed all others.

Uncertainty, along with pain, filled his eyes as he followed her movements across the cabin, where she began picking up discarded shirts, belts and breeches, hoping to annoy him, but also to settle her nerves. She must tread lightly, for her son's life depended on this man.

"Stay your fussing, my lady." He moved toward her.

She picked up one of his shirts and handed it to him.

A slow smile lifted one side of his lips. "Does my bare chest offend you, my lady?"

She gave him a curt look. "Don't be a dolt. You surely know your effect on women."

"I only care for my effect on you." He tossed the shirt over his head and studied her. "We said much to each other in that cave." He ran a gentle thumb down her cheek.

Ignoring the sensations swirling through her, she turned away, unable to look at him. "'Twas merely the stress of our impending deaths that brought forth such silly declarations."

Silence invaded the cabin, save for the creak of timbers and splash of the sea.

Cadan marched to his desk and poured another drink, quickly gulping it down.

Clasping her hands together, she took a step toward him, her heart crumbling. "We are vastly different, Cadan. I want marriage and children and to live a Godly life. And you have made it plain you want none of those things."

His shoulders tensed, and he finally turned to face her, his face a mask of pain and anger. "Quite right, Lady Fox. You are dismissed. I'm sure you are tired." He gestured toward the door with his glass.

Panic soured in her throat. "You still intend to rescue Matthew?"

His intense gaze pierced her harder than any sword. "You have my word."

Nodding, she left, closed the door, and began walking away. The pain in her heart dragged down each step, prompting her to run back into his arms and declare her love. Spinning about, she was about to do just that…

When the loud crash of glass shattering against the bulkhead rang through the hall. She hesitated, unsure whether he'd hurt himself or his temper had taken over. Opting for the latter, she sped away.

Chapter 34

Pain throbbed, luring Cadan from his sleep. *Pound! Pound! Pound*! Blow after blow struck his head. Who was hitting him? Swatting the air around him, he felt naught, naught but air. The rush of water against the hull reminded him where he was, but the agony in his heart begged him to slip back into unconsciousness. He rubbed his eyes. The pounding continued. Struggling to rise, he swept his feet over the side of his bed and sat, instantly regretting it. The cabin spun around him as queasiness crept up his throat.

Morning sun speared the stern windows and set ablaze pieces of glass shattered over the deck. Lady Fox had betrayed him, tricked him, declared her love and then had withdrawn it like a vast treasure once given but then snatched away. And like all noble women, she'd merely played with his affections to get what she wanted. *Just like Elyna.*

Even worse, Cadan was the biggest fool of all for falling for it yet again.

How she must be mocking him, laughing at how easily she'd caught him in her web of seductive deceit and lies. Just like Elyna. Memories of his wife standing half-dressed in their bedchamber filled his mind. He'd just caught her with Allard, his blade at the villain's throat. And all Elyna could say was how sorry she was, that she never loved Cadan, that she loved Damien Allard.

He raked back his hair and drew a deep breath as Zada skittered over and stared up at him with an incriminating eye. "What now, my lizard friend? Are you to betray me as well? Leave me and run off with the lady?"

"Talking to a lizard now, are we?" Pell's voice startled Cadan, and he glanced up to see his quartermaster enter the cabin.

"Door was ajar," Pell said when Cadan cast him a punitive glare. "You look like you've been to Davy Jones' Locker….and back."

Cadan slanted his lips and with difficulty rose to his feet. The ship bucked over a wave and he stumbled slightly, placing a hand on the bulkhead to steady himself. Empty bottles of rum lay scattered on his desk, and a wave of unusual guilt crashed over him. Aye, after Gabrielle had left, he'd drank far too much. 'Twas the only way to dull the pain stampeding his heart, gouging out new gaping wounds and opening up old ones as it went. But now, Lady Fox's words taunted him. He must remain sober, alert, and at his best if he stood any chance of getting Matthew back.

What was he thinking? 'Twas far more important to get his revenge on Allard and retrieve Dempster's treasure! Then why was Matthew's safety the first thing that had come into his mind? Why, when the lad's mother had lied to him, betrayed him?

Pell's gaze took in the shattered glass covering the deck, and he crossed arms over his chest. "The lady did something to displease you, Captain?"

Cadan gave a sordid huff. "You could say that."

"Seemed you two were getting along well when I left. Perhaps too well for you to be left alone with her."

Cadan stared at his friend. "Things are not always what they seem with women like her."

Zada leapt onto the stern window seat, settling in a stream of warm sunlight.

"Women like her?"

"Noble, educated, coddled, spoiled."

"She is not Elyna."

"She is exactly like her." Cadan snapped a fiery gaze at his friend.

Pell moved to the stern, glancing out over the turquoise sea, sparkling in the sun. "One thing I have recently learned is that God orchestrates the events of our lives, the people we meet, the situations we encounter, all for our good, if we allow it. If we submit to Him and not fall into the pit of our own emotions and flesh." He breathed out a heavy sigh and looked at Cadan. "Gabrielle is the best thing that has come your way in a long time, Cadan. That much I know. Seek Him and His will, and you won't be disappointed."

Chuckling, Cadan leaned on his desk. "What's this? Returned to preaching, have you?"

Pell smiled and fingered his cross. "You could say that. Been talking to God again and found I rather missed Him."

"Even after he took your son and wife?"

"Turns out I needed Him even more when that happened."

Cadan stared at an empty bottle of rum. "I must still be besotted, for I can make no sense of your ramblings."

Pell approached and laid a hand on Cadan's shoulder, bringing his gaze up to his. Gone was the usual sullen despondency. In its place, joy and peace flooded his eyes, his very demeanor.

"Revenge will kill you, Cadan. This revenge on Damien and now on Gabrielle. 'Tis a cancer that rots a man's soul. Let it go."

Cadan stiffened his jaw but did not respond. How could he? He could never let Damien go free. He must pay for what he'd done.

"I'll have Omphile brew that tea that aids your rum-induced affliction." Pell started away. "Then you are needed above, Captain. We are making good speed toward Saint-Domingue and should encounter Allard soon."

"You finally gave your life to de Laud?" Omphile's tight embrace was accompanied by tears of joy streaming down her ebony skin.

Returning her hug, Gabrielle couldn't help but smile, though she'd been doing no smiling during the long night. In truth, she'd shed so many tears, she doubted she could produce a single drop moving forward.

Omphile released her and backed away, gesturing toward the tray of food she'd brought to break Gabrielle's fast. "Sit, eat, an' tell me all about it."

Gabrielle pressed a hand over her stomach. "I fear I'm not hungry, but I thank you for the food."

"What's de matter, Child?" Taking her hand, she led Gabrielle to sit on the cot. "I's mean 'sides you missin' your babe, but we's gonna get him back real soon."

Gabrielle studied her friend. She'd told her once that Gabrielle would see Matthew again, and it had come true. "Did the Lord tell you that?"

Omphile sat on the chair beside the bed. "Not in so many words. It's jist more o' a sense."

Nodding, Gabrielle clasped her hands together, studying the beam of sunlight oscillating over the bulkhead. "You were right, Omphile. I never really knew God. I followed His rules and did everything right because of my parents. Now I know He's real." She looked up and pressed one hand over her heart. "I sense Him in here, and He spoke to me!"

Omphile clapped her hands together. "Then all will be well now, you'll see."

Gabrielle shook her head. "But ever since I gave myself to Him, everything has gotten so much worse! Cadan hates me now, and I still don't have my baby...my poor baby." Apparently, she was not out of tears after all, for more filled her eyes. "All I ever wanted was to get married and have a family, and that dream seems farther out of my reach than ever."

"Nothin' is impossible wit' God, Child, nothin'. Mebbe He jist wants you to trust Him, even when dere seems no hope." She took Gabrielle's hand in hers. "You put Him at de helm o' your ship, now best t' let Him take you where He thinks is best."

"A sail! A sail!" The unmistakable shout filtered down from above.

Gabrielle glanced up, every sense alerted, her heart daring to pick itself out of the mire of despair and crawl onto hope.

Leaping to her feet, she opened the door and darted from the cabin before Omphile could protest.

She emerged from the companionway to a gush of salty wind that tore her hair from her pins, the rays of a hot sun, and an excitement buzzing over the ship that sent pirates darting about. Commands to raise and adjust sail bellowed from the quarterdeck where a quick glance told her Cadan stood beside Pell.

Their eyes met briefly, but she quickly turned away, not wanting to renew the pain in her heart. Moving toward the railing, she gripped the damp wood, leaned over it toward the sea, and attempted to see the ship they were chasing. 'Twas too far away to tell if it was Damien.

Shielding her eyes from the sun, Gabrielle watched as the topmen scrambled across yards to unfurl topsails. Soon the canvas dropped, flapping impotently before it caught the wind in a thunderous snap. The *Resolute* listed to starboard, and Gabrielle tightened her grip on the railing as the ship, under a mountain of snowy canvas, rippled through the sea.

Wind blasted over her, and she closed her eyes and lifted up a prayer for the safety of the crew and for Matthew to soon be in her arms unharmed.

Would God answer her prayers now that she knew Him? She couldn't say. And at the moment, all she could do was hope.

Omphile appeared at her side and laid her hand atop Gabrielle's. Minutes passed like hours as the *Resolute* bucked over the waves like a wild stallion, flinging salty spray back over her. Squalls of foamy water swept past her feet before heading out the scuppers back to sea.

Finally, when she could stand it no longer, she glanced up at Cadan, his boots spread apart on the heaving deck, his white

Holland shirt flapping in the wind and his eye pressed to the scope.

He lowered it and bellowed a command that sent hands to trim the sails for maximum efficiency. Olin relayed further orders to the crew, sending them aloft once again.

Cadan's intense gaze locked upon hers. Without even speaking, he understood the question her eyes must have shouted at him, for he replied with an understanding nod.

Her body froze with both fear and excitement as she spun back around.

It *was* Damien's ship. *And* her son. *Oh, Lord. Please!*

Within minutes, as they closed the distance between them, she clearly spotted Damien's ensign and the familiar lines of the *Nightblood.* Yet instead of raising all sails to the wind, Damien's pirates raced over the deck, jumping into ratlines, and running out guns.

He intended to fight.

Terror clogged Gabrielle's throat. She gasped for a breath. Matthew was on that ship! One shot from Cadan in the wrong place could rip him to shreds.

No sooner did that horrifying vision blaze across her mind than a loud boom! quaked the sea. A plume of gray smoke hovered over a minion gun on the *Nightblood*'s stern just as Cadan shouted, "All hands down!"

Chapter 35

Gabrielle dropped to the deck, pulling Omphile down with her. The smell of salt, sodden wood, and tar filled her nose as fear filled her heart. An eerie whine scraped over her, followed by the sound of wood splintering, and she glanced up to see the four-pounder shatter the quarterdeck railing into a hundred splinters before plummeting into the sea.

Pushing against the deck, she stood and searched for Cadan. Had he been hurt? Nay, there he was, rising behind the binnacle along with Pell.

His curse stung the air, followed by a rapid jet of commands. "Hands about ship! Ready gun crew! Load and run out guns! Furl tops and main!"

Shorten sail? Gabrielle spun to see the *Nightblood* had slowed considerably and was coming around on a port tack, bringing her guns to bear.

Without thinking, she pivoted, clutched her skirts, leapt up the quarterdeck ladder, and marched to Cadan.

"You do not intend to engage him!?" she shouted over the wind and the creak of blocks and grind of booms as sails were adjusted.

He raised the scope to his eye. "How else to get Matthew back?" His unruffled tone enraged her.

"Pray. I'd like him back in one piece!"

He lowered the glass and raised an incriminating brow. "What do you take me for, my lady? I am no fool."

There was pain in his eyes, sorrow, and a spark of fury. But it made her bite her tongue. She'd come to know this man and doubted he would kill an innocent child for his own gain.

But you've been wrong about men before.

That sickly sweet accusing voice returned, the one that always had a shred of truth encased in an anchor of darkness that pulled her down to the depths.

"Now, get below!" He gestured toward Omphile. "Take Omphile and go back to your cabin. That's an order."

Lifting her nose in the air, she spun about, made her way back down to the main deck, and retook her position at the starboard railing. If that man, that insolent, *obstinate* pirate thought she'd go hide when her son's life was at stake, he didn't know her very well.

Though in truth, she rather surprised herself. She'd never been brave. She'd always been the one cowering in her cabin when her father encountered an enemy. When had she changed?

The *Nightblood* swept down upon them, sails bulging and guns blazing. In minutes, with the wind advantage, Allard would be able to tack and loose a broadside that would sink them to the bottom of the sea. What was Cadan's plan? He made no move, gave no orders to evade the oncoming ship.

Wind punched her face, yanking more hair from pins and sending it flailing behind her. Gunsmoke, brine, and fear stung her nose.

A spurt of gray smoke belched from the *Nightblood*'s gundeck, its blast pounding the sky in thunderous echoes. Gabrielle was about to drop on all fours when the shot splashed into the sea mere yards from where they stood. Close. *Too close.*

Still, the *Resolute* continued on her present course, rising and plunging through the sea, stripped to mizzen and sprit for the coming action. Soot and his crew prepared guns fore and aft as pirates brought up powder bags from the magazine.

"Mebbe we should go below, Miss." Omphile's eyes blazed with terror.

Pushing hair from her face, Gabrielle yelled over the crash of wind. "I won't leave my son."

Omphile nodded and, instead of leaving, pressed her hand atop Gabrielle's again.

The *Nightblood* was nearly in position to loose a broadside! What was Cadan thinking? Still, when she glanced at him, he stood firmly on the quarterdeck, surveying the scene as if he were out fishing and not about to be fired upon and lose everything.

"Helm, hard a-starboard!" Cadan commanded, and with creaking cordage and rattling blocks, the *Resolute* swung a weather, her starboard side dipping into the sea. Gabrielle barely had time to cling to the railing as her feet slipped beneath her. She flattened against the bulwarks. Foamy claws reached up the hull, desperate to drag her into the sea.

The pounding *boom! boom! boom!* of the *Nightblood*'s broadside sent a ripple through sky and sea. Gabrielle's heart stopped. Were they to be ripped apart right here on the deck? Was she never to see Matthew again? Panic gripped her, stealing her breath.

Completing the tack, the *Resolute* leveled just as three of the *Nightblood*'s shots splashed into the sea off their larboard side. A fourth shot, however, struck the hull above the water line. Black smoke rose from the charred hole, and Cadan quickly dispatched Moses down the hatch to inspect the damage.

Yet no sooner did the *Resolute* complete the turn to starboard, than Cadan issued command after command to brace about for a hard turn to port.

Soot and his crew hovered around the cannonades lining the larboard railing while Cadan ordered archers to the tops, slow matches in their hands.

Before Gabrielle could realize the brilliance of his plan and begin to scream in terror that Matthew could be injured, the *Resolute* wove around and ran astern of the *Nightblood*.

"Fire!" Cadan shouted, and Soot and his gunners unleashed a barrage of hell and confusion, raking the *Nightblood* across the stern. Twangs and zips brought Gabrielle's gaze up to see archers firing flaming arrows at her sails.

Gray smoke swept over the deck. Coughing, Gabrielle batted it aside and tried to peer through the haze at Damien's ship, heart in her throat. Men darted across her decks in a frenzy. More yellow flashes shot from her stern chasers as a loud, continuous thunder of swivel guns erupted. Shots zipped over the *Resolute*'s quarterdeck, some crashing into the railing and deck. The rest, however, splashed into the water as they sped out of range.

Dashing over the deck to the port side, Gabrielle peered at the *Nightblood*. The stern railing was shattered, her mainmast damaged, and fire erupted on her mainsail. Within minutes, a loud crack split the air, and the mast toppled in a tangle of flaming sailcloth, cordage, and shattered spars. Screams and shouts pierced her ears as pirates rushed to lower buckets into the sea and put out the fire.

None of the *Resolute*'s shots had hit below deck where no doubt Matthew would be. She dared breathe a sigh of relief, though there was still danger from the fire.

Cadan appeared beside her. She knew 'twas him before she looked his way. His presence never failed to stir her blood in ways no one ever had.

"They will put out the fire quickly, my lady. Never fear."

How did he know what she was thinking? She turned to thank him, but he had already left, marching fearlessly across the deck, shouting commands as he went.

The *Resolute* made yet another sharp turn to port, bringing her broadside to bear.

"Ready the larboard guns!" Cadan shouted.

Gabrielle stormed toward him. "You wouldn't!" She gripped his arm.

"He'll raise the white flag." Cadan assured her, placing his hand over hers.

She tugged on him, terror prickling down her spine. "But he knows you're bluffing. He knows you won't fire below decks and risk hurting Matthew."

"He knows no such thing." His tone lacked the comfort and confidence she sought, transforming her fears into nightmares. Turning from her, he glanced at the *Nightblood*, black smoke billowing from her burning sails. "Signal them to heave to and surrender!"

Gabrielle could only wait and pray as, shielding her eyes from the sun, she stared at the enemy ship. Damien was no fool, but neither did his pride allow for such a demoralizing defeat.

However, moments later, Allard's white flag rose and the remainder of her sails lowered.

Soon the *Resolute* swept alongside the *Nightblood*, keel to keel, not five yards between them. Captain Damien Allard stood amidships, hands fisted at his waist, red plume fluttering from his hat and a defiant scowl on his lips.

His gaze pierced Gabrielle with a spear of hatred before he shifted his eyes to Cadan, offering an unspoken challenge that could not be dismissed.

The charred remains of sailcloth, now soaked with water, hugged the deck beneath broken pieces of a mast and a web of lines and cordage.

"Go below." Cadan slipped beside her, shoving pistols and knifes into his baldric. "He's not going down without a fight."

Gabrielle glanced back at the *Nightblood*. Where moments before only a few pirates had been on deck, now there were dozens, all armed, all growling in their direction.

"Grapnels!" Cadan shouted and four of his men whirled the iron hooks above their heads and tossed them across the gap betwixt the two ships. They struck the deck of the *Nightblood* with a clank and a scrape of splintering wood. Then heaving the ropes, the pirates groaned under the strain as they wrenched the ships together with a thudding crunch that sent both vessels aquiver.

Gabrielle swallowed. She was about to be in the midst of a fierce battle. Some would die this day. Some would be dearly wounded.

But all she could think about was getting to her son.

Cadan had no time to forcibly lock the women below as a barrage of musket shot from the *Nightblood* peppered the deck. At least they had the good sense to duck behind the bulwarks as shots zipped and whined about them. Whipping his cutlass from his baldric, he shouted. "To battle, men!" and led the way over the railing. His pirates, blades and muskets drawn, followed like a flood of rats, swarming in the waist and under the booms amidships.

The air filled with flying cutlasses, hissing and clanking, and the occasional pop of a pistol or scream of the injured. Cadan had but one enemy in mind—Damien. But where was he? Pirates attacked him from right and left, but he would not be deterred. Swinging his blade about him, he cleaved it down upon one assailant, then snapped it up to strike another. One man leveled a pistol at him, a toothless grin beckoning him on. Before the man could shoot, Cadan plucked his boarding ax and knocked it from his hand, then struck the man's head. He toppled to the deck.

To Cadan's right, Pell engaged with another pirate, knocking him across the jaw with the hilt of his cutlass before firing his pistol at another. On the foredeck, Moses made quick work of two pirates attacking him, while Soot crammed his barrel-like body into another, sending the pirate over the railing into the sea. The rest of his men, blades whirling aloft and pistols smoking, held their own. Nay, more than held their own. They were winning. In truth, only Damien's injured men littered the deck.

Fiery rays from the sun beat down on Cadan's back as the stench of blood and death filled his lungs. Another pirate charged him, grimacing and growling like a dog. Their blades clashed in the air with a mighty clank, but with a quick snap to the left, he tore the sword from the man's hand and thrust it to the deck. Eyes wide, the coward scampered away. In truth, as Cadan scanned the ship, most of Damien's men had been bested, some had even tossed their weapons down and raised their hands, preferring surrender to death.

One glance at the quarterdeck revealed Damien, unaware of his impending defeat, engaged with one of Cadan's men. He made a quick move to the right, bringing his blade about so fast, Cadan's man had no defense. The rapier pierced his side and with a groan, he fell to his knees.

Chest heaving, sweat gleaming on his brow, Damien scanned his ship, his look of bloodlust quickly transforming to panic when he saw that he had lost.

Now was the moment Cadan had longed for, had dreamt of for so long. Taking the quarterdeck ladder in two leaps, he charged Damien.

A flash of green fabric caught his eye, spirals of golden hair, a bundle in her arms… and before he could warn her, protect her… do anything! Damien grabbed Gabrielle and held a knife to her throat.

Fury like he'd never known fired through every cell in Cadan's body.

"Back off or I'll kill her!" Damien seethed.

Matthew began to wail. Terror flashed from Gabrielle's eyes as Damien shoved her against him, blade tight on her neck.

Foolish woman! Why had she not stayed on board the *Resolute*?

Halting, Cadan tightened the grip on his cutlass, breath coming hard and fast.

"Tell your men to stand down!" Damien raged, eyes wide with fear and hate.

"Hiding behind a woman again?" Cadan said. "Why not fight me like a man?"

A few chortles followed by grunts of approval emanated from the pirates on both sides.

Cadan waved his blade over the mob. "'Tis obvious we have won fair and square. By the pirates' code, you must grant me the victor's rewards."

"And what, pray tell, are those?"

Cadan glanced over the crew. "I could, by rights, kill your men and steal your ship. However, all I want is you, the woman and her child, and the treasure."

Damien chuckled, inching backward with Gabrielle. "You're mad." The knife drew a trickle of blood down her neck, and 'twas all Cadan could do not to rush the man and knock him to the deck.

He turned to face Damien's crew. "What say you? Your lives and the ship or Davy Jones Locker for the lot of you?"

The pirates seemed to be pondering the choice as whispers filtered among them. Finally, one man emerged, a more polished man than the rest, standing tall, wearing somewhat clean attire and his black hair slicked back.

"According to the pirate code you speak of, we offer a resolution. A duel to the death between you and Captain Allard. Winner takes all."

Chapter 36

Everything within Gabrielle wanted to scream *No!* to the pirate's offer. A duel to the death? She could not bear it. She could not bear to lose Cadan, not when it was her fault. In truth, not ever! Oh, why had she been so foolish? If she had only waited, prayed, sought the Lord, Cadan and his men would have won, and she'd have Matthew back safe.

Pressing fingers over the blood on her neck, she glanced at the burly pirate who now held Matthew. He was not supporting his head as he should, and Matthew was wailing so loudly she feared the beast would toss him overboard. But every time she approached to help, the man whose head resembled a cannon ball growled at her.

On the main deck below, Cadan and Damien prepared to do battle, as pirates on both sides retreated toward the railing or clambered up on the fore or quarterdeck for a better view.

The stench of sweat, gun smoke and blood tainted the salty breeze. Across on the *Resolute*, Omphile stood, hands clasped together in prayer. She'd tried to talk Gabrielle out of her foolish quest, but Gabrielle would have none of it. Now, look what a muck she had made of things.

I should have prayed, asked you what to do, Lord. I'm sorry. Please, help Cadan win. Please save Matthew.

He's not listening to you anymore. He's tired of your rebellious ways.

The words struck her in the gut with their truth. How many chances would God grant her before she learned to trust Him?

Innumerable.

Gabrielle looked around for the source of the voice, but no one stood nearby. Still, the peace and love it suddenly brought gave her no doubt as to the source. Could God be that merciful, that forgiving to His children?

Cadan tore his shirt over his head and tossed it aside. Whirling his blade before him, he jerked hair from his face and grinned at Damien.

Damien, on the other hand, remained in his purple doublet over a suit of silver brocade, one side of his lips quirked in a victorious grin, while he took an imperious stance on the deck as if he were playing a sport.

The two men couldn't be more different.

Her gaze swept back to Cadan. She loved him. She knew that now. Despite that he had kidnapped her and used her as bait, despite that he drove her utterly and completely mad, he was a good man, brave and resolute, a champion of justice, and yet chivalrous and tender when need be.

And she didn't ever want to live without him.

Matthew ceased wailing, and she glanced his way, fearing the worst, but he remained in the pirate's arms, snuggled against his filthy waistcoat.

Oh, Lord what is to become of us? She closed her eyes for a mere second, but when she opened them again, the pirate who had been her guard appeared. He stood with authority and confidence between her and Matthew, a most peaceful look on his face.

"Who are you?" she asked him, not expecting an answer, for he had never spoken to her before.

But he turned her way and smiled. "I've been assigned to guard you and the child."

His voice was smooth like silk and carried with it a peace that now filled his eyes.

She didn't know what to say. "Who assigned you?"

"The Captain."

She glanced back at Cadan, taking his fighting stance.

"Cadan?" she asked, looking back at the pirate.

Smiling, he began to fade from view. "Nay. the Captain of Heaven's Armies." And then he was gone.

The Captain of Heaven's Armies? The Lord Jesus?

Gabrielle's knees turned to pottage, and she gripped the railing, lest she fall. So God had indeed sent an angel to protect her. Even when she'd been angry with Him. Even before she'd turned to Him and trusted Him.

Such love! She never knew such love existed.

Lord, I've been such a fool.

The clang of swords brought her gaze to Cadan and Damien, who had begun to fight. Fear trounced her joy. Fear for Cadan. Fear for Matthew. Fear God would not answer her prayers.

Nay! Perfect love casts out all fear. Isn't that what the Scriptures said? How could she be afraid when she was now God's daughter? She glanced at Matthew. Wouldn't she do anything for her son? Even die? Wouldn't she do anything and everything to help him, anything that would be for his ultimate good?

Of course!

Trust Me, Daughter.

She smiled, even as the mighty clang of blades rang through the air, even when everything—her very life—was at stake, even when all seemed lost. She smiled because she finally had a real relationship with Almighty God. He spoke to her, and she to Him. She could trust Him with everything, come what may, for they were only passing through this life. Eternity was all that mattered. And everything the Lord allowed was for the purpose of getting as many people there with Him as possible.

Drawing a deep breath, she lifted up a prayer for Cadan and turned to watch the fight, her heart soaring with hope.

Cadan leveled his blade at Damien, narrowing his eyes upon his nemesis, the one man who had hurt him more than any other, the one man who had ripped everything from him—his wife, his honor, his freedom.

Now his time had come. Cadan would get his revenge, and Damien would go to the bottom of the sea where he belonged.

But first Cadan would wipe that insolent sneer off his lips.

They lunged for each other, blades clanging. Pirates shouted curses and obscenities from all around them, flinging insults at their enemy and encouragements to their foreseen victor.

With a quick step to his left, Cadan spun around and slashed Damien's waist, slicing his purple doublet.

Growling, Damien leapt back, prancing back and forth, eyeing Cadan with disdain.

"Had enough?" Cadan asked.

"I've only just begun, *mon ami*. Prepare to die!" Damien rushed Cadan, spinning his rapier back and forth so fast, 'twas hard to see.

Cadan stumbled backward, diving and ducking as fast as he could.

Gabrielle gasped. The pirates cheered, clearly entertained by the expert swordsmanship.

Backed against the railing, Cadan fended off each blow, the hiss of their blades filling the air. He would not let the man defeat him. He could not! Gathering up his remaining strength, he let out a mighty growl and met Damien's final blow with a clang that would wake the dead.

It woke young Matthew, for he began to howl.

Hilt to hilt, they pummeled each other, Cadan now driving Damien back. Sweat stung Cadan's eyes and he blinked it away.

Damien leapt to the side, spun around, and cleaved his rapier downward onto Cadan. Pain seared his arm as the blade sliced through his skin. The metallic smell of his blood joined the scents of salt and sweat.

Gabrielle shrieked. The pirates shouted with glee.

Grinning, Damien plunged his blade toward Cadan's heart.

Cadan leapt to the right. Agony wrenched his side as the rapier slashed through him once again.

Gabrielle screamed.

He gripped the wound, blood trickling between his fingers. The sky spun. The deck lured him downward. Stumbling backward, he blinked, forcing himself to focus, to not allow the terror rampaging through him to win.

Damien cast a supercilious grin of victory over his crew.

Just enough time for Cadan to swing to his right and bring his cutlass from behind him in a move that sent Damien reeling backward.

He lumbered, rapier spinning, and Cadan quickly slammed the hilt of his blade onto Damien's hand.

His blade fell to the deck.

Moans and groans, along with huzzahs blared from the crowd. Matthew continued to whimper.

Shock screeched from Damien's face as he struggled to retrieve his blade, but Cadan kicked him in the gut, knocking him to the deck.

Helpless, he stared up at Cadan like a lost puppy.

Cadan pointed the tip of his cutlass at Damien's heart. "You stole my wife, you branded me a traitor, had me tortured and imprisoned for five years. Now, you will pay with your life. Down to the depths with you, you odious cur!"

Clearly trembling, Damien said naught, just stared at Cadan with pleading eyes. His pirates cursed and spit in his direction.

"To the devil wit' ye, ye foppish frog!"

"Toss the yellow-dogged maggot overboard!"

The cutlass quivered in Cadan's hand.

Do it. Run him through! He deserves it!

The voice raked over Cadan, prompting him to do what he'd longed to do for so long.

But a vision of Smity's body floating in the water appeared in his mind, along with the sense of evil and darkness that had surrounded the man. Revenge had destroyed Smity, had filled his days with misery until it finally stole his life.

How ugly it was…. this revenge, this desperate need to mete out the same punishment that he had suffered. In Smity's case, the harm had not been done on purpose. In Damien's case, it had. But did that make revenge any better? Or was it just a path that ended in destruction?

"Kill 'im! Slice 'im thru!" the pirates began to chant.

Sweat streamed down Cadan's back as the hot sun fired rays upon it.

Then there was Pell, who'd never sought revenge, but who now returned to a God of forgiveness. Cadan could not deny the new joy filling his quartermaster. Hadn't he said revenge would rot his soul?

Vengeance is Mine. Come back to me, My Son.

He knew that voice. 'Twas a voice that had oft spoken to him as a lad, back when his mother was alive and would read the Bible to him and tell him about a loving God who had died to set him free. He had believed it back then, had embraced the love of a Savior who would never leave him.

Now, he realized he was the one who had left the Lord.

Suddenly, his hatred for this man dissolved like the foam atop an incoming wave spreading across the sand. Gone. Dissipated.

Pity replaced it, pity and sorrow for a man whose evil heart would send him to hell if he did not change his ways and turn to God.

Cadan withdrew his blade.

The pirates grumbled and cursed, and Cadan swept the tip of his cutlass their way. "Anyone else care to do battle?"

Instantly, Damien's men grew silent.

"Pell, lock Damien in the hold of his ship. Soot, Moses"— *where was Moses?*—"and the rest of you, lock the weapons below, disable the cannons, and release Damien's men." Cadan studied the pack of fierce slovenly pirates. "You will allow us to leave unhindered, and the ship is yours."

Nodding, the pirates cheered.

Damien struggled to rise, his face a mask of fear and contempt as Pell grabbed his arm and hauled him away.

Soot approached, scratching his head. "Why not take 'is ship too, Cap'n?"

"I want naught to do with the *Nightblood* or anything belonging to Damien," he shot back, but then glanced behind him where Gabrielle slowly descended the quarterdeck steps, Matthew in her arms.

In truth, there *was* something of Damien's that he very much wanted to keep.

Cadan strode into his cabin, feeling lighter, happier, filled with more joy than he had in many, many years. Tossing his baldric and weapons onto his desk, he turned to face Pell, Soot, and Moses entering behind him.

With medical satchel in hand, Moses ordered Cadan to sit while he checked his wounds. After dressing the cuts on his arm, he gestured toward the one in Cadan's side. "Dis one needs stitches, Cap'n. It's gonna hurt a bit." His dark eyes met Cadan's.

Cadan nodded.

Above deck, footsteps thundered. Olin's shouts ricocheted in the wind, ordering the pirates to make all sail and get as far away from Allard as they could. Not that they had anything to fear from that daft blackguard, for his crew seemed rather elated to be rid of him as captain.

"That were some fight, Cap'n," Soot exclaimed, plopping his large body into a nearby chair.

Pell crossed arms over his chest, his eyes alight with admiration. Or was it pride? "You could have had your revenge, Captain. Whatever stopped you?" Yet by his understanding look, Cadan would bet his friend already knew.

Moses poured rum over his wound, and it took all of Cadan's strength to keep from shouting in agony. "Lost interest,

I guess," he managed to squeak out as he reached for the nearest bottle of rum. But for some reason, he found no craving for it on his lips. Hmm. Odd, that.

The needle pierced Cadan's skin. He grimaced. "What of other injuries? How is my crew?" He'd seen a few of his men fall to the deck during battle.

"Jist four o' dem, Cap'n," Moses replied. "Minor cuts. Wilson were shot in the arm, but it went clean through. Already took care o' dem."

Another pierce of the needle, and Cadan fought to maintain consciousness.

Even so, he thanked God none of his crew had been killed.

One more stab of the needle. Sweat broke out on Cadan's forehead. His breath came fast.

"Almost done, Cap'n." Moses' tone was apologetic.

A sudden, terrifying, horrible thought blasted through Cadan, shoving aside his pain. The treasure! He'd forgotten to get the treasure! He started to stand. Moses forced him back down. Pain radiated from his side, but he no longer cared.

Finally, Moses finished, tied off the stitches and wrapped a bandage around Cadan's waist.

"Thank you, Moses." Cadan nodded at the large man, then leapt to his feet and marched to the stern windows. Beyond the sparkling sea, the bare masts of Allard's ship could barely be seen on the horizon. How could he admit such a failing to his crew? They'd feed him to the sharks!

"What's wrong?" Pell asked.

Cadan spun around. "The treasure. It's back on Allard's ship! Turn the *Resolute* about at once, Pell. We must return and get it."

No one moved. All three men stared at him, smiles on their faces.

"I gave you an order!" Cadan fisted hands at his waist.

Soot moved to the edge of his chair. "We's got the treasure, Cap'n."

"What?"

"Aye." Pell nodded his head toward Moses. "While you and Allard were dallying with your blades, Moses took a few men and hauled the treasure from the *Nightblood* over to the *Resolute*."

Smiling, Moses gathered up bloody clothes and instruments. "Weren't hard t' find it an' even easier t' sneak it past everyone."

Soot chuckled. "Them were all watchin' the fight, hollerin' an' punchin' their fists in the air, they never saw a thing!"

Laughter bubbled up in Cadan's throat and he shook his head. "Well done, men, Well done!"

"What is well done?" Gabrielle, Matthew in her arms, swept into the cabin, one brow arched over blue eyes alight with playfulness.

Here was the reason he'd forgotten the treasure. He'd been so concerned about getting her and Matthew to safety and far away from Damien that no thought of anything else had entered his mind.

But suddenly as she stood before him, the sunlight brushing over her, setting her skin aglow like pearls and her hair like spun gold, he realized that she was the only treasure he wanted. Her scent of rose, sunshine, and a hint of sass wove around him, and 'twas all he could do not to take her in his arms.

"Cap'n Allard's treasure, Miss." Soot rose to his feet. "Moses got it while the Cap'n an' that fiend were fightin'."

She gave a curt smile. "Then, Captain, you must be pleased to finally have your treasure."

She had no idea. Nor did he wish to disclose his intense love for her, for she'd made her own sentiments quite plain.

"I am," he finally said.

"But what I don't understand is why you didn't kill Damien? You had him. 'Twas your dream, was it not?"

Cadan rubbed the back of his neck and sighed. "Let's just say the Almighty had a word with me." He glanced at Pell, who returned his nod with a smile.

Gabrielle blinked, her pert little nose twitching.

"Ye mean God?" Soot scrunched his face.

"Aye, and He showed me how ugly revenge was. In truth, he showed me many things."

Pell approached and clapped him on the back. "Finally."

"Hallelujah," Moses added.

Soot scratched his head. "Well, I'll be a pickled sardine."

Gabrielle, shock still flashing from her eyes, turned to Soot. "God loves us all, Soot. I know you've wondered that of late."

Huffing, the master gunner turned to leave. "Too much talk o' God in a pirate's cabin fer me."

They all laughed as he headed out the door.

"I best check on the wounded." Moses nodded toward Cadan and left.

Fingering his cross, Pell kissed Matthew on the head. "And I have a ship to steer." He winked at Gabrielle before he, too, marched out, closing the door behind him.

Leaving Cadan alone with Gabrielle.

Her eyes searched his as she gave a sad smile. "I know you fought Damien only for the treasure and your revenge, but still, I owe you a great deal for saving my son. Thank you." She turned to leave.

Cadan grabbed her hand. "Stay, Gabrielle. Please."

Chapter 37

Gabrielle should leave the captain's cabin. *Immediately.* She should not be here alone with this man, not when every inch of her longed to stay, not when her heart swelled at the very sight of him, at the very sound of his deep voice, at the look of love pouring from his eyes. She sailed upon dangerous seas, and if she turned to face him, she feared she'd go down in the storm.

Father, help! This was her weakness—love, marriage, family—but she knew God's plans were the best. Yet how could those plans include a man, a *pirate*, who wanted none of those things, who, despite his recent mention of God, had denied Him over and over?

Hear him out, Daughter.

Closing her eyes, she turned to face him, and instantly regretted it, for he still wore no shirt and his muscles, tight from his recent battle, rolled and bunched across his chest and arms and rippled down his belly. Dark hair hung in strands to his shoulders, stubble lined his chin and jaw, one bloody bandage was tied around his left arm while another circled his waist. He looked every bit a vicious pirate captain, a man who would kidnap a woman for treasure. Yet…something in his eyes, in the way he looked at her defied all that.

"Yes, Captain?"

Yawning, Matthew stretched out one arm and opened his eyes, gurgling, drawing both their gazes.

Smiling, Cadan approached, and the most surprising thing happened. Her son reached out his chubby hand toward him.

"May I?" Cadan held out his hands.

Gabrielle stared at him, frozen, unable to form a rational thought. But before she could make sense of it, she handed him to Cadan.

The pirate, all muscle and strength, nestled Matthew against his mighty chest as if the child were made of cotton. Cooing, Matthew smiled up at Cadan and continued to run his little fingers over the stubble on Cadan's chin.

If the sea turned to chocolate and the clouds to whipped cream, Gabrielle couldn't be more shocked. In truth, all she could do was stand and stare at the affection drifting between this enigmatic pirate and her son. Swallowing a burst of emotion, she fought back the tears burning behind her eyes. So, Cadan *had* been the one to care for Matthew in her absence. She'd not thought it possible, this man who commanded a ship of cutthroats, who was an expert swordsman and even better at sea battles, a man who loathed children. Or so he'd said.

Cadan eased a finger over Matthew's cheek, and her son grabbed hold of it with his tiny hand and clung to it, refusing to let go.

The ship rolled over a wave and Gabrielle reached for the desk to steady herself while Cadan maintained his balance with ease.

"I see you have bonded with my son," she managed to squeak out.

"We spent some time together, aye." He smiled back down at Matthew. "He'll make a good pirate one day."

Gabrielle raised her chin. "He will do no such thing."

Cadan chuckled, then moved to a teakwood chest perched against the bulkhead and laid Matthew inside.

Alarmed, Gabrielle followed him, but found her son cocooned in a bed of linen shirts and cotton coverlets. "You made a bed for him?"

Cadan stared down at Matthew. "Aye. He slept here many nights."

Gabrielle shook her head. "I don't know what to say, Cadan, save thank you for taking such good care of him."

"I've grown quite fond of him." His eyes met hers, and for the first time since she'd known him, vulnerability burned within them. Followed by an intensity of feeling that forced her to turn aside.

Heart pounding, she moved to the stern windows, staring at the oscillating blue sea. Zada looked up from his sunny spot on the window seat, and Gabrielle scratched his head, surprised at how she'd missed the silly lizard. "What is it you want, Captain?" She kept her tone stern, detached.

She felt rather than heard him slip behind her, his masculine scent swirling about her, his presence cocooning her in warmth, protection, love, fear…a plethora of conflicting emotions.

"I owe you an apology, Gabrielle. I wronged you greatly. I used you and your child for my own greed and revenge. 'Twas evil of me. I know that now."

The words drifted around Gabrielle, refusing to land on her reason, refusing to enter her heart and take residence. For if they did…?

"And how do you know that?" she retorted, keeping her back to him, for she feared what she'd do if she saw sincerity in his gaze.

He heaved a deep sigh. "Let's just say I've come to my senses, I've returned to God, my Creator and Redeemer. And He has shown me how ugly both greed and revenge are."

Was this a trick? A ploy to loosen her restraints, break down her walls? But to what end? She must see for herself. *Father, show me the truth,* she prayed before she slowly turned around.

Cadan stared at her with eyes bursting with love. "The Lord's plans are best if we trust Him and follow Him."

Narrowing her own eyes, she backed away, studying him, his expressions, his stance, the intensity of his gaze. "Captain, I fear Pell has taken over your body."

He chuckled and reached for her, but she retreated further, her back hitting the bulkhead. "I can hardly believe it. Do you speak the truth?"

He gave a sad smile and nodded. "Finally. Alas, I don't blame you for not believing me."

Several minutes passed as the gentle purl of water against the hull serenaded them. A humility she'd never seen before crossed Cadan's eyes, a humility that could only come from knowing God. "I'm happy for you, Cadan," she finally said, "for I, too, have turned to the Lord." She glanced back out the windows. "I realized I never knew Him, yet I blamed Him for all the bad things in my life."

Approaching, Cadan took one of her hands in his. "Seems we both had much to learn."

She nodded, smiling, their eyes meeting once again, his searching hers as if he longed to peer into her soul. And oh, how she wanted to grant him entrance, how she wanted to fall against that mighty chest, to melt into his strength, to receive his love.

But just because he claimed to know the Lord didn't mean he sought marriage or children. Tearing her hand from his, she wandered about the cabin, chest thundering, and blood racing. She should leave before he broke her heart, tore away what remained of her restraint. She stumbled over a pile of tossed garments and bent to pick them up.

His boots thundered over the deck, and before she knew it, he clasped both her hands, removed the garments and tossed them onto his bed.

Sunlight angled in from the windows, waving over the stripes on his back, and she resisted the urge to run her fingers over them, if only to ease his pain.

"So, you forgive Damien?" she asked.

Facing her, his jaw stiffened, and he huffed. "Working on that, but yes, with God's help."

Matthew cooed and gurgled from the chest. "Then what of my son?" Though clearly, Cadan harbored no resentment for him, she needed to hear it from his lips.

"He's but an innocent in all this. What kind of monster would blame a child?" Sincerity, along with shame, clouded his expression as he raked back his hair.

She tore her gaze from his. "Very well. However, if you wish me to continue visiting your cabin, Captain, I do have one request."

He grinned. "Anything."

She retrieved a shirt lying atop his bed and handed it to him. "If you please?"

His lips curved in a rakish grin. "Does your attraction mean I have your forgiveness?"

"It has naught to do with it, but you have my forgiveness, nonetheless."

"Then I have the perfect solution for this problem you have." He raised one brow, a seductive twinkle in his eyes.

Huffing, she shook her head. "Yes?"

He brought both her hands to his lips and kissed them. "Marry me."

The room spun. Her pulse raced. And she would have stumbled and fallen if Cadan hadn't kept a firm grip on her hands.

"Not the reaction I hoped for," he said.

Pulling her hands back, she gaped at him. "I thought you never wished to marry again. I thought you hated children."

"I find, Lady Fox, those sentiments no longer inhabit my heart. Not since you came into my life."

"And you want more children?"

"If you are their mother, I want a household of them! I love you, Gabrielle. I'll love you forever." He caressed her cheek with the back of his hand.

Tears spilled from her eyes as her heart swelled to near bursting. "I love you too, Cadan." She fell into his embrace, and he lowered his lips to hers.

Life and love and hope and promise all swirled together in that kiss as her body responded with a yearning she'd never known, a flurry of sensations that made her insides melt, and a tempest of desire for a life with this man.

After several minutes, they parted, their breath coming fast and filling the air between them.

Withdrawing, he cupped her head in his hands. "Shall I take that as a yes, Lady Fox?"

She smiled. "A resounding yes!"

Footsteps thundered above, followed by shouts and the distant *boom* of a cannon.

"Cap'n!" Soot burst through the cabin door. "We's bein' fired on! Ye's needed above!"

Of all the bad timing! With Gabrielle's kiss still lingering on his lips, Cadan leapt up the companionway and marched to stand beside Pell at the tiller. Plucking the spyglass from his quartermaster, he leveled it on his eye.

"Two points to starboard, Captain," Pell said. "She snuck up on us from behind that cay."

Anger tightened Cadan's jaw. "Who was the lookout? She should have been spotted long before she got a shot off!"

Swishing brought his gaze around to see Gabrielle and Omphile coming on deck. He'd told her to stay below, but of course she never listened.

"Sorry, Cap'n!" Olin shouted from the main deck. "We was celebrating our victory an' all the treasure we got, an' I guess we weren't …."—he gulped—"Sorry."

"No excuse!" Cadan barked back, but he'd have to deal with them later. Wind whipped over him, bringing the scent of the sea, men's sweat, and gun smoke as the *Resolute*, with the wind on her quarter, crested a mighty wave.

"Three sails, three sets of sail!" The lookout in the crosstrees shouted. *Three*? Alarm stormed through Cadan as he focused the scope on the horizon. Indeed, three ships headed straight for them.

A jet of yellow smoke shot from the lead ship's bow. *Boom!* Cracked the air and billowed over the sea.

"Down!" Cadan shouted, but before his crew could respond, the shot flew over their bow and splashed into the sea. A warning, no doubt.

"She's signaling for you to dip yer colors, Cap'n!"

Blast it all! Cadan would not surrender. He glanced at Gabrielle gripping the quarterdeck railing. He would not see her or Matthew harmed, or any of his crew. *Father*? He looked up to heaven and sighed, wondering how long he'd be punished for his crimes.

No answer came. Just the arrows of a hot sun piercing his chest.

Raising the spyglass yet again, he studied the oncoming ships, focusing on their ensigns. Not British or French or any nationality, but rather from the black flags covered with threatening pictures, they were Brethren of the Coast—pirates! A fleet of them. Why had he not heard of a roving fleet of pirates in these waters?

"Soot, ready the gun crew and load and run out the guns! Beat to quarters!" Cadan barked, sending his pirates scattering to their tasks. The fleet had the weather gauge, which did not bode well for Cadan's success. Still, if he could cripple the first ship's guns, he might be able to tack a weather and outrun the others.

"Wait!" Gabrielle laid a hand on his arm, and before he could stop her, she grabbed the scope and held it to her eye, expertly focusing on their incoming foes.

"'Tis no enemy!" she cried with glee. "'Tis my Father!"

Cadan stared at her, aghast. "And just *who* is your father?"

She bit her lip as wind tossed her golden curls behind her. "I suppose I should have told you sooner." She gave him a sheepish look. "Captain Edmund Merrick."

Pell chuckled. Omphile gasped.

Cadan had no words. In truth, that name spun a web of confusion in his mind. Aye, he knew who Captain Merrick was. There wasn't a sailor in all the Caribbean who didn't know that name. But Lady Fox was his daughter? The daughter of an Earl? The daughter of the most famous missionary-pirate ever to sail these seas? He stared at her, baffled. Yet suddenly her knowledge of sailing and ships made sense.

"He's coming up on our starboard side, bringing his guns to bear, Cap'n!" Olin shouted.

"Guns primed and ready, Cap'n!" Soot added.

Cadan glanced at the men manning the guns, then at the oncoming ships. At their present speed, Cadan could tack to port and loose a broadside, but not before Merrick could do the same. Did he even know his daughter was on board?

He looked at Pell. "What say you?"

"If 'tis Captain Merrick, he means you no harm. He's a Godly man."

"Please!" Gabrielle tugged on his arm.

I've sent him.

Had God just spoken to him? Yet the peace it brought was unmistakable.

"She gives the signal to reduce sail and lie to, Cap'n!" Barnett yelled.

Cadan rubbed sweat from the back of his neck as he balanced his boots on the heaving deck. What to do?

"Stand down," he finally ordered Soot. "Lower our flag, Olin!"

"But Cap'n!"

"Do it!" Cadan shouted, then leapt down on the main deck, uttering a string of orders that lowered all sails and brought the ship around.

Now was the test whether he'd heard from God or not. Merrick had a reputation as an expert at sea battles. He'd also been known to sink pirates to the depths. Even worse, what would he do to Cadan when he discovered he had kidnapped his daughter?

Gabrielle couldn't remember a time she'd been this nervous to see her parents. She'd always been such a good, obedient girl. In truth, she'd rather enjoyed watching her brother Alex and her sister Reena suffer punishment after punishment for their rebellious antics as children. Whilst she received naught but her parents' approval and praise. Heart racing, she watched as the *Redemption* luffed alee then came even on the *Resolute's* keel. Pirates from both ships hitched the two mighty crafts together with grappling hooks and ropes.

Her father had ordered sharpshooters to the tops where they leveled muskets down upon Cadan's crew should they decide to attack instead of surrender.

Scanning the all-too-familiar deck, she spotted Sloane, then Jackson and Brighton, her father's trusty crewmen, all armed to the teeth. Where were her parents? She searched the deck of the ship that had been her home for most of her life. There. Dressed in his usual leather breeches stuffed in Hessian boots and a leather jerkin covering a white cambric shirt, her father stormed across the deck, cutlass in hand, pistols and knives stuffed inside his baldric. His intense gaze surveyed the *Resolute*, his blade lowering when he noted they'd laid down their arms.

Cadan stood amidships, hands fisted at his waist, waiting to meet him. Not an ounce of fear was evident in either his expression or stance, though she knew he must be nervous.

Finally, Merrick's gaze swept to Gabrielle, standing on the quarterdeck.

A lump formed in her throat. Would he be shocked to see her? Would she see joy, love, or condemnation on his face? She deserved condemnation for her actions, for running away with Damien, for not trusting God.

But, instead, he smiled. And in that smile, she saw love, not anger. Longing, not condemnation. Her heart melted. The look of relief that beamed from his face made her want to leap down the stairs and run into his arms.

He gestured behind him and Charlisse, Gabrielle's mother, emerged from the crowd of pirates, her gaze following her husband's up to Gabrielle. Squealing, she threw her hands to her mouth and started for the railing, but Merrick held her back. True to form, her mother wore breeches of her own and a leather doublet over a cream-colored shirt. Pistols and a small knife were stuffed in her belt. And though gray streaked the hair at her temples, the rest flowed in blonde curls down her back. Seems they had anticipated a battle, and her mother never shied away from joining her husband.

Lud, but Gabrielle had missed her. Had missed them both.

Sails flapped impotently in the wind above them as Merrick led a small band of his pirates over the bulwarks and dropped onto the deck of the *Resolute* with a resounding thump. His men pointed blades and pistols at Cadan's crew.

"I am Captain Edmund Merrick of the ship *Redemption*. And you are?"

"Cadan Hayes, captain of the *Resolute*." Cadan replied.

Drawing his cutlass, he pointed it at Cadan's throat. "And just what, pray tell, are you doing with my daughter?"

Horrified, Gabrielle leapt down the quarterdeck ladder. "Nay, Father. He has done me no harm!" She charged him and placed a hand on his arm, but he nudged her aside.

"We heard he kidnapped you!" Merrick's face reddened in rage.

"Nay!" Gabrielle glanced at Cadan. "Rather, he saved me. Please, Father, Lower your blade."

Squealing, her mother jumped over the railing and joined them, flinging an arm around Gabrielle and drawing her close.

Finally, Merrick withdrew his cutlass, still eying Cadan with suspicion. Gabrielle flew into his arms, soaking in his scent and strong presence. Her mother joined them, and they all embraced, tears spilled down Gabrielle's face. "I have so much to tell you. So much has happened."

"We would hear it all, daughter." Merrick kissed her forehead. "Your brother and sister are most anxious to see you." He glanced at the *Ransom* and *Reckless* drifting in the sea behind the *Redemption*.

"And I, them, Father! I have missed you all so much."

"We were so worried for you, darling!" Charlisse cast a wary glance at Cadan before embracing Gabrielle again. "We heard…we thought you'd been kidnapped, and we've been searching for you for months."

Gabrielle wiped her tears. "You have? I thought you'd be angry with me."

Charlisse slipped a strand of Gabrielle's hair behind her ear. "My precious baby. Never."

Her father cupped her chin. "We will always love you."

Renewed tears spilled down her cheeks, and she shared a glance with Cadan, who stared at the reunion with both shock and joy.

"Lower your weapons." Turning, Merrick ordered his men, and with a few grumbles they sheathed their blades.

"I have something to tell you." Gabrielle took a step back. "*Someone* to show you." Fear threatened to steal her newfound joy. How would her Godly parents react to Matthew?

Chapter 38

Two months later

Heart tight, breath heaving, Gabrielle took her father's hand as he assisted her up the companionway of the *Resolute* and onto the quarterdeck. Her mother hurried behind her, gathering the train of lace that spread out behind Gabrielle's wedding gown. A breeze ripe with salt and tropical flowers wafted over her, sending curls dancing over her neck. Halting at the railing she glanced across at the foredeck where pirates crowded to witness the proceedings, men from both Cadan and her father's ships, Sloane and Jackson among them. Sloane, looking just as strong as ever in his seventies now, winked her way. She smiled in return.

Cadan's crew lined the quarterdeck. Soot, Hellfire in his arms, gave her a knowing grin. Beside him, Durwin fumbled his hat in his hands and barely met her gaze. Cadan had released him from the hold, forgiven him, and given him a position on the ship, though not first mate. He'd have to earn that title.

Below, garlands of colorful tropical flowers were draped over railings and hung on the bulkheads while gardenias and roses littered the deck, filling the air with their sweet scent. A canopy of white lace stood near the starboard railing while beyond, the *Redemption*, the *Restitution*, the *Ransom*, the *Reckoning*, and the *Reckless* rocked idly in Kingston Harbor. Morning sun showered a sparkling blanket of saffron and silver over the rippling waters that led to the city of Kingston beyond.

Spread across the main deck, attired in their finest, stood her family—her brother Alex, his wife Juliana and their son Caleb, her sister Reena and her husband Frederick. Lady Isabel and Kent, Frederick's parents, stood to their side, while next to them Rowan and Morgan were chasing a young Rose over the deck. Her family, her growing family, for she'd learned that Reena was with child—her first—and Morgan ripe with her second.

A fiddle began playing and all eyes raised to her.

But her thoughts, her heart were on Cadan. She shifted her gaze to the canopy, but she couldn't see him beneath it. Sudden terror wrenched her heart. Was he there? Was she to be jilted once again?

Her father must have sensed her fear, for he smiled and extended his elbow. "Shall we?" Dressed in black breeches and tight-fitting doublet with metallic lace trim, he looked more handsome than she ever remembered.

Her mother slipped beside her. "He's there," she reassured Gabrielle with a smile. No one would ever guess the lady was well over fifty years, for despite the gray streaks brightening her hair and a few lines at the corners of her eyes, she had a vibrancy, an inner joy that captivated all who met her. And brave. The lady was the most courageous person Gabrielle knew. This day, however, she'd abandoned her breeches for an embroidered gown of purple silk with belled sleeves and a veil of silver lace.

Gabrielle stared down at her own ivory gown with quilted petticoat, hanging tassels, and rose-colored trim. She ran a hand over her smooth satin bodice and fingered the curls dangling about her neck from her elegant coif, embedded with pearls. Her hands shook. Her mother grabbed them. "'Twill be all right, precious." Then bending, she gathered up Gabrielle's train of gossamer lace, and together, her parents escorted her down the ladder and onto the main deck.

Closing her eyes for a moment, she finally dared to open them and look up.

Cadan was there! He gave her that smile of his that sent her heart reeling. With his hair slicked back and tied behind him and in a suit of black taffeta, he almost looked like a gentleman. Almost.

Of course her father had spent the last two months interrogating the man, testing him at every opportunity, chastening him, berating him for his treatment of his daughter, and ensuring his faith in God was real. Yet Cadan passed every test, trial, and punishment, for Merrick had finally deemed him worthy of her.

He gave her a nod of assurance, his eyes beckoning her onward.

Pell stood behind him, a Bible in his hands. To the right, Moses wrapped an arm around Omphile's shoulder, and Gabrielle couldn't help but grin at the newly engaged couple. But 'twas the precious bundle in the woman's arms that drew Gabrielle's loving gaze. Matthew.

After adjusting Gabrielle's train, Charlisse moved and took the babe from Omphile and nestled him close. She and Merrick had welcomed Matthew with open arms and all the love they had to give to a new grandchild.

Even after Gabrielle had told them her sad tale, even after they knew how the babe had been sired, and by whom, they still welcomed him, along with Gabrielle, back into the family. It reminded her of God, who welcomes all who come to Him asking forgiveness.

Drawing a deep breath to steady her nerves, she swerved her gaze back to Cadan. One side of his lips quirked in a sultry smile as he gestured her forward.

Was this really happening? Was she marrying the man of her dreams? The man God had chosen for her?

Thank you, Lord! Joy leapt inside of her. Would she always be this happy?

She turned to her father beside her. "After this, Father, what do we do? What is God's plan for us?" She hoped it included more children for her and Cadan, but she was open to whatever the Lord wanted.

He patted her hand in the crook of his elbow and grinned. "Why, daughter, we follow where the Lord leads. On to the next adventure. All of us." He waved his hand proudly over his children and grandchildren. "What a privilege it is to serve the King of Kings. We must do all we can to tell as many people as possible of His love and the purpose and joy that comes from being in His Kingdom."

"Indeed, Father. Indeed." Her eyes grew moist.

"But for now? Your groom awaits." He nodded his head toward Cadan.

Smiling, Gabrielle allowed her father to lead her to stand beside him. Cadan took her hands in his, gazing at her with such love and devotion, she nearly swooned.

A breeze stirred the lace of the canopy, bringing the scent of the sea and of Cadan. A bell rang, birds squawked. But the only thing Gabrielle cared to hear were the sacred vows Pell asked them both to repeat.

By the time Cadan lowered his lips to hers, she knew that although this was the happiest day of her life, it was only the beginning.

About the Author

AWARD-WINNING AND BEST-SELLING AUTHOR, MARYLU TYNDALL dreamt of pirates and sea-faring adventures during her childhood days on Florida's Coast. With more than thirty books published, she makes no excuses for the deep spiritual themes embedded within her romantic adventures. Her hope is that readers will not only be entertained but will be brought closer to the Creator who loves them beyond measure. In a culture that accepts the occult, wizards, zombies, and vampires without batting an eye, MaryLu hopes to show the awesome present and powerful acts of God in a dying world. A Christy and Maggie award nominee and two-time winner of the RWA Inspy Reader's Choice Award, MaryLu makes her home with her husband, six children, four grandchildren, and several stray cats on the California coast.

For a peek at the characters and scenes from the book, visit my The Resolute Pinterest Page!

Read the other books in the Legacy of the King's Pirates Series! *The Redemption, The Reliance, The Restitution, The Ransom, The Reckoning,* and *The Reckless*!

If you enjoyed this book, one of the nicest ways to say "thank you" to an author and help them be able to continue writing is to leave a favorable review on Amazon! Barnes and Noble, Goodreads, Bookbub (And elsewhere, too!) I would appreciate it if you would take a moment to do so. Thanks so much!

Comments? Questions? I love hearing from my readers, so feel free to contact me via my website: https://www.marylutyndall.com/ Or email me at: marylu_tyndall@yahoo.com

Follow me on:
Blog: https://crossandcutlass.blogspot.com/
Pinterest: http://www.pinterest.com/mltyndall/
BookBub: https://www.bookbub.com/authors/marylu-tyndall
Amazon: https://www.amazon.com/MaryLu-Tyndall/e/B002BOG7JG
Instagram: https://www.instagram.com/marylu_tyndall/

To hear news about special prices and new releases sign up for my newsletter on my website Or follow me on Bookbub!
https://www.marylutyndall.com/
https://www.bookbub.com/authors/marylu-tyndall

Other Books by MaryLu Tyndall

THE REDEMPTION
THE RELIANCE
THE RESTITUTION
THE RANSOM
THE RECKONING
THE RECKLESS
THE FALCON AND THE SPARROW
THE RED SIREN
THE BLUE ENCHANTRESS
THE RAVEN SAINT
CHARITY'S CROSS
SURRENDER THE HEART
SURRENDER THE NIGHT
SURRENDER THE DAWN
FORSAKEN DREAMS
ELUSIVE HOPE
ABANDONED MEMORIES
SHE WALKS IN POWER
SHE WALKS IN LOVE
SHE WALKS IN MAJESTY
VEIL OF PEARLS
WHEN ANGELS CRY
WHEN ANGELS BATTLE
WHEN ANGELS REJOICE
TEARS OF THE SEA
TIMELESS TREASURE
WRITING FROM THE TRENCHES
THE LIBERTY BRIDE
PEARLS FROM THE SEA
THE HIGHWAYMAN'S BARGAIN